Acknowledgments

WITHOUT THE DEAR friendship and creative collaboration of Farrin Jacobs, whose book-editing jobs I've been living vicariously through for years, *Blood Is the New Black* would not have existed. Farrin and Joe Veltre at Open String Productions are responsible for the book's conception and have been delightful and patient throughout the process, and I appreciate all their help. Also, thanks to Allison McCabe at Three Rivers Press for her dedication in editing, and Heather Proulx for running logistics.

In addition to the professionals, I'd like to thank several friends who went above and beyond in helping me finally finish a novel. Miranda Purves read the manuscript, provided much-needed moral support and made her trademark *charmant* suggestions at the darkest hour. Zoë Wolff, my favorite editor, rightly felt that Kate really ought to be more freaked out than I'd originally written her and gave much other useful advice. Without Jeff Howe's vigilance and care, the book would have been later than it already was. The multitalented

Dr. Kay Hooshmand-Parsi answered all kinds of amusing questions on slash wounds and bloodless bodies for me, and Olga Frolova was instrumental during some early plot discussions . . . in Russian. Of course, the biggest thanks of all goes to my husband, Ivan Isakov, who has been endlessly cheery and supportive, who was always willing to discuss and advise, and whose favorite book this is.

Also thanks to my parents, Sam and Marilyn Stivers, who have been wonderful, as always, and cancelled not one but two European vacations to accommodate my writing schedule. And *spaciba* for their understanding to my dear in-laws, Yuriy and Mila Isakov, and friends John and Julia Quinn, whose New Year's 2007 trip got covered in *Blood*.

Finally, I'd like to thank my editors-in-chief—none of whom are remotely vampires. Dominique Browning at *Mirabella* instilled in me a sense of the magazine world's glamour and was the model for Kate's bedazzlement by her boss. Cyndi Stivers (no relation!) at *Time Out New York* is the inspiration for Lillian Hall's miraculous abilities with the red pen. And Lamar Graham at CondéNet taught me—when I was but a green delinquent—how to write. May they all avoid Nolita dressing rooms and live to a ripe old age.

BLOOD IS THE NEW BLACK

Valerie Stivers

HODDER

Copyright © 2007 by Open String Productions

First published in Great Britain in 2007 by Hodder and Stoughton
A division of Hodder Headline

The right of Open String Productions to be identified as the Author
of the Work has been asserted by her in accordance
with the Copyright, Designs and Patents Act 1988.

A Hodder paperback

1

All characters in this publication are fictitious
and any resemblance to real persons, living,
dead or undead, is purely coincidental.

A CIP catalogue record for this title
is available from the British Library.

ISBN 978 0 340 93396 1

Printed and bound by Mackays of Chatham Ltd, Chatham, Kent

Hodder Headline's policy is to use papers that are natural, renewable
and recyclable products and made from wood grown in sustainable
forests. The logging and manufacturing processes are expected to
conform to the environmental regulations of the country of origin.

Hodder and Stoughton Ltd
A division of Hodder Headline
338 Euston Road
London NW1 3BH

Blood
Is the
New Black

Prologue

'M CROUCHED UNDER a desk in the assistants' bullpen. I
know they know I'm in here. I'm sure they can smell me or
sense me or whatever it is they do. I knew working at *Tasty*
might suck, but I didn't expect that to be true in a literal sense.
I mean, vain I was ready for, but vampires? I'm starting to get
goose bumps, like the first time I could feel someone watching
me from behind the copier. The faint footsteps I heard earlier
are coming closer. Right about now, the clack of stilettos is
pretty much the scariest sound I've ever heard. I'm not exactly
sure which vamp those stilettos belong to, but I'm sure they're
headed my way.

I have the stake. I have nowhere else to hide. There's only
one thing to do.

Wait for her to find me.

1

Clothes to Die For

"DARLING, YOU REMEMBER Lillian Hall. You met
her last month when you were in New York with
me. Remember? In Bryant Park? The one who
took such an interest in you? Well, I just bumped into her in
Milan—she was staying at my hotel, which I thought odd
because the editors are usually at the Ferragamo, but that's
beside the point. I could hardly believe it myself, but she
offered you an internship at *Tasty*."

My heart drops. I clearly remember Lillian Hall—a cold,
gorgeous, acerbic woman who scared the crap out of me.

"You are familiar with *Tasty*, yes? It's the hottest young
women's magazine in America. Lillian Hall took it over and
re-launched it six months ago. The circulation has gone
through the roof," my aunt rattles on without pause. Her telephone manner is rapid-fire at the best of times.

I used to have a theory that my aunt Victoria arranges things
for me out of guilt, because she knows where my mother is
and isn't telling me. But now I try not to think that way. I try to

think of her as a woman who married very well later in life, chose not to have children, and regrets that a little.

"This is my last summer before med school. Are you honestly suggesting that I drop everything and get a job at a fashion magazine?" I ask. "Wouldn't that be flighty of me?"

"Believe me, darling," Victoria says, "you are in no danger of being flighty."

I don't quite know what to feel. As my aunt well knows, fashion and I have a long, tortured history. My mother, Eva, was a designer, and her successes and failures in that field led our family to . . . well, where things ended up.

With Eva being who she was, I grew up sewing. And I still do frequently go all *Pretty in Pink* and knock out a sundress or repurpose a thrift-store find into something original. I'm also more aware of the world of high fashion than most twenty-three-year-olds with no money, living at home with their dads, and taking the MCATs are. I jest. I'm completely, obsessively aware of the world of high fashion. I moon over unaffordable brands like Alberta Ferretti, Thakoon, Mint. I love how Zac Posen constructs his garments. I respect how the folks behind Martin Margiela deconstruct theirs. And I think Marni makes clothes to die for.

However, I'm not going to follow in my mother's footsteps. I want a career where hard work guarantees you a job, safety, respect. Where you're in no danger of being called "contrived" or "out-of-step" in the newspaper. Where you don't spend all your time trying to impress a bunch of shallow bloodsuckers.

"I'm flattered," I tell Victoria. "But there are lots of people who would . . . enjoy that environment more than I would."

There is a long, chilly pause during which I remember that Victoria pays my student loans.

She sighs. "This kind of opportunity doesn't come twice. Oldham Inc.—that's the media empire that publishes *Tasty*— gets hundreds of résumés for every position. And they don't even look at them. A rich plum like an Oldham internship is only achieved through connections. Lillian noticing you was kismet."

It was eerie, actually. Victoria had taken me to a benefit dinner in Manhattan—she's a society dame; her every bite raises money for something—and on the way out of the Bryant Park Grill we crossed paths with Lillian, a small, delicate, lugubrious, black-haired woman with skin so translucent, it immediately had me pondering medical conditions. Victoria knew Lillian because Victoria knows everyone. She said, "Darling!" Lillian said, "Darling" back in a tone faint with ennui. Diamonds and rubies glittered on her trim white hands. My aunt said, "This is my niece, Kate McGraw."

And Lillian said "Oh?" and proceeded to stare at me so keenly and for so long it became awkward. I was wearing my own design (blue-flowered, mini, adapted from a fifties house-dress), but that didn't seem to be the point of interest. Under those icy blue eyes I felt cold and small and somehow . . . hunted. Then—and this is the weird part—she gripped my chin with her hand, said, "I've been waiting *forever* to meet you," and swept past us in a blast of icy air.

"I think she must have confused us with someone else." Victoria looked bemused. "I don't know her all that well."

And there it rested, until today. Now my aunt starts turning the screws. "You've never validated your aesthetic skills or your

creativity because of my sister's dreadful behavior. I understand that. But once you go to medical school it will be too
late. I wouldn't want you to feel unfulfilled for your entire life
and not know why. . . ."

Me neither. "I already have a life plan," I say. "I did premed
at Brown. It's too late."

"Plans are made to be canceled." Victoria is not your usual
mother figure.

"I'm the wrong style of person for that job. I wouldn't have
anything to wear." *I didn't just say that!*

Victoria senses victory. "You don't give yourself enough
credit. The clothing you make for yourself is quite cute."

"Right now I'm wearing a dress made from a pillowcase."

"You've done something fabulous with it, I'm sure."

"I live in Monticello, New York. I work as an EMT. I witnessed the Jaws of Life being used last night."

"Then you're ready to step fearlessly into the jaws of death,
aren't you? Don't tell me you'd let the complexes your mother
has instilled stop you from doing something you really, secretly
want?"

She's manipulating me, and it's working.

I close my eyes. "Does this internship pay?" I ask.

"You get a stipend. And moreover, since it's in New York, I
was looking forward to you coming to live with me for the
summer. It would be lovely to spend a little time together."

She can't know that living with her was a teenage dream of
mine. A long-held, secretly cherished desire. Even had it been
possible, I couldn't have done it because the years of the mil-
lennium were a rough time for my dad. I needed to stick

around the house to keep an eye on him. But Dan McGraw is doing much better these days, and I am somewhat of a free agent.

Just like that, she's got me. How much damage can one summer do?

2

Gargoyles

TWO WEEKS LATER, in early June, a yellow taxi deposits me, two huge army duffel bags, and a rolly suitcase with a sewing machine in it on the pavement of West Seventy-second Street. In front of me looms a tall stone building encrusted with gargoyles.

I've arrived at Aunt Victoria's.

The New York City heat and humidity are postapocalyptic. My hair—a salon blow-out of freshly hennaed auburn locks—is sticking to my neck. I'm sure I've already sweated off my pricey berry-stain cheek coloring. The makeup, the hair, and my short crimson manicure are all attempts to get in the groove for the new job. Too bad I'm still gawky, pale, flat-chested, and have many of what my new employer would no doubt term "figure flaws." I feel visually wrong every time I come to New York.

My duffels are stuffed with every semi-decent thing I've sewn for myself in the past few years, plus some Eva 4 Eva sample dresses my mom left behind. They're so heavy I'm forced to drag them between two parked cars and onto the sidewalk. I've stopped to rest when a man in livery dashes out of the building and hefts them for me, informing me that Mrs. Rogers had told him to be on the lookout.

I've been here before, and I'm familiar with the doorman concept, but it never ceases to intimidate.

Of course, around here a doorman is the least of my worries. Victoria's husband, Sterling Rogers, is a real-estate developer, and they live in a spectacular, split-level, floor-through penthouse with a wraparound terrace and moody views of the Manhattan skyline. This vast, sprawling apartment is decorated mainly in charcoal gray and black, with spot-lighting to pick out the museum-quality art, the rare orchids, and the framed prehistoric teeth and jawbones that Sterling makes a hobby of collecting.

The elevator door dings and opens directly into the stunning living room. A wall of glorious air-conditioning rolls over me, and I delight in the miracle of evaporation while digging in my pocket for a five for Miguel, the doorman. I hand it to him, wincing with uncertainty. Do you tip doormen?

"Bellissima! Welcome! You've survived the bus station!" my aunt cries, gliding out from another room.

I've insisted that my living expenses this summer will come out of my savings. Thus, the bus into the city, where I then had to splurge for the taxi.

Victoria, as always, looks glamorous. Her hair is stick straight, dark brown, and bobbed; her lipstick bright red. Both emphasize her angular face. She's always been the tall, severe beauty to my mom Eva's girl-next-door.

"Hi, Aunt Vic." I hug her. "You look *charmant!*"

See. I'm practicing.

"Thank you, dear. But a young woman should never compliment an older one on her appearance."

"Why not?"

"It only serves to emphasize the difference in their ages. And most women will think you're mocking them."

Victoria is famous for her pearls of un-maternal wisdom. My best friend, Sylvia, fascinated by socialites in general and my aunt in particular, writes them down in a notebook.

Victoria takes my clammy hand in her cold one. "Come say hello to Sterling, dear. He's off to Japan this evening."

Her husband is a tall, gloomy, silver-haired man with large ears and a slight stoop. I suspect there was a pituitary imbalance somewhere in his past. Sylvia, who has seen a picture, says he looks like Count Dracula. It's true but mean, since Victoria is crazy about him.

My memories of my aunt from childhood are of somebody with problems. My mother thought Victoria was always dating the wrong men (and sleeping with them too quickly, if I dare to read between the lines). And then, boom, Victoria met Sterling and overnight became fabulous and started dealing art. I get the feeling that she knows how lucky she is, and is always grateful for it.

We find the apple of her eye in the master bedroom, arranging a silk handkerchief in the pocket of a made-to-measure blazer. British, I surmise, by its slanted side pockets and a flash of bottle-green lining. Vic kisses him and straightens the hanky.

"Kate," Sterling says, giving me a plate-sized hand to shake. "You must be excited about your internship. Victoria tells me it's quite prestigious."

"I can't wait." I give it all the enthusiasm I can muster. I'm not sure *excited* adequately describes my feelings. I'd go with *anxious* or *terrified*.

"Lillian Hall is an acquaintance from the Seventh on Seventh benefits," Sterling continues. "They use one of our buildings as a party space. She's a wonderful woman. Razor sharp."

"She seemed focused," I say, recalling how Lillian's pale, android-blue gaze raked me from head to toe. It's true that I could almost *feel* Lillian noticing that I'd gone for a dress with a waist, while everyone else that night was wearing "baby means business" tents, trapezes, and bubbles.

"Lillian is *exceedingly* clever," Victoria agrees. "I hope you'll have a chance to watch her in action, though I can't imagine she'll spend much time with the interns."

"Speaking of time, dear . . ." Sterling taps his watch. Victoria and I retreat from their bedroom.

We head down a red-painted hallway hung with Fuseli sketches, turn left at the museum display cases filled with shark teeth, and open a carved Chinese door.

"We're putting you in the William Blake room," Victoria says. She winks at me. "In his youth, Sterling was a *prescient* collector."

Behind the door is a medium-sized room done in the same Gothic-Asian aesthetic as the rest of the apartment. The walls are black; wooden-slat blinds cover the windows; a spread of red velvet blankets a low platform bed whose side tables are vintage Chinese hatboxes topped by orchids in bloom. Over the bed, hanging in a pool of light, is a watercolor of a harried-looking man with a flowing white beard, holding his arms imploringly up to heaven.

Luscious.

"Will it do?" Victoria asks. "We have the other guest room I could put you in."

"This is wonderful," I say. "Very dramatic."

"I'm so glad you like it." She smiles at me. "Please don't open the blinds during the day. Glare is bad for the art. You won't mind terribly, will you?"

"Of course not." I'm secretly disappointed. I'd been looking forward to enjoying the views.

Vic helps me to drag my bags in and start unpacking. Actually, she unpacks while I loll like a teenager on the red velvet spread and let her.

"I won't be back until late," she volunteers, "so we should run through the schedule for tomorrow."

"We're not having dinner together?" I'd imagined that on my first night in the city we'd do something stereotypically urban like ordering in Japanese.

"Oh, you know how clients are!" she says airily. "Tomorrow you'll be reporting to Lexa Larkin. She edits the society pages and does most of the celebrity wrangling for *Tasty*. Unofficially, she's in charge of buzz. And she's running a contest at the moment that she needs help with."

My heart sinks a little. Buzz? As a noun?

"Usually, you'll start work at nine-thirty in the morning, but for tomorrow Lexa has asked that you arrive just before eleven o'clock. That's when they hold their Monday features meeting. You'll be able to jump right into a room full of fashion elites."

Victoria pauses for a moment to hold up a sky-blue silk top made from a Vintage Vogue pattern. "This is a good color for you," she says. "It goes with your eyes."

She puts it on a hanger, front and center in my new closet, where she's placing the items she particularly likes, organized by color. Like the rest of the women in our family, she has a good aesthetic sense.

"I don't know the exact address, but you won't be able to miss the building. It's two fifty-story towers of black glass just off Columbus Circle—they look like they've been twisted and fused together. Rem Koolhaas designed them for the Oldham family in the late nineties. There isn't a more impressive corporate headquarters in Midtown. You'll love it!" She beams at me.

"Sounds epic," I say gamely. "But if I don't have to be there till eleven, I'll see you in the morning, right?"

"Hardly, darling. I'm a late sleeper."

AFTER STERLING leaves for the airport and my aunt flits out for the night, I'm left alone in the gorgeous, rambling apartment. I poke my way down the red hallway, gingerly opening doors, looking for a room that might have a TV in it. Eventually I find what I recognize to be Victoria's study. I was in here once a few years ago while she wrote me out a check.

I'm drawn, unwillingly, to the wall where she's hung framed photos. Most of them are of her and Sterling in locations of jet-set leisure. Boating on the Irrawaddy River in Burma, posing with sherpas in Bhutan, strolling on Isle de la Cité in Paris, where they have a second home. But there's a section of photos of family, and within that, a large one documenting my mother's career. Here's Eva, modeling one of the first professional sample dresses for her Eva 4 Eva line. It's the mid-nineties and her hair is cut in long, soft layers. The dress is in the lingerie-slip style, made from paper-thin silk. Eva sewed on the bias, which is difficult to get right, especially with slippery fabric, but her creations were always perfect. She could pattern-match along the seams and not waste a scrap. Wearing the dress, standing outside on our front lawn, she looks happy.

Those were the early years, back before she became consumed by her career. There are photos of her riffling through the racks in the first store to stock Eva 4 Eva, snapshots of her at home sewing bridesmaids dresses for Vic and Sterling's wedding—and a tragic one of me as the flower girl at same. At thirteen, I was already grown to my full five feet nine inches.

Even in photos, you can see the changes in Eva. As success came her way, her smile got tighter and a groove appeared between her eyebrows. She'd started "playing the game." She had to go to Fashion Week twice a year in New York. Then she had to go to Paris, London, and Milan, too. She got an advertising budget and had to oversee her own shoots, often on location in European cities. She had less and less time for her family.

Until she didn't have any time for us at all.

A couple of years after Eva left home, I went through our house, took down all the pictures of her, put them in a box, and stuffed it in the back of my closet. I can't do that at Victoria's, of course, but I resolve to avoid this study where they're hanging. I ease away and shut the door after me.

I eventually find a home-theater setup with a wall-sized

screen, but watching it by myself seems too lonely—so I call Sylvia.

Sylvia Rand and I were inseparable at school. We lived together from our sophomore year at Brown and were the kind of friends who can generate news for each other between falling asleep at night and meeting for breakfast in the morning. After graduation last year she moved home to L.A. to take a job as a stylist assistant for cheesy E! Network makeover shows. I did what seemed responsible and moved back to my hometown, where my EMT job awaited. The separation has sucked.

"Aii, *asshole!*" she says, in lieu of a greeting. She must be driving. "Sorry, honey. Are you at Victoria's?"

"I am."

"Take lots of pictures for my graphic novel."

"I will." Sylvia, a pudgy, dreamy girl with a face whose prettiness she doesn't appreciate, has been painstakingly illustrating this dark masterwork since school, though with the job she doesn't have much time anymore. The novel is a vaguely sadomasochistic tale of angels and demons in a fancified version of the Roman Empire. I'm not sure of its sales potential.

"I was just thinking about you," she says. "Have you read every fashion magazine cover to cover this month? Plus all the Web sites? Because Nico"—that's her boss—"says Lillian Hall is notorious for reading every publication before anybody else. There are stories about her being out all night during Fashion Week, going straight to work, and still, without picking up a paper, knowing what was in all the trades. She plucks it from the ether, like one of those cell phones that knows to reset itself at daylight saving time."

"Don't you hate it when your cell phone is smarter than you are?"

"Honey, always."

"I've also been asking around about Oldham," she continues. "People call it 'the Evil Empire' and the building is 'the Dark Tower.' 'A bad thing?' you ask yourself? Not at all! It's the most glamorous publishing company in the world. They pay well. But they also like to fire people in publicly humiliating ways. It's a rite of passage."

What have I gotten myself into?

"I'll try to skip that rite."

"Honey, you're going to do great. Now tell me what you've decided on wearing. . . ."

3

Ice in Her Veins

A FEW BLOCKS from Oldham Inc., I start to sense that something isn't quite right.

When I first set out from my aunt's place to walk to work, the New York City morning bustle provided a pleasant diversion from my gut-wrenching nervousness. I even took a picture for Sylvia with my phone—a *Tasty* billboard, proclaiming THE MORE YOU SHOP, THE *TASTIER* YOU ARE! But closer to the office, I notice the icy stares from other women. They check out my face, my body, my clothes, all with a look that says, *I'm judging you, but don't think I give a shit.* I catch someone's eye. She stares without acknowledging me, as if I am a channel she's watching—a boring one. I walk past rows of waiting taxis, vendors hawking the *New York Post,* and quilted silver carts selling coffee, doughnuts, and fried-egg sandwiches. Every few minutes a different tall, thin girl in an unbelievably chic outfit sweeps by me, put-together blondes in ladylike, knee-length black pencil skirts or skinny black trousers with heels. A variety of high-collared, cap-sleeved cotton blouses are on display. As are gym-enhanced female biceps and icky toe cleavage. At the corner of Fifty-seventh Street and Seventh Avenue, I look up, and up, and up . . . until dizziness threatens. I'm staring at a towering, black-glass structure that can only be Oldham's headquarters. "The Dark Tower" is apt.

What am I doing here? I feel ice in my veins, a stab of pure fear.

Followed by a stab of pure self-consciousness.

I really, really don't want to go in there.

Last night, after hanging up with Sylvia, I decided that if I was going to work at a style magazine, I should express my style. My collection of Eva's sample dresses provided possibilities, and after looking at those old family photographs, I was ready to cut something up. For my *Tasty* debut, I've chosen a silk sheath dress with a red-and-white print reminiscent of an Arab kaffiyeh. Eva's version was floor-length but I've chopped it to be thigh-exposingly short, and cinched it with a wide fake leather belt. I matched it with a pair of cruelty-free cloth shoes, and a red velvet ribbon tied around my wrist. I look . . . very different from everyone in the vicinity.

Was I totally insane?

I approach the building, feeling all eyes are on me. These blonde clones will turn as one and strike me dead for violating dress code. I stop short at the mountain of black glass's revolving maw and step to one side. I'll just gather my nerves a bit. Hurrying toward me is a woman in her late thirties, who looks realistically imperfect and stressed out. Her blonde hair is in a sloppy ponytail, and she clutches a thick, disorganized stack of papers against her chest with the same hand that's holding her iced coffee. The papers are sliding. I leap forward to help her.

She springs away, obviously terrified of me. The papers slip out of her grip, pinwheeling in the breeze across the flagstone plaza.

"Oh, shit!"

"I'm so sorry! I didn't mean to scare you!" I say, crouching down (carefully, because of the short skirt) to gather some of the papers. "I just noticed that your papers were sliding and I thought I should help."

"An act of altruism at Oldham Inc.?" the woman says. "You must be new."

"Brand. Spanking." I admit.

Together we scramble after the loose papers.

"It's my first day in a sense, too," she says. "I'm just coming off maternity leave—for my third child, if you can believe that." She seems to check me out for the first time, then adds, "No offense, but you don't seem like the Oldham type."

How could she tell?

"I know. It's a long story."

"Oh?" she says, and takes the last of the papers from me. "Well, good luck!" And she disappears through the revolving door.

Maybe people here aren't so bad.

A gazelle-like blonde gives me the once-over, and actually laugh-snorts right to my face as she walks by.

Scratch that. These girls are going to be monsters.

I wait outside for another few minutes as the river of blondes turns to a dribble—people arrive at work very late here, but I guess ten-thirty is the cutoff. Then I step into the belly of the beast. The lobby is a shining obsidian expanse of polished stone, humming with activity. There's a newsstand, a café, and lots of fit, tooth-whitened people standing around chatting. At a central podium, a scrum of security guards oversees the entrances to two banks of elevators labeled 1–25 and 26–50. Regular employees cruise confidently through the barriers, waving a plastic card at a sensor. Outsiders like myself line up self-consciously at security to plead our cases. I find myself afraid to catch anybody's eye, paranoid I'll be recognized — by whom and for what I have no idea.

Fortunately, I am on the day's list and am issued a tempo-rary pass without ceremony. I try to hold it in my hand but the guard insists I stick it on my clothing. Thus branded, I ascend to my new office.

The elevator doors open on the thirty-seventh floor into a space lit the glowing white of a near-death experience. Giant billboard-sized replicas of *Tasty* covers adorn the walls. I scut-tle past the gaping void of Jessica Simpson's exposed navel, up close the size of a manhole cover. The less said about Keira Knightley's bulging, man-sized teeth, the better. By the time I hit reception, I can feel the naked fear of all the job candi-dates, hopeful fashion designers, and freelance writers who have waited here, shivering on the immaculate white leather furniture, rehearsing their speeches in their heads. "Hi?" I say to the attractive young guy sitting at a low-walled desk in the center of the space. My voice squeaks upward with uncer-tainty, turning "Hi" into a question. I try again. "HI." A little loud, but it will do. "I'm Kate McGraw. I'm a new intern here to see Lexa Larkin."

The receptionist — he's wearing a Fake London T-shirt and nail polish — introduces himself as Felix, checks some lists, spins a strange occult-looking carousel, and informs me that I have paperwork to fill out.

"It will be just a second, don't you worry," Felix says, rummaging through a filing drawer. He's smiling, but the smile doesn't reach his eyes, which are wary. He digs up a packet of forms thick as September *Vogue* and hands it to me.

"Sorry," he says, "Human Resources isn't totally computerized yet. You'd think since they've been around since the dawn of time and . . ." He trails off. "Never mind, I talk too much."

"Oh, not at all." I wonder what he's worrying about. "But can I take these with me and return them later today? I'm supposed to be in the eleven A.M. meeting and it's ten to eleven now and I'll never get this done in time."

Felix looks dismayed for me. "I'm so sorry," he says. "But they are *sooo* strict around here. I don't dare let you through those doors if you haven't filled out your paperwork."

I sit down and start writing as quickly as possible. I need addresses of the past five places I've lived, phone numbers of former bosses, the date of my last physical and much, much more. I'll never finish it before the meeting. Suddenly I'm sweating again despite the air-conditioning.

"Could you call Lexa Larkin and let her know that I'm here at least?" I ask him.

"Sure! Of course!" he cries. He punches a few numbers and then hangs up, making a rueful face at me. "I'm *sooo* sorry," he says. "They must all be in the meeting already." Is he secretly gloating?

A very un-*Tasty*-looking delivery man walks in, wheeling a handcart stacked with coolers. "I'll be right with you," Felix tells him, managing to smile and give me a get-lost vibe at the same time.

Twenty-five minutes later I thump the stack of papers—completed to the best of my ability—on the desk.

"Great," he says, without looking at them. "I'll walk you in now."

Into the middle of a meeting? "That's okay. I don't want to interrupt. I'll wait," I say.

Felix takes my arm in a steely male-polished grip and starts walking. Heartbeats later he flings open a door, announces, "New intern Kate McGraw," and literally shoves me into a room full of people. Angular, black-clad people clustered around a massive table in rows of chairs three deep. All heads turn toward me. I have never been so aware of my bare thighs or the freckles thereon.

"Miss McGraw," says a petite, glossy-black-haired woman at the head of the table. "Attending the editorial meeting as an intern is a privilege. Be on time."

Lillian—for it is she, Lillian Hall—fixes me with a stare. It feels as if time has stopped and it's just the two of us in here and for a second I go completely cold, just like I did when we met before. I bob my head. I could not possibly speak at this moment. In her element, she's even more beautiful and ethereal-looking than I remembered. She has two tapered, ebony pincers of perfectly straight, shoulder-length hair, that alabaster skin, and those brilliant eyes. She seems ageless, like a movie star at her peak.

A no-nonsense-looking blonde who sits next to Lillian smiles blandly. I recognize, with horror, the woman who dropped her papers downstairs, to whom I admitted that I'm not really the Oldham type.

Lillian and everyone else is staring at me. What is this, humiliate-the-late-new-girl day? I want to curl up and hide inside my stupid minidress. After a long silence, the blonde takes pity on me and motions toward the back of the room.

"Take a seat."

I stumble past numerous stiletto-clad feet and sink into an empty chair.

The meeting continues. I stare at my lap. Blood pounds in my ears. There's a mortifying chance I might cry. I knew that I would suffer if I ever dipped a toe into the poison reflecting pool that is the fashion industry. I saw what happened to my mother. How could I have been so stupid?

Around me, they're discussing violence in fashion shoots.

"A little blood on the clothes, yummy models, a crime-scene-tape bow. I'm really seeing it."

"Blood-spattered is a trend!"

"Adorable! Love it!"

"Cute! The bows are inspired."

"But we have to be careful."

"We don't want to become a scapegoat for teen violence."

"Instead of death, what about an afterlife theme for this portfolio? We'll have the models wear angel wings on the grounds of a castle, meant to represent heaven—"

"Enh, wings are so cliché."

After a while I overcome my feelings of disgrace and begin to peek around.

Lillian is wearing her jawbreaker rings and a rigorously

tailored, high-collared black suit jacket, the first few buttons undone to show an almost sexy amount of bare skin. She makes everyone else seem too dowdy, too fussy, too cheap, too something. I don't notice I'm staring until she's suddenly staring back at me. And my blood freezes. Again. What is it with this woman? I mean, it's pretty cold in this room — the staff members who are sitting in the outer rings are clutching their sweaters and shawls — but this is *different*.

Just before I break free of her arctic gaze, she smiles at me — at least I think she does — revealing bride-white teeth. Sharp ones. Sharp like "My, what sharp teeth you have, Grandma." It happens so fast I can't be sure I didn't imagine it. The smile. The teeth. Even the staring contest. I must have imagined it.

Taking only the quickest of glances, so as not to make eye contact with anyone else, I scope out the room. Though not as gorgeous as Lillian, everyone is either classic-pretty or so well-groomed that looks don't matter. Particularly striking is a Persian-cat-faced woman with a British accent. She has a puffy, white-blonde updo and oversized black glasses and wears a plunging black V-neck that sets off her bony sternum like plastic wrap on a chicken breast. Really, she's so skinny I'm concerned for her heart rate.

My eyes are also drawn to a waify girl with huge, almost buggy gray eyes who looks younger than I am, but sits around the table in the inner circle. She's ostentatiously taking notes and nodding in agreement when Lillian or the Brit speaks.

A piece of paper appears on my lap. I do a quick reconnaissance to make sure no one is looking, and unfold it. It says, "Are you fashionably late?"

I turn my eyes toward my neighbor. Sturdy, pale, with rumpled dark hair. Wearing army pants, he's probably in his late twenties.

I flip the piece of paper and write, "Ha."

He plucks the note from my fingers and balls it up. I take another quick glimpse at him, getting an impression of intense, deep-set brown eyes. Then I force myself to look away and ignore him for the rest of the meeting.

This is hard, but not as hard as it might be, because the next topic under discussion is something called the Tasty Girl Contest. My ears perk up. Victoria mentioned that I would be working on a contest.

"What's the status?" the brisk, preppy woman I ran into downstairs asks the room at large. "Are we running this in October?"

It's only June, but the staff is already sewing up October.

"It's been a brilliant success, darling. The readers are really keen. We have more than a thousand entries," the British woman replies. "Annabel knows the details."

"Two hundred and sixty-six logged and twelve full mail buckets waiting to be sorted," Annabel, the young, officious girl, jumps in.

"And, remind me, what is this little contest?" a statuesque black man sitting on Lillian's other side asks. He's wearing an inside-out blazer, sewn so the seams and the linings show — probably Dutch, Central Saint Martins grad, circa 1995 — over a monogrammed white shirt that reads *SLS*. While talking, he doodles on a tablet with a lavender V5 pen.

The British cat lady fluffs up; I suspect she has already told him many times about this contest. "It is a *modeling contest*," she says. "Readers from all over your country have entered. We are going to pick the ten *Tasty*-est"—here the Brit giggles at her own wit—"and then fly them to a bloody great location for a photo shoot."

Her sycophant, Annabel, adds, "We'll break the next Han, the next Dasha, the next Iekeline!"

The Brit continues, "I've arranged for two simply brilliant chums from England to do the photography and the styling. Giedra Dylan-Hall and her consort Kush. Of course you've heard of them."

There's a flutter around the table. Even an inexperienced person such as myself can surmise that picking the photographer is outside the cat lady's job description.

"*The* Giedra Dylan-Hall? I'm so sorry, sweetie." SLS's voice drips poison. "We don't have the budget for that."

This turns out to be a fatal mistake. His rival pounces. "I worried that you might be running a little over budget. So I asked Giedra to do it simply as a favor to me. And she agreed."

"Free photo shoot? I'm sold," the manager-type woman I met outside says.

SLS tries a different tactic. "Do you honestly think we have ten *readers* who are worthy of being in our pages? Aren't you setting your sights a little high?"

"Pick one or two winners," a skinny, tiny woman with streaks of premature gray in her short, dark hair chimes in. The color contrasts strikingly with her pale, youthful face. She must be one of SLS's allies. "That would be stronger from an art perspective."

"I agree that finding ten will not be so easy," says a smoky-voiced woman with masses of curly brown hair and a painted-on beauty mark. "We did a casting call yesterday that made me want to put my eyes out with a Polaroid."

The Brit curves her apricot-glossed lips into a smile. "We *have* to have ten winners," she purrs. "Surely art direction and photography can compensate for any minor flaws in the models." She appeals to the black man. "You always say, 'The shoot's about what's behind the camera, not what's in front of it.' Don't you?"

"That *is* a maxim of mine," he admits grudgingly.

"So?"

"So let's move on," Lillian interrupts. "Have we secured Trey for the October 'Ask a Man' feature?"

"His people are getting back to us," the Brit replies. "I'm sure he'll be keen."

Lillian looks coldly at her. "Mmm . . ." she says. "If his commitment isn't written in blood, get me a few other options." She looks around at the table, displeased. "Let's plan a little further in advance, ladies. You should all have excellent time-management skills by now. Next week we're going to start mapping out November. I want warm, winter ideas. Boot stories. Coat stories. Maybe a few bathing suits for the Caribbean over Christmas break."

"Ice-skating!" Annabel blurts, and then looks around anxiously, as if she's overstepped her bounds by making a suggestion.

Lillian raises an eyebrow. "Dead on," she says. "Ice-skating feels fresh. Now, let's everybody put our thinking caps on and come up with ten or fifteen more of those. It's our job to track down the trends wherever we may find them."

"Until next Monday, folks," the manager lady says, motioning that the meeting is dismissed. "Happy hunting!"

THE BRITISH blonde is Lexa Larkin, my new boss. Up close, she's even freakier looking. Her white-blonde hair swirls out from her face like meringue; her manicured hands are limp and weak-looking. She says, "I've never had an intern without previous fashion experience. You should know that I have grave reservations about this. You'll find that I'm very honest and direct with people. It's one of the reasons I'm so successful."

"I appreciate your honesty," I reply, uncertainly.

She squints at me through her glasses.

This exchange takes place in the hallway outside the meeting, right where everyone can overhear. In fact, they can't avoid overhearing because there is no background noise, no sudden babble of people being released from two hours of sitting still. People stride away silently, heads held high, looking like models walking down a runway. Every one of them is specter-thin and dressed to kill. My homespun red dress stands out like a blood-soaked rag in shark-infested waters.

"To be frank—and I'm always frank," Lexa says, "you're too old for a career change."

"But . . . I just graduated from college last year," I stutter. "And Lillian offered this job—"

At the sound of Lillian's name, Lexa flinches.

"I am up for whatever you need me to do. I've had lots of work experience. I was an EMT, so I'm used to a fast-paced environment—"

"We all do charity work, darling," Lexa says dismissively. "But *I've* been in fashion since before there was a Fashion Week."

I find this hard to believe.

"My years in the industry have given me an encyclopedic knowledge," she continues. "I know the name and specialty of every French frock-maker worth her salt since the 1750s. Have you heard of Rose Bertin? Or the Marquise de Flambeau? She dressed Madame de Staël."

"No, but I'll Nexis them!"

Two very similar looking girls passing us roll their eyes at Lexa. She smirks back.

We start with a tour, whisking from the conference room back toward reception, down a long central corridor lined with cubicles. Editorial takes up half the floor. The other half, Lexa says, is for "the publishing side of the masthead." I understand from her tone that they are subhuman. As far as I can tell, our half of the floor comprises a huge central space with three rows of cubicles—one row for Fashion, one for Research and Copy, and one for Lifestyles and Features. At the end of each row are the closets (Beauty, Fashion, Accessories). And in each closet is a desk (where the "closet assistant" sits; there is such a job). Long hallways run all the way around the perimeter, where Photo and Art are located, and where the bigwigs have actual offices with doors and windows. Shane Lincoln-Shane, the art director (the imposing man who spoke in the meeting; the lavender pen is his trademark), is in one corner office and Lillian is in the other.

The all-white theme of the reception area continues into the interior. Snowy, high-gloss paint seals the wooden floors.

White canvas covers the cubicle walls. Work spaces are personalized with design-classic desk lamps and cleverly collaged bulletin boards. Most chairs are backed with bright cushions in a fabric expressing the occupant's personal style. Aromatherapy is big. We pass through distinct scent zones of lavender, gardenia, rose. My eyes itch.

Lexa points out the off-limits areas: The first no-no is Lillian's palatial corner office. I peek inside as we dash by, catching a glimpse of Oriental rugs and dark antiques that contrast dramatically with the white space. The offices on either side of Lillian's are empty. The diminutive but terrifying editor-in-chief, Lexa explains, "doesn't like a lot of foot traffic." It makes her "cranky."

Lillian's assistant, a gorgeous light-skinned black girl named Bambi, marooned in a cubicle in front of Lillian's door, is hiding behind her computer whispering into her phone. She stares at us with wild, hunted eyes.

"Don't be mad, Shallay," she pleads. "I'll find out as soon as I can." Then she slams the phone down and starts typing frantically. On the ledge of her cubicle are three towering, exotic flower arrangements addressed to Lillian.

When we're out of Bambi's earshot, Lexa tells me that Lillian fires her assistants every couple of weeks, so remembering Bambi's name isn't essential. "There was a brilliant girl during our re-launch who lasted for a few months," she tells me. "Oddly enough, that one survived Lillian but was fired for an impropriety with the company Web server. It's such a *shame* when a young person is fired from her first job." She smiles at me blandly, lips like peach-frosted pillows in her white face.

On that cheery note, we continue our tour of the thirty-seventh floor, walking down a long hallway away from Lillian's office. I'm eager to see the view, but the perimeter walls are taken up by offices, through whose open doors I see windows with the blinds drawn tightly shut. There's a problem with monitor glare, Lexa explains.

The art department is the number-two off-limits locale. Shane Lincoln-Shane can be thrown off his game by the slightest of interruptions.

"If you see Shane Lincoln-Shane coming, hide," Lexa instructs me. A previous intern once made the mistake of asking him where the bathroom was. She was intercepted by HR on her way out of the stall and canned, right there in the can.

After Shane's area is a big open room for the designers and photo department—I'm introduced to the Susan Sontag–gray-streak girl from the meeting; she's Matilda, the head designer—and then we come to what Lexa calls "the fashion closet," across from Photo. It's a huge room, bigger than the whole art department, where clothes that designers send in for shoots wait to be either used or returned. Appallingly, I want to spend hours in there, examining the decadent goods. I even think I see a rack of Marni for fall. The brand's melted-candy colors and funky tailoring make it my favorite label—though I don't have the money to have a favorite label.

I feel increasingly pale and squishy as I meet my new coworkers. Everyone is so poised and pretty and lint-free. Their blacks match. They all greet me with slight, polite surprise. As if it's obvious from looking at my vintage dress and cheap accessories that I don't fit in here.

I wish I didn't care. But I do.

One of the last times I saw my mother comes to mind. She'd already rented her apartment in New York—the one we later found out never existed—but she was home for the weekend.

I was sixteen and wanted Eva's help finishing a top I'd been working on. I was planning on going to a party that night and needed it to make an impression on my crush, Will Crossman (sarcastic, black-haired, pot-smoking high-school god, Will Crossman)—at least that was the fantasy. In reality I should have known I wouldn't talk to him. And I was way too shy to make an impression on anyone. Nonetheless, when Eva came home later than planned, I was already annoyed with her. And then she got a phone call from a friend insisting that she come back down to the city for a party where important industry people were going to be. I was outraged when she agreed to go.

I followed her around the house, berating her for letting me down and for letting my dad down—"Don't you think your husband wants to spend the weekend with you?"—while she mechanically tried on outfits and did her hair and nails. She looked pale and tired. She'd been having problems with short-ness of breath, which she claimed was brought on by the stress of her career. I must have criticized her for caring so much about how she looked. She told me, bitterly, that I didn't understand how hard you had to try to fit in if you weren't born into the world of money.

I've always remembered that, not because what she said was wise—I thought it was stupid—but because of how unusual it was for her to speak sharply to me. Now, for the first time, I can see how she felt. Trying to be one of these *Tasty* girls could suck you dry.

I trail Lexa away from Photo and Fashion, past the Copy/Research row, past Features, around the corner past Beauty and the beauty closet, and into her dark office. Lillian, three doors down, is a little too close for comfort. Also, it's as cold as a meat locker, and like everyone else, Lexa has her white canvas blinds drawn, despite what must be an incredible view.

My new boss flips on a lamp, snaps her fingers, and points to the chair in front of her barren desk. Her chair-pillow is peachy-pink raw silk. Instead of a fluorescent light, she's hung a peach-and-gilt chandelier (of the million-tiny-lampshade variety). I perch on the guest chair (no pillow) nervously. On one wall she has a framed poster of an advertisement for the magazine with the "The More You Shop, the *Tastier* You Are" slogan. Sitting next to her computer is the same clear plastic cup with a straw that I noticed on a couple other of the senior people's desks. It's filled with crimson fluid. Lexa seizes this and starts slurping.

If everyone stays so slender by drinking this smoothie, maybe I should try one.

"Is there a Jamba Juice near here?" I ask.

"It's beet juice," she tells me dismissively.

The straw rattles in the bottom of the cup. Lexa openly and noisily licks her lips, then takes the straw out of the cup and squeezes the last few drops onto her outstretched tongue. You'd expect someone who looks so posh to have better manners.

I'm officially not looking forward to working with her.

And then without a chance to ask about what my responsibilities will be, I'm whisked out of her office by her assistant, Annabel, the officious, pop-eyed girl from the meeting. (OK, like everyone else around here, she's actually very pretty, in a sleek, patrician kind of way.) "You must feel really honored to work here," she says, emphasis on *you*. "I'll show you where the interns sit. And if you have any questions, save them for next week. I'm preparing a binder for new employees that explains everything. It's already two hundred pages." She glares at me as if the binder is just for me.

Two doors down from where Annabel sits in a half-walled cubicle outside Lexa's office is a small, windowless room lined floor to ceiling with filing drawers—another kind of closet, I assumed when we passed it the first time. Now Annabel knocks on the open door. Seeing who it is, the room's two occupants leap up.

They must be the other interns.

"Is that DVF?" asks a tall, size-zero girl with perfect, limp brown hair that looks like she slept on it and woke up looking fashionable. Except, because of her heavy, peaches-in-syrup Southern accent, she pronounces it "day-vee-ehff."

Annabel is wearing a short-sleeved, pearl gray cashmere cardigan over a wrap dress that I, too, suspected was Diane Von Furstenberg.

"The dress has a seventies vibe, but the sweater is patrician," pronounces the other girl. "Very TriBeCa." She has black hair and wears pearls.

"TriBeCa?" Annabel says. "You're saying I look *downtown?*"

My fellow interns hasten to assure her that they didn't mean *downtown*-downtown. They meant original but classic.

"I don't know," Annabel says. "Should I return it for a solid color?" She is carrying a pen in her hand, and starts anxiously clicking it.

The black-haired girl jumps in, attempting to save a bad situation. "Is there anything we can do for you, Annabel? We'd love to help out."

Annabel thinks for a minute. "Nothing right now. I have to get back to work. Lexa is *really* relying on me."

She's totally forgotten me.

"Uh," I say. "So I'm supposed to sit here?" I point to an empty desk.

Annabel flips her hair—shoulder-length, highlighted—and departs.

Once she's gone, the others don't pretend to be nice.

"There are only supposed to be two interns," the brunette says, pronouncing it "intuns." So much for Southern hospitality.

"We had a beanbag in here before," the black-haired girl says, "but they got rid of it to make room for your desk." She looks like she did lots of hazing at her sorority.

"Kate McGraw," I say, and smile weakly. "Nice to meet you. Sorry about the beanbag."

The tall, Southern girl is Nin Casey. She's nineteen, a former model, and has an adventurous sense of style—at the moment, she's wearing daisy-yellow bloomer shorts with knee-high brown boots and an eyelet blouse designed, I suspect, by Catherine Malandrino. She's taking a year off from college to work here, and by her own testimony doesn't want to go back. Her father is a prominent Atlanta real-estate developer.

The other one is Rachel Rosen. She tells me, "I just graduated from Columbia J-school with honors. I've written lots of pitches, I have tons of clips from the fashion trades. It's only a matter of time before I get a byline in a book with a big circ."

Rachel also hastens to add that she won a student-writing competition the prestigious *New Yorker* ran. She has been granted special dispensation by the corporate powers that be to "keep blogging."

"The higher-ups like it because it creates a link to the MySpace generation," she tells me.

Nin says, "You link to MySpace?"

I guess she's so rich and stylish and pretty, she doesn't have to be smart.

I can't decide if I hate these girls or want to be them, or both.

Rachel and Nin are surrounded by white plastic mail buckets heaped high with manila envelopes. These are the Tasty Girl Contest entries.

Nin tells me, "There's really not enough work for three of us."

Is she kidding? "Didn't Annabel mention logging entries in the meeting?" I ask. Prying extracts the name of a disorganized Quark file they've been working on. "You could do this in Excel," I suggest. "And network it so we can all work at the same time."

Rachel says, "We didn't learn Excel in J-school. Most pubs use Quark."

"Yes, but to keep track of all this information, it will be easier if we use something sortable." I demonstrate how an Excel file works.

"I love grids," Nin says. "They're so boxy."

"I can easily cut and paste all your data into this, and—"

"Okay, you do that," Nin says. "We're going to the caf."

They both depart for lunch in the famous Oldham cafeteria—designed by the architect David Rockwell—and I cut and paste the pitifully small amount of data they've compiled. Then, uninvited, I start opening envelopes (some of which are inaccurately addressed to *America's Next Top Model* at our street address). In addition to head shots and application forms, the girls have answered lengthy medical questionnaires and provided an essay on the topic "What Makes Me Tasty?" And here I thought modeling was all about looks.

At four P.M., my only breaks have been going downstairs twice for cigarettes, first for Lexa, second for the beauty editor, she of the fake freckles and tousled roller curls, who sits next door to Lexa. (Our intern closet is across from the beauty closet, from which wafts a smothering, fluffy pillow of conflicting scents.) On principle I don't normally buy cigarettes. I've been known to ask, "Drop something?" when people throw their butts on the ground. But I was so bleary-eyed from entering names, addresses, ages, and contact information into the computer that I was delighted to be given the errands.

Nin and Rachel follow my lead logging entries, all the while discussing what's new on their favorite media-gossip blogs. I learn that there are several devoted to Oldham's magazine empire, including a popular one called www.StakeOut.com, which is trained solely on *Tasty* and prints the most outrageous rumors. Today StakeOut claims that Lillian turned the tables on PETA and left a dead animal on the organization's doorstep. There's also a site called www.RejectPile.com, where horror stories from people who've interviewed here are posted. At five-thirty the jaunty blonde I'd run into this morning while lurking outside stops by.

"I'm Lauren, the managing editor."

Her ponytail is even messier than it was in the morning and the creases around her eyes seem deeper. She's carrying an armload of eleven-by-seventeen photocopies.

"How are you doing, Kate?"

"I'm so sorry about this morning," I say.

She leans on my desk, pitching her voice low, which I appreciate because the last thing I need is for my humiliation to be exposed to Nin and Rachel.

"Look," she says, "this isn't always an easy place to work, especially when you're new. But if you hang in there, even for a couple of weeks, it *will* get better."

"Thanks. That's nice to know."

"I have a good sense of people. And I think you'll do well."

I don't see why anyone would think that, but I'm grateful to her for saying it.

"Can I do anything to help you out?" I try out the intern refrain.

She sighs. "I only wish you could. But I'll tell you what: I'll keep you in mind. Maybe I can find a story or project for you. I know some of the editors aren't focused on providing the interns a rewarding experience. Do you like to write? You want to take pictures? You want to style a model's outfit for a photo shoot?"

"I'd like to write," I answer. I've liked writing from the time Eva and I used to go through fashion magazines and make up silly headlines together. And at school I squeezed in as many writing courses as was possible given my concentration.

"Okay," she says. "Why don't you come up with some ideas for stories you'd like to see in the magazine. I can't promise you that there will be an opportunity, but I'll do my best."

"I'll do my best, too," I say, hoping it will be good enough.

4

A Fight to the Death

HOW WAS YOUR first day?" Victoria asks.

It's Monday night and my aunt has, at my request, ordered Japanese delivery for us. She's also wearing Japanese—Junya Watanabe—and looks clean-scrubbed and girlish, sitting cross-legged on her living-room sofa. A button on the wall has lifted a painting, disgorging a flat-screen TV. This, for her, is a "splurge night," since Sterling hates takeout and televisions.

She looks so happy I can't tell her the truth, which is that I'm an outcast.

"Busy!" I reply. "And I'm kind of the new girl. The other interns have both been working at *Tasty* since Lillian took over last year (and changed the name from *Shop Girl*). One of them is still in college, but she says she'll drop out and take a staff job if they offer it."

"I told you what an incredible entrée you've been given, darling," Victoria says. "Internships are the new first jobs. Some people intern for two or three years before becoming assistants. It's common in the art world, too."

I struggle to dip my rainbow roll in soy sauce without losing control of the slippery fish. "I'm sure things will get easier," I say.

Victoria nibbles on a piece of pickled ginger. "I should think so, darling. How is the Larkin woman? She's a tabloid sensation in England. Solidly D-list, but she thinks she's B. Those are the worst kind—so insecure."

I don't want to admit that Lexa hates me. But Victoria reads it on my face. She puts down her barely touched dinner and, in a rare moment of maternal warmth, pats me on the shoulder.

"You really ought to have new shoes."

She abandons her dinner and comes back bearing a dusty-pink box with the words *Miu Miu* printed on the top. Inside is a pair of jewel-encrusted blue velvet wedge heels. "These are from last season but they'll go with simply everything."

Words to live by.

I SPEND longer than I'm really proud of on Tuesday morning, mixing, matching, and strategically snipping, but Vic is right. Our feet are the same size and, counterintuitive as it may seem, the jewel-encrusted blue velvet wedge heels go with most things in my wardrobe. I settle on wearing the heels with one of Eva's early pieces over a newly short-short jean miniskirt. The talk in the meeting about the "blood-spattered" trend reminded me of this particular dress: a pearl silk nightie edged in white lace and splashed with red paint.

I totter-clomp into Oldham right on the dot of nine-thirty

and go through the rigmarole with security again. The lobby is much less crowded at this time of day, and on the *Tasty* floor it's positively crypt-like. Felix the receptionist greets me like a long-lost sibling, hopes vociferously that I didn't get in trouble for being late yesterday, and asks if I don't just *love* my fellow interns. "They're such sweeties, you must feel right at home." He is a master of insincerity.

I agree that Rachel and Nin are treacle-pops and receive a featureless gray plastic card that, in the future, will get me through the security barriers downstairs.

No one else I know is in yet. Lexa's door is shut. Annabel's computer is on but she isn't at her desk. Even Nin and Rachel are nowhere to be found. But there are plenty of Tasty Girl applications to sort, so I get started, working as fast as I can in the hopes of finishing sometime before I have to go to school in the fall.

Nin arrives close to ten, also wearing wedge heels and a jean miniskirt. I consider bringing this up as a conversation starter. But I don't. As the day wore on yesterday, I understood that we are to be mortal enemies. The life of an intern is a constant struggle for interesting work. When I say *interesting,* I mean test-driving crème blushes and untangling the belts in the accessories closet—two scorching-hot assignments my rivals gloated over yesterday afternoon while I stayed in the intern closet with the letter opener. The tasks sound silly, but they aren't treated that way. And when you're as ambitious as Nin and Rachel, it's important that you spend the day making connections and doing favors for people. Between the two of them, they had worked out a method of sharing the spoils. Now that I'm here, it's a fight to the death.

Nonetheless, I greet Nin politely and observe, "The office starts pretty late."

She shrugs one bare, brown shoulder. "People get in at different times."

"My last job was working as an EMT. We had to get in at six-thirty."

"An EMT?" (pronounced "ay-em-tay"). She swivels in her chair to face me. "How *did* you get this job?"

I should lie and impress her, but I can't. "I met Lillian through my aunt, and she offered it to me. I don't know why."

"And who might Auntie be?"

"She's an art broker. She arranges deals for private clientele."

Nin regards me skeptically. "She's not involved in fashion? Does she have well-known designers as clients? Like, did she source the art for Elie Tahari's new place in the Hamptons?"

"Nothing like that." I shake my head. "Her clients are mainly in Europe."

"Very mysterious."

Nin repeats the story to Rachel when she gets in at eleven. And then, at eleven-thirty, they—almost nicely—suggest that if I'm bored opening envelopes, I could go score some page-proof distribution off Annabel's desk. "They're in her out-basket," Nin tells me. "We take them around every day."

Maybe they've decided to accept me.

I happily comply, since I'm itching to get out of the closet.

Annabel and Lexa still aren't in, but Beauty and most of the other desks along our corridor have filled up. I pick up the stack of proofs and set out.

The first inkling of trouble comes when I put my shoulder

to a door that I believe will lead me toward the fashion department and it's locked. I shove again, puzzled.

"You realize that's Art?" a passerby asks me. She's a ruddy,
middle-aged woman with unfortunate pigtails.

I've gotten turned around and stumbled upon the forbidden
lair of Shane Lincoln-Shane.

"I didn't, thanks." I walk casually away from the door,
shaken by my brush with disaster. "You don't happen to know
were I could find Kristen Drane, the fashion director, do you?"
I ask the woman. The tiny Chihuahua in her arms bares his
teeth and growls in my direction.

"Marc Jacobs, stop that," she says.

"Isn't he cute?" I say.

"He's a *she*," she says, scolding. "That's Kristen's assistant, Reese, right over there." Marc Jacobs bursts into frenzied
barking.

Now I remember. Kristen Drane's office is on one of the
long rows and is directly across from the kitchen, which strikes
me as a strange location for the office of a fashion director.

Her assistant has sunken dark eyes and a concave, Art Nou-
veau visage. She's wearing a high-necked, black Victorian
blouse, riding boots, and black shorts. She sighs when I walk
up. Her chair-pillow is a twisted botanical chintz of artichokes,
lizards, and thorns on a midnight-blue background.

"Hi, Reese." I find myself employing a hushed whisper, in
tribute to her sullen beauty. "I'm Kate, the new intern. I have
two stories for Kristen."

The stories are titled "Match Your Meds: A Designer for
Every Designer Drug" and "Oh Myla! or Icky Vicky? What
Your Panties Say About You."

Both stories are in quiz format. Nin told me this morning that it was Lillian's genius to combine self-discovery multiple choice with fashion spreads. A page I'm delivering to a different editor asks, "Are you tickled pink, feeling blue, or going mellow yellow?" A quiz follows, and each "Results" section is accompanied by silhouetted crop-tops, wedge sandals, over-sized sunglasses, vintage costume jewelry, and so on in pink, blue, or yellow. The brands are youthful, pricey, and trendy. The other galley I'm carrying is a beauty spread that determines if readers are ready for orange lipstick. Sample questions: Can you touch your toes? Do you like salt-and-vinegar potato chips? Were you terrorized in junior high by an elderly dancing mistress? Do you think your friends are honest with you?

I notice that the byline on the "Oh Myla!" story is Reese Malapin's.

"Did you write this?" I ask her.

"Yes, I wrote it. I went to Harvard. My senior thesis was a Marxist critique of the tiny bow on women's panties."

Her charcoal eyes blaze at me with disturbing intensity. I get the feeling that Reese Malapin is a girl with an axe to grind. And I don't want to be anywhere near her when she starts swinging. Tiny starbursts of broken blood vessels cluster on the knuckles of her right hand. A sign of bulimia. She sees me notic-ing and defensively tucks her hands away under her folded arms.

"Okay! Well, I'll just give this one to Kristen, then." I push Kristen's door open. Reese cries out a warning, but too late.

There's a person stretched out on the floor just in front of the desk.

She's waxen pale, with her arms folded over her chest in a

pose that looks more eternal-rest than cat-nap. I jump and shriek. The thing about fear—which I wrote a term paper on for Neurobiology 101—is that your body reacts before you have time to process what you're reacting to. Signals first pass through the amygdala, which gives the command for increased heart rate and breathing and muscle tension, and then travels on to the cortex, where you figure out if it makes sense to be afraid, or if it's a false alarm.

I know that there's nothing scary about seeing an editor sleeping.

I have plenty of time for my brain to process the signals and tell me "false alarm." But seeing her there is panic-inducing. The reaction is so purely physical that I find myself frozen, waiting for it to pass. Reese snatches the page proof from my hands and drags me away from the doorway. We stare at each other, stricken.

"Did you wake her?" she hisses.

"I don't think so!" I don't know what's wrong with me, but my flesh is one continual crawl.

"You almost got us both in *huge* trouble. Don't you know—"

Lexa has appeared on the scene. Gently, she draws the door to Kristen's office shut. Then she puts a limp, icy hand on my arm.

"Kate, I've just had my morning routine disturbed by two phone calls about you. Complaints."

All the assistants within earshot are paying very close attention.

"What kind of complaints?"

"That's in confidence, Kate." She's gently guiding me away

from Kristen Drane's office, back toward our end of the floor. "One of the reasons I've been so successful is that I always suss out the lay of the land when I arrive in a new job. I suggest you do the same. Get to know your surroundings before jumping right in with people. You should know who an editor is and what her section is about before you ever knock on her office door. Know what someone has written in the last issue before you start a conversation."

"I've read the last issue," I protest. "I just . . . I guess I didn't pay attention to the bylines or, um, the masthead."

She sighs. "*Real* magazine people read the masthead first."

My cheeks burn. She's right. I wouldn't have walked into a hospital job without first knowing who the staff is and what they specialize in.

"It won't happen again."

As Lexa silently escorts me back to my desk, I notice how many of the senior-staff offices are dark with a cracked-open door, just like Kristen's was. And most of the assistants I pass are whispering on the telephone, as if they're trying not to wake a sleeper.

"Lexa, is there something I should know about people's sleeping habits?"

Her look says that putting up with my stupidity is a great trial to her.

"How the senior editors spend their mornings isn't your concern. But as a rule of thumb, don't go knocking on doors before noon. People get started early on Mondays for the features meeting, but other than that we're a late office."

We're back at the intern closet. News must spread like wild-fire because Rachel and Nin—who I'm assuming set me up

for a result exactly like this—are both looking smug. In part-
ing, Lexa decrees that I concentrate solely on sorting the
applications for the Tasty Girl Contest. She promises to have
another mail cart full of them delivered just for me.

Mail carts around here are the size of pallet-loaders.

WHEN THE screaming starts I lurch upright in my chair. The
scream sounds again, rising hysterically until it's suddenly cut
off. Rachel and Nin are both away from their desks. Slowly and
quietly, I get up and look down the corridor.

Nothing.

I wait for the sound of running feet, but all is silent save for
the bleeping of phones and chatter of a distant fax machine.

Grabbing the heaviest metal object I can find, a three-hole
punch, I head for the source of the noise. It sounded like it
came from Lillian's end of the floor.

All is calm by Lexa's area—Annabel's computer is on, but
she is not at her desk. All's well in Beauty, too.

I sneak quietly toward Lillian's area, feeling silly, but also
genuinely concerned. Those sounded like real screams of
panic and terror. Lillian's door is shut. Around the corner, I
catch a flash of Annabel's highlighted ponytail, with two pens
stuck into it, disappearing into an open doorway. There are
muffled sounds of a struggle. "Shut up! You're causing a
scene!" I hear Annabel say, breathlessly.

Raising the three-hole punch, I dash over to the door,
which turns out to be to a supply closet. Annabel, mottled with
exertion, is pinning Bambi, Lillian's assistant, against the wall.
What in the hell is going on here?

"What in the hell is going on here?" I ask.

Annabel's buggy gray eyes roll toward me. "I'm glad you're here!" she cries. "Tell her to shut up! If anyone finds out, it'll be on StakeOut, and the magazine will be embarrassed!"

Bambi's cries grow louder when she sees me.

"Shut *up!*" Annabel lifts Bambi slightly off the ground, by the neck.

I'm surprised that Annabel is that strong. I'm also surprised that the first thing she thinks of in a crisis is what the blogs will say.

"Bambi, quiet!" I command. "Annabel, put her down right now!" I use my best scene-of-an-emergency tone, perfected in my previous life as an EMT. I may not know how to dress, but I sure can bark commands.

Annabel drops Bambi, who slides down the wall, hyperventilating. Her asymmetrical, goddess-drape jersey dress falls off her shoulder.

"Get me a paper bag," I tell Annabel, and push past her into the closet.

"Don't go in there!" Annabel cries. But it's too late. I've seen what Bambi saw.

Lying on the floor of the supply closet between some plastic bricks of the May issue and a circular step stool is the body of the Chihuahua I'd seen earlier. Marc Jacobs. Her diamond collar has been torn off and cast aside. *Oh my GOD.* I check the dog's vital signs, but Marc Jacobs, as they say, is over.

Remaining calm—sort of—in a medical emergency, I put my arm around Bambi and coax her out of the closet, gently pulling the door shut behind me.

"Someone called for a reprint of our April story on French

braiding," Bambi sobs, burying her tear-streaked face on my shoulder. "I opened the door and even before I flipped on the light I knew something was wrong."

"And the dog was like that?" I whisper.

"Yes. The closet is always locked. I don't know how he got in there."

"Annabel, go get Lauren. Quick!" I order, keeping my voice low. If Lillian's not here, I'm assuming the managing editor is next in line. At least that's what today's assiduous perusal of the masthead told me. "I'll make sure no one goes in."

Annabel nods, instructs me to cover Lillian's phone, and clatters off down the hall on her ladylike stilettos.

"Maybe he had a heart attack? I heard a lot of yapping. I didn't think anything of it," Bambi chokes out.

Sounds like Marc Jacobs to me. "Actually, he's a she. How long ago was she barking?" I ask.

"Around half an hour ago. But then she stopped and I forgot about it."

That's odd. Even a body as small as the Chihuahua's shouldn't have cooled so rapidly. Also, I saw two tiny white specks on her neck. They looked like dry white sores, or puncture wounds. But if they were puncture wounds, they ought to be bloody, and they weren't.

I need to look at them more closely.

"Bambi, sit down, try to breathe deeply," I tell her, pulling open the supply closet door.

Annabel stops me.

"Lauren's not at her desk!" she says, handing me the paper bag I asked for. She must have run all the way there and back. Fast.

I give the bag to Bambi, who obediently puts her face into it and starts breathing.

"Well, who else can we call?" I ask, distressed. A *Tasty* newbie, I'm the last person who should be handling this crisis.

"Um." Annabel is cracking under pressure. "I'm not sure. I've memorized the employee handbook but this wasn't covered." And then, seeming to notice me for the first time, she says, "Hey, is that an Eva McGraw slip dress you're wearing over that miniskirt?"

"You know who Eva McGraw is?" I'm shocked.

"I wrote a paper about that dress. It's a design classic." Her fashion-magazine chops kick in. "But it was longer."

"I re-sewed it."

"You re-sewed an Eva 4 Eva slip dress?" Annabel asks, looking truly horrified. "Didn't you know it's a collector's item?"

"No. I didn't know that."

"How'd you get that dress?"

"Eva McGraw was my mom." I can't believe that just popped out of my mouth.

Annabel's eyes widen. "*That,*" she says, "is very interesting."

"But please don't tell anyone." The last thing I need is people around here finding out about Eva.

"Hey," says a male voice. "I was just passing by and I heard screaming."

Intuitively I know who it is before I turn around—the guy from the meeting. And it is he—chiseled, scruffy, wearing destroyed khaki pants and a T-shirt that says *Hasselblad*. Today his eyes look like the color of melted caramel. He smiles slow and twinkly when he sees me. I'm not sure if he remembers me, or is just a flirt.

"Don't worry, darling, we're fabulous," says Annabel. She gives him an appreciative grin. "False alarm!"

"I work for Shane Lincoln-Shane," he says. "I know screaming when I hear it. And this was not the 'You photographed the model in the wrong top, you idiot' type of screaming. This was the real thing."

"Everything is *fine*," Annabel says.

But everything isn't fine.

"Can you look at something?" I ask, beckoning him toward the supply closet.

"With pleasure," he says. Despite the circumstances, the way he says *pleasure* causes a swoony feeling in my stomach. His eyes flick beyond me and go dark when he sees Marc Jacobs, forlorn and stiffening on the closet floor.

"Fuck," he says.

And then, to my great relief, he takes charge. He locks the closet door. He calls publisher Marion Morales's assistant from Bambi's phone. "Delores, it's James Truax. Listen, we have a problem over here and we're going to need you to track down Marion. You know where she is right now? Do you have her cell phone number? You're going to need to call it."

James Truax is calm and competent in a crisis. He takes it for granted that he can tell Annabel and me what to do. (All *I* do is tell Bambi when she can stop breathing into the paper bag.) Even when Oldham security shows up, he gives them instructions in how to keep people away from the area. No one did anything when the screaming was going on. But now, after things have quieted down, an awful lot of people seem to be stopping by to "distribute pages" or "just to see if Lillian's in."

Anthea Ferrari, a dark-haired woman who is the corporate

PR director, arrives twenty minutes later, harried, grouchy—and, by her own testimony, half microdermabraded. James greets her and graciously takes up a position on the sidelines next to me. We watch as she sends Bambi home for the day. We eavesdrop as Marc Jacobs's pigtailed owner—a contributing editor by the name of Susan Craigs—is found and informed. Some corporate bagmen dispose of the body. And too quickly, there's no reason for me to linger in the presence of James Truax. I want to express my thanks but end up standing there stupidly, staring at him. "I'm Kate McGraw, by the way," I finally blurt out.

"I know," he says, then adds, "Oh. James Truax. I'm in Photo."

I hold out my hand and we shake, awkwardly. *Why did I do that?*

James Truax from Photo has a firm grip, but not too firm. He seems tall, though he isn't much taller than I am. And something about the way he's making eye contact with me sparks the ridiculous idea that he's trying to impress me. I drop his hand. Another awkward pause falls between us. I start walking back toward my desk, and to my surprise, he follows me.

"How is your second day?" he asks.

"Great." Suddenly I can't keep up the pretense. "Just great. I've been scorned, publicly humiliated, tattled on, and now . . . whatever all that was about."

He shakes his head. "I'll tell you a secret. I am from a state called Ohio. Perhaps you've heard of it?"

I'm smiling.

"You have? Good. You're ahead of most of them. That woman you work for doesn't know Ohio from Idaho. And to her, if you're from an upstart colony and your family isn't super-rich, you're a nobody. You don't exist." He says this lightly. "If she's giving you a hard time, that means she's threatened by you. And that's not always a bad thing. Keep her on her toes and you'll go far."

He's very certain of himself. I haven't met many people like that. And though I'm not sure why Lexa would be threatened by me, I like his way of viewing things. "Well, okay. I'll take your advice," I say. "It shouldn't be too hard to keep getting into trouble. I can do that when I'm not even trying."

He laughs. "I'll do better than give advice. Why don't I buy you a drink?"

I'm about to analyze the connotations of this statement when he adds that we'll be meeting up with his roommate, Rico.

"We'll give Marc Jacobs a fitting send-off," he says, "and Rico can fill you in about Oldham. He's the accessories editor for *A Man's World*, and he got me this job. He's living proof that not all fashion people are assholes. I think this is you."

We've arrived back at the interns' closet. He looks into the room as if he's seeing it for the first time. It doesn't look good, since it's waist-deep in applications by wannabe Tasty Girls. I guess that mail cart Lexa promised arrived in my absence.

"They didn't splurge on the working conditions, did they?"

"There used to be a beanbag. But they removed it to make room for me. To popular dismay."

He laughs. "You definitely need that drink."

I open my mouth to say no thanks—drinks with a hot coworker sounds too high-stress—and agree to meet him downstairs at seven-thirty.

Fortunately, Nin and Rachel are still away from their desks and don't witness the invite or my acceptance.

Anthea Ferrari forbade us to talk about what happened to the poor little dog, on pain of legal consequences. But after several hours of logging applications, I decide this doesn't include Sylvia. I call her and fill her in. Since she's a devoted dog person, she gets so agitated she has to pull over her car in the parking lot of a Pinkberry.

"Honey, that's so fucked up," she says when she can talk. "Couldn't you have called an ambulance?"

I'm not sure they have veterinary ambulances. They should.

"The most disturbing part is I'm not convinced it was an accident," I tell her.

"What?" Graphic-novelist Sylvia is always ready to entertain a twisted plot. "Why?"

"I don't know. I just get a bad feeling from this place."

Speaking of that feeling, it's now seven P.M. and the floor is almost dark except for the pool of light from my desk lamp. "I went to the restroom just before I called you, and I could have sworn someone was watching me from behind the photocopier. And earlier today there was a cute blonde digging through the *trash* in the kitchen. She was collecting empty cups of this gross beet drink they all like. It's like they're wild animals."

"Well, you know how important intuition is," she says, seriously. "If you're really worried, I think you need more information. Investigate the scene of the crime. And keep your eye on everyone."

"Okay."

"And don't work too late."

"I have to. My only chance of impressing my boss is to get these contest entries sorted in record time." Since she's been depressed lately about being single I don't tell her that I'm waiting around for a maybe-date with an alarmingly hot coworker.

5

Thirsty

JAMES TRUAX IS waiting for me on the black-flagstone plaza, leaning up against a concrete planter, hands shoved into the pockets of his khakis. "Quick, let's go."

"What? Why?"

"Shh . . ."

"You're kidding, right?"

He doesn't answer me, but briskly walks down the street. Two blocks away he says, "Okay, you can talk now."

"What's the big rush?" I ask. I'm expecting him to say something about Marc Jacobs, or the vow of confidentiality we both signed hours beforehand.

"I try to stay out of the work tabloids," he says. "And Stake-Out isn't above writing about the photo assistant leaving with the new intern."

"Oh." An awkward pause descends. "That's ridiculous," I say.

He agrees. "It is. Especially since everyone knows I make it a rule not to date fashion chicks."

"Are you calling me a fashion chick?" This is a first.

"Are you implying that you want to date me?"

"No!"

He starts laughing. "Don't sugarcoat it for me."

"You know what?" I say. "I don't think I'm in the mood for a drink after all." I stop on the street corner and fold my arms against a slight chill in the balmy, evening air.

"Oh, come on. Don't be mad. I was just kidding you."

"I'm not mad, I'm tired. I've had a long, weird day. I just want to go home."

"All the more reason for a drink. Come on. Forgive me. I'm poorly socialized."

Somehow I doubt this. I suspect James Truax gets whatever he wants. The light changes and I follow him across the street. "If you're so against fashion girls, why did you want to have a drink with me?"

"You held up pretty well today. I didn't see any of those debutantes you work with getting Bambi to breathe into a paper bag. So what's your story?" he asks me. "Why did you jump in there like Meredith Grey in couture?"

"These are homemade clothes, not couture. The reason I knew what to do with Bambi was because in my real life I've been working as an EMT and I'm enrolled in med school in the fall. I'm going to be a doctor. Why do you work at *Tasty* if you're so anti-fashion?"

"I'm a photographer. The job helps me make connections. And it also pays pretty well, so I can save up money to go shoot what I really want to shoot."

"What do you really want to shoot?"

"Nothing you would be interested in."

"You just met me, how can you know what I'm interested in?" I say, surprised—and impressed—by my skill with the sassy comeback. If you didn't know me better, you'd think I was flirting.

"The next art project I'm planning is in Guatemala."

"I built houses in Guatemala one summer with Ameri-Cares," I volunteer smugly, "the summer after my senior year in high school. It was one of the best jobs I've ever had."

We've stopped in front of a narrow storefront lit with a neon Heineken sign.

James Truax makes eye contact for a second. I'm mesmerized by his dark stare.

"Here we are." He opens the door and then waits for me to walk through it, chivalry unusual for a man his age. He puts his hand on the small of my back to guide me past a long bar to a darkish area with carved wooden booths.

Waiting in one of the booths, smoking—I didn't know you could still do that indoors—is a guy wearing a fedora and a natty white blazer over a cotton tank top that says *Bundeswehr*.

"Sit down, kittens, and tell me everything," he commands, blowing a cloud of smoke into our faces. "I hear there was a dogicide at *Tasty* High?"

This, I gather, is Rico. James summons the waitress for drinks. I whisper to him, "We signed a nondisclosure."

Rico hears me.

"Puhleeze, darling. You aren't going to start being loyal to Oldham, are you? The bosses would mix cocktails with our blood if it served their purposes."

"I don't know. I'm the my-word-means-something type." Though I told Sylvia.

"Kate's idealistic," James says. "Rumour has it she graduated from Brown a year ago."

"That's soooo sweet." Rico exhales another cloud of smoke. "Here's what we'll do, darling. *James* will tell me everything, and then the kitty cat will be out of the bag through no fault of your own, and we can discuss freely."

James launches into the story, and after a brief struggle with my conscience, I help him. Innocence-on-a-technicality isn't really my style.

"Very weird," Rico proclaims, delighted. "So what's our theory, gang? Do we suspect the contributing editor of some foul neglect of her puppy?"

James shrugs. "I don't know her."

"I met her in the hall earlier today," I say, "before the thing happened with Marc Jacobs—the dog's a she, by the way. I don't think she neglected her dog. She seemed protective of her. And the corporate people were sure it was an accident."

"Of course, accidents can happen to anyone," Rico leans over the table to whisper conspiratorially. "But so can scandals, and they're much more fabulous. If the contributing editor is innocent, the guilty party must be a staffer."

Rico obviously *loves* gossip.

"Lillian is a dark horse, don't you think?" he continues. "And those vamps she's brought on board with her, brrr . . . Wouldn't want to meet one of them in a dark alley—or a darkened supply closet."

"I don't know. I don't really know anyone yet."

"Not knowing someone never stopped Rico from talking about them," James interjects.

Rico rolls his eyes. "Were you aware that two *Tasty*-affiliated people have died since Lillian topped the masthead? *Now* what do you think of her?"

"He also likes to read the gossip blogs," James adds.

"Jimmy!" Rico scolds. "Do you want your new girlfriend to have a bad impression of me?"

"Rico. Do you want me to do your next batch of head shots for free?"

This appears to be a potent threat because Rico says, "Sorry. I know you're not his 'girlfriend,'" putting the last word in air quotes.

James scowls.

"I've barely even seen Lillian," I quickly interrupt. "I'm just an intern."

"And James hasn't filled you in?"

"I don't concentrate on office politics," James says.

"Well, darling, there are some unwritten rules about Lillian Hall. One, don't ride in the same elevator with her. You haven't, have you?"

"No."

"Thank God. You might yet survive. Two, she can't stand the smell of garlic. That's why none is served in the cafeteria."

"I haven't been to the cafeteria yet."

"Good. Three, no one bigger than a size six is allowed on the floor. Never, ever invite a fat friend up to *Tasty*, or suggest an overweight person for a job."

"That's horrible."

"That's fashion, babygirl. Four, she always sits in the same chair in the conference room, at the fashion shows, at Carnivoré, and anywhere else she goes. But no one on staff tells newcomers *which chair it is.*"

"Are you trying to make me paranoid?" I glance at James, wondering if this is all an elaborate leg-pull.

Rico seizes my hands. "I'm trying to save your skin. Or at least your job. Are you listening to me?"

"I am. When in doubt, remain standing until Lillian has already sat down."

"Also, you should always be able to answer the question 'What was she wearing?' Lillian expects total sartorial recall. Like, Susan Craigs, the Marc Jacobs girl, stumbles distraught onto the scene in . . . ?" He snaps his fingers and says "Snap" at the same time.

"Pigtails." I'm good at this game. "Paul & Joe floral demi-sleeve blouse from two seasons ago. Paper Denim & Cloth miniskirt. Stackable blue rubber bracelets. And . . . some kind of strappy slip-on heels with the plastic-looking base. Maybe Gucci or Louis Vuitton. Overall, I'd say she was rocking a kind of eighties-resort look."

Rico raises an eyebrow. "I'm impressed. I wouldn't have suspected that you would have TFR—Total Fashion Recall."

James, on the other hand, looks at me like I've grown two heads.

I shrug. "I don't *buy* international luxury brands but I like to read about them."

"So if Susan Craigs is 'eighties-resort,' what am I?" Rico asks.

"Gay Casablanca," I blurt, hoping he won't be offended.

He's not. "Mmmm. Bogart. I love it. And what's yours?"

"Oh, I don't know. Recycle-iste? Almost all my clothes are repurposed from something else."

"How about Lillian Hall?"

"Lillian's got the best style. She always looks pulled-together, but also kind of dangerous. Victorian editrix."

Rico calls for another round of drinks because, "Marc Jacobs would have wanted it that way."

Once we're working on our second round, Rico becomes even more confidential.

"Did you tell her, honey, about the *other* mysterious violent incident to happen at *Tasty* this year?"

"Honey" in this case means James, who stares at him curiously. "What incident?"

"Hello!" Rico cries. "You were there! The casting call gone awry?"

James nods, explaining, "One of the models hurt herself at a casting call."

Rico and I both wait for further detail but none is forthcoming.

"Straight men are *the worst* storytellers," Rico sighs. "His boss was doing a casting call, so, as usual, there are about fifteen or twenty gorgeously androgynous young women clustered around Art and Photo. The casting was for a bathing-suit story, the girls were being Polaroided in their underwear, and there was a lot of confusion as people were getting dressed and undressed. The girls were using an empty office to change. And between one thing and another no one saw what happened."

"What happened?" I can't help it. I'm hooked.

"We still don't know!" Rico says salaciously. "But when the elevator doors opened at A *Man's World*, Roger Whiteman, 'The Elegant Gentleman,' was greeted by the sight of a disoriented teenaged model wearing only Victoria's Secret 'Pink' and a sheath of bright red blood. Roger Whiteman is gay and about seven hundred years old, so you can imagine how shocking it was for him."

"*What?*" I can't shake the sense that Rico is putting me on. "What happened?"

"All we know is that the security camera in the elevator and the one in *Tasty* reception show the same thing. The girl pulled her *Carrie* move before she left the floor. She claimed she didn't remember a thing."

"What was the source of the bleeding?" I ask.

"It was horrible, darling, tiny incisions all over her arms and torso. A few of them quite deep. No one knows what caused them."

"And what did the police say?"

"You know how corporations just *hate* photographs of the police storming into their headquarters. It was all handled in-house. And I think it was decided that she'd done it herself to get attention."

"She was a confused girl," James says. "She probably saw some brutality-chic photos and thought she'd found a creative way to get herself in the game. The difference between a fashion spread and a trailer for *Saw III* is becoming less and less obvious. Some people say it's Lillian's influence."

"But then why go get on the elevator in your underwear, before you've had your picture taken?" Rico asks.

"I don't know about the details." James turns to me. "Take my word for it. There's nothing to worry about."

"Nothing to worry about as long as you're not in the fashion business," Rico adds. "There was that other lurid murder this spring where two girls died in the Jean Saint-Pierre atelier. You remember?"

I shrug apologetically.

"I guess you wouldn't have heard about it out in the provinces. They hushed it up pretty well."

"Do you think you should be engaging in this kind of distasteful speculation?" James interrupts. "Kate's new in the office. Does she need to hear all the gory details?"

"Yes," I say.

"Yes!" Rico says.

James shakes his head and busies himself stirring his drink.

"Jean Saint-Pierre has a simply breathtaking atelier in the Fashion District in one of those former warehouse buildings with huge windows, pressed tin ceilings, and wooden floors. This spring he decided to forgo a show in favor of having a one-day open house. I don't approve, but more and more designers are doing it that way.

"Anyway, it was a huge success. Fashion came out in force. And everyone agreed that the collection returned the focus to the body but without giving up the volumizing elements that have made Jean Saint-Pierre so re-relevant with the past few collections."

"Lexa was wearing Jean Saint-Pierre on your first day of work yesterday," James says. "That black top."

I look at him, surprised that he noticed.

"I have a good visual memory," he disclaims.

"Oh, sweetie," Rico says laughing, "That's what they all say."

"Is that what it's called these days?" I ask.

James comfortably tells us to go to hell. "Finish the story for Kate," he prompts.

"Two people excused themselves for a smoke in the stairwell and never came back. No one noticed. They weren't big names. One was a buyer for a Midwestern department chain. Another girl was from *Yarn Daily* and was lucky to have been on the list. A seamstress found them the next day, stuffed behind some rolls of crepe de chine. Their throats had been cut and the buyer was missing her Birkin bag."

"That's . . . grisly. I can't believe it. What did the police say?"

"Chiqua, the police only investigate things on TV. In the real world they say 'Huh?', scratch their asses, and move on to the next problem. I think they got the seamstress deported."

THE DING of the elevator door opening into Victoria's apartment doesn't seem so muted when I get home at one A.M. I hope I'm not waking her up.

I jimmy my shoes off and sneak into the living room, wishing there was someone to tell about my first evening out in New York City. The flat-screen, however, is once again hidden behind the Caspar David Friedrich painting and there are no signs of life. My aunt may not even be home. Walking past the door to the master bedroom confirms my suspicion. The door is open, the spot-lighting illuminates the scary succubus painting hanging over the bed, but its red velvet cover—matching the one in my room—is unrumpled.

Victoria stays out awfully late for a fifty-year-old woman.

Feeling a little less proud of my own "wild" evening, I curl up in bed with a notebook and a pen and work on that list of stories I might want to write that Lauren asked me to prepare until I fall asleep.

6

Hot, Young Blood

F A PERSON sets her mind to it, she can open and log contest entries pretty fast.

I show up early the morning after drinks with James and Rico and work at a breakneck pace. Rachel and Nin periodically help out, and by noon the empty mail buckets are stacked up in the hallway outside our door and I have a densely populated Excel spreadsheet in hand. We're done.

"Let's go give this to Lexa," I suggest to Nin, who is at her desk. Rachel is on some errand related to her blog. I still haven't summoned the courage to ask her what the blog is about or what the URL is.

"We're away from our posts, I see," Lexa says when Nin and I knock on her open door.

Annabel's head pops up; she looks outraged. The girl is on her hands and knees cleaning out the space under Lexa's credenza while trying not to be run over by her chair.

"I'm sorry I haven't been able to watch them better today," she apologizes.

"We just came to let you know that we're done. And we brought you this." I hand over the spreadsheet.

Lexa peers at it through her glasses. "Well done," she says grudgingly. "We'll schedule a meeting . . . at a convenient time . . ." she trails off and starts snapping her fingers. Annabel leaps to her feet and races out of the office, returning in a flash with Lexa's appointment book.

"Tomorrow you're judging the accessory awards all afternoon," she says, looking worried.

Lexa keeps snapping.

"You could do it *exactly* at noon?" Annabel volunteers.

"Get Art and Photo in the meeting. And book the conference room," Lexa commands. Her squinty green eyes pass over Nin and me where we remain trembling on her threshold. "As a reward," she tells us, "interns can come to the meeting."

"Lexa is great about mentoring." My eyes meet Annabel's wide, gray ones. She's given no hint of it in her tone, but just the same I detect sarcasm.

When we've left Lexa's office, I tell Nin I'm heading for the ladies' room, but instead I approach Lillian's area. With Rico's horrible stories percolating in my brain, I want — no, need — to revisit the scene of the crime.

The supply closet door is locked.

In Bambi's chair sits a delicate-looking girl with a tiny nose ring. She introduces herself as Sari. Since it's very unlikely anyone has told Sari about the events of yesterday, I ask her if she has a key for the supply closet. She doesn't, but helpfully suggests that there might be one in Lillian's office.

"Can you come back later?" she asks. "She's not in and

I shouldn't go in there. It's my first day and I barely had a chance to meet Lillian."

Even better.

"Oh!" I beam at her. "Lillian's really nice! I'll just go in and get it myself. She won't mind!"

I sidle into Lillian's huge corner office, disappointed to see that even here the blinds are drawn tightly shut. The room is nice, though. Lillian has Oriental rugs and instead of a desk, she uses an antique hardwood table. Interestingly, a fresh beet juice already sits on its polished surface. I wonder where it came from, since Sari's too inexperienced to know her boss's favorite beverage. A brief perusal of the desk's spick-and-span surface doesn't turn up any keys. Nor are there any keys on a heavy black glass conference table stacked with fashion books. On the wall facing the table is a bulletin board thick with photos of Lillian at various events—Lillian receiving awards, Lillian in period costume, press clippings with Lillian's name highlighted. Lexa has something similar in her office, but less populated. There are no keys tacked to the bulletin board. A big crate takes up one corner. I walk over to it, surprised to discover that it smells like earth. I am both fascinated and repelled by the dank, musty smell. What the hell could be in that?

"Can I help you?" a flat voice asks.

Lillian Hall, the woman Herself, has silently materialized right behind me.

For a second I'm too shocked to do more than gawk down at her. A tiny mink stole—complete with the head and feet—curls around her drooping marble-white shoulders. She's wearing huge ruby earrings in addition to the rings and a corset-looking top. Very S&M princess on Zoloft. It is only now that I realize I'm much taller than she is.

"What are you doing in my office?" she sighs, as if the answer can be of no interest to her.

I've never been a particularly apt liar, but inspiration strikes. "I wanted to come thank you in person for arranging this internship for me."

"Sit down," she intones.

I sink into one of the tall-backed chairs as if shoved.

Lillian walks over to the door and looks out, toward Sari.

"You're fired," she says. "I won't have an assistant allowing people into my office when I'm not here."

Sari starts crying.

I try to get up but have no strength. "It's my fault, Lillian," I blurt. "I told her it was okay." Oh my God. First the beanbag, and now this. I am a menace.

Lillian shuts her door. "She shouldn't have listened to you, *cherie*."

"I told her you wouldn't mind," I say. "I said you were nice."

Her face remains blank but it looks like the corner of her mouth almost twitches upward. "Then you lied." She looks marginally more animated. "You are your mother's daughter. Not many interns would dare to come into my office."

She knew Eva? I want to know when and how, but tell myself this isn't the moment to ask. "Don't fire Sari for my mistake," I plead.

Lillian sighs heavily. "Don't bore me," she slurs. "I'm so sick of being bored."

Moving as if she's floating—how does she do that?—she approaches me and pulls up a seat. For a few long minutes she just stares. I'm reminded of Rico's warning not to share her elevator. Could it really be dangerous to be alone with her?

She edges her chair a little closer to mine. It's amazing how bloodlessly pale she is. Round blue eyes. Heart-shaped face. She's wearing a strange, strong, swampy-smelling perfume. At least I hope it's perfume.

She's so close that her bare knees touch mine. I'm pressed all the way back in the chair. What does she want with me?

"You're so fresh and young," she sighs. "So alive. I can *feel* the life in you. All that hot, young blood pulsing through those tender little veins."

I wonder, for a crazy second, if she's going to kiss me — her perfect, poreless face is so near mine and the strange smell has intensified. It might be her breath. Is Lillian a lesbian? Her lips part. I catch a glimpse of the sharp, white teeth I'd noticed before, and shiver.

The moment passes.

She gets up and retrieves her beet juice. "How old do you think I am?"

A Victoria-rule comes in handy: Take your honest estimate of a person's age; double the number of the decade and then subtract it from the honest estimate, to achieve a polite under-estimate. So if you think a woman is twenty-nine, you double the decade to get four; subtract four from twenty-nine and tell her you think she's twenty-five. If a woman looks sixty-five to you, say she looks fifty-three. And so on. It's like the frat-boy equation that the youngest girl a guy can respectably date is "half your age plus seven."

"You look twenty-nine," I tell Lillian, cutting down my esti-mate of about thirty-five. I'd think she should be even older than that, but her skin is way too smooth. "But I don't think you can be, because you're the editor-in-chief."

This is the right thing to say. Her mouth definitely turns upward this time.

"I feel eight hundred and fifty years old. It doesn't show?"

"Not at all," I say. And then, with sincerity, because this is true: "You don't look old in any way. You could be a super-model."

"As the years go by, I find myself having to spend more and more time in spas. Not to keep my looks, but to remain fresh and, how shall I say, *alluring*."

"You can do acupuncture, spa treatments," I tell her. "Though from what I've read, getting enough vitamins makes a huge difference in a person's energy levels."

She goggles like I've lost my mind, then bursts into rusty-sounding laughter.

"I could write down the names of a couple of good multi-vitamins for you—"

"That won't be necessary. Thank you. I have a vitamin-rich diet. Though I don't get to eat as much as I would like."

"Who does?" I sympathize.

"You really have no idea!" She laughs again. The tiny hairs on the back of my neck known colloquially as hackles flutter. There's something very weird about this woman. My gut is telling me to get out of here, and fast, but some other, perverse part of me feels sorry for her. She seems lonely, a feeling I understand these days. Maybe all these stories about how scary she is are a self-fulfilling prophecy.

"Can I help you out at all?" I ask. "Now that you've fired Sari, would you like me to answer your phone until you find a new assistant?" The words are out of my mouth before I can think better of it.

She's surprised by the offer, I can tell, but after thinking for a moment, she likes it. "Yes," she says slowly. "That has . . . possibilities. Lexa will be miffed that I'm stealing you away from her, but she'll survive," she says, and smirks. "You can fill in until HR sends another temp over. And from now on you will cover for my assistant during her lunch break."

"I'm honored." I'm horrified. What have I gotten myself into?

I'm on my feet and bolting for the door when she calls after me, "Just one thing, Kate. Stay away from that supply closet."

IT'S JUST my luck that Lexa is waiting for me in the hallway when I finally get back to my desk an hour later, after covering Lillian's phone until a temp arrived to replace Sari. My heart sinks when I see my boss's blonde pouf.

"Hi, Lexa!" I try cheerfulness. "Have you come to see the finished work?" I point at the four towering stacks of Tasty Girl applications, in folders and sorted by state.

She sinks her claw into my upper arm. "Into my office. Now."

She half-drags me down the corridor, moving so fast it's hard for me to keep up. Those fashionably emaciated limbs pack incredible strength.

She shoves me in front of her and I stumble in the darkness, tangling briefly with her guest chair before catching my balance. This is crazy. I've never heard of a job in the modern world involving physical abuse at the hands of one's employer. Except for celebrity assistants and Naomi Campbell's maids.

Lexa clicks on the lights.

I draw myself up, trying to regain some dignity.

"What are you bloody well trying to accomplish?" Lexa shrieks. "What were you doing in Lillian's office?"

She looks unhinged.

"Nothing, I—"

"I warned you to stay away from her. She'll blame me! You don't have a sodding clue. . . ."

"She wasn't mad, Lexa. I swear, it's okay."

I remember Sari's fate and hope that this is true.

Lexa stops short. "She wasn't mad? How about displeased?" she asks.

"At first maybe a little. But she asked me to answer her phone until Human Resources could send over a temp assistant. That's why I've been away from my desk for so long. I'm sorry." My explanation tumbles over itself.

"You mad cow. I'm under a lot of *pressure*, Kate. New country. New publicists. New paparazzi. Those American spelling rules. A person in my position has to do everything *right*. I can't afford to make mistakes. I've only been mentioned in the gossip columns *three* times since I crossed the pond. Do you know what that means?"

"I'm sorry. I'm sure it must be difficult for you," I placate her.

"You have no idea. And you Yanks are so strict. The rules of conduct here are much more severe than in the U.K."

I don't know what she's talking about, but she seems to be calming down. "If you don't want me to answer Lillian's phone, I don't have to."

"Are you trying to get me fired?" Lexa screams. "Of course you have to do *exactly* what Lillian tells you to." Air hisses out from between her teeth. "You are a disaster," she spits. "I knew it from the beginning. You can't be trusted. You'll answer Lillian's phone, but other than that, you'll stay in that intern room, at your desk, not getting into trouble, for the rest of the summer. Don't bother coming to that Tasty Girl meeting tomorrow. No more meetings for you at all. And I don't want to see you talking to another editor, ever again. Full stop."

"But—" I protest.

"Now get out of my office."

LEXA IS clinically insane. That's clear to me now. But knowing that doesn't help. I'm trembling with the shock of the confrontation. My eyes brim over. So no one else sees me crying at work, I slip into the ladies' room. It's always deserted.

Except, of course, for today.

Annabel is leaning over a sink, crying. She's wearing a striped, short-sleeved cashmere sweater and patterned skirt from, I jealously suspect, Thakoon. The fair skin on her neck and chest is broken out in big red welts.

"Are you okay?" I ask, dashing the tears from my eyes.

"I'm fine," she sniffles. "I just came in here to be by myself for a minute."

"But you're covered in welts," I persist.

"They *promised* me it wouldn't be this way anymore. I have these allergies that were supposed to be cured, but they aren't yet."

Medically, this is an unrealistic expectation. You can treat allergies with drugs or procedures like sinus drainage, but you can't cure them. "What are you allergic to?"

"Everything. Pollen. Dust. Cosmetics." She laughs bitterly. "And before I was promoted to being Lexa's assistant, I worked in the beauty closet. My eyes have been itchy since I started working here." For emphasis she rubs her bloodshot gray eyes. "This morning Lexa made me sort out some products for her to take home."

"That's awful. She knows you're allergic?"

Annabel suddenly looks wary. "She knows. But it's complicated. She thought it would be okay."

Talk about protecting your abuser. I must look as disapproving as I feel because she sniffle-laughs. "Don't worry about me. I'm fine."

She's been rude to me ever since I started working here, but in this moment she seems vulnerable.

"You know what you need?" I offer. "Cortisone cream. You should go buy some."

"No thanks. If I ride the elevator down looking like this, someone will take my picture and post it on a blog. I'd rather itch. Hey," she says. "Is this another Eva 4 Eva ensemble?"

"It is." But I don't want to talk about Eva. "About that cream . . ."

"Wait a minute." A calculating look crosses her face. "Do you want to go to a party tonight? I have a plus one."

"What kind of party?" My hand is already on the door handle. I thought Annabel was being nice to me because no one was looking. I'm surprised—and suspicious—that she wants to be seen out in public with me.

"Saks is celebrating the return of the flare-legged jean. You'll get a couple of free pairs."

Free pairs of three-hundred-dollar jeans?

She misinterprets my expression.

"Don't worry. Saks always has good swag. They give me a Coach bag every season." She shrugs disinterestedly, as if Coach bags are peanuts to her.

Swag, I've already learned, is the magazine editor's term for the barrage of free luxury goods sent to them by corporate PR people. So much of it comes in each day that various departments have "giveaways" to get rid of it. Nin and Rachel are obsessed with this feature of the job, and have told me all about their various scores.

A party where they're giving out jeans but the crowd is too glamorous to be impressed sounds stressful to me. Also, I was just out at a bar until after midnight last night with James and Rico. I really don't think I should go. I deflect the issue. "Flare-legged jeans are back?"

Annabel rolls her eyes and sighs disgustedly. "I know! Jeans just got skinny!"

"I think it's too soon," I opine. "Fashion won't go for it."

"They're just trying to confound us," she says. "It's annoying."

Hey, this is just like talking to Sylvia! I can do this!

"But we can still go to the party."

It's one thing to talk fashion nonsense, but another to go to a real fashion party. "I don't know." I try to come up with an excuse she'll accept. "I'm not really dressed for it."

Annabel surveys me. "I don't think this is so bad," she says.

I assume that from her it's high praise. I'm wearing my mesh and rubber eco shoes and an Eva 4 Eva chemise-top black silk slip dress with a tattered, irregular hemline, under a forties thrift-store mini-jacket. I've tied a black velvet ribbon around my wrist. "I don't know." I hesitate. "Will other people from work be there?"

"*Everyone* who is anyone will be there."

That's what I was afraid of.

"Take off that jacket."

I shrug free, exposing my pale arms, little moles, dark arm hair, and other fashion faux pas. I'm extra-regretting that I didn't wear a bra this morning. True, the only kind of support I need a bra for is of the moral variety. But still.

Annabel continues her scrutiny. "The ribbon is a little too high-contrast."

I remove it.

"What's up with the shoes?"

"They're from recycled tires. They're environmentally responsible."

"Oh! That's great, then. Green is the new black."

I can't tell if she's kidding.

STAKEOUT POSTS a story about the sudden death of our contributing editor's dog around four. I'm back at my desk, quietly taping Lexa's expense receipts to sheets of blank eight-by-eleven paper, when Rachel says, "This is outrageous. Why does StakeOut always pick on us? They're saying someone here killed a dog?"

I jump guiltily, giving myself a paper cut. I keep my voice neutral. "You guys think it's just a rumor? About the dog?"

Rachel sighs. "It's obvious what's fake and what's real on that site. If you had an instinct for news, you would know that."

Reluctantly, I type in the URL for StakeOut. I'm hoping it can shed some light on a deeply disturbing event.

ONE BITCH DOWN . . .
Starving Minions at *Tasty* Make Puppy Chow

We have no confirmation on this, but it's juicier than a
big rare steak, and bloodier, too. We hope it's true. Is
that so wrong? This is what we've been waiting for since
our favorite lady vamp took the reins at *Tasty:* a moment
when Miuccia's monsters show their true colors. Brace
yourselves, soldiers of the light: Yesterday afternoon at
Oldham, contributing editor Susan Craigs (author of *My
Closet, Myself*) was seen in the lobby with Marc Jacobs,
her (female) Chihuahua. Two hours later Craigs, dog-free
and looking drugged, was spotted leaving the building
in the company of two burly dudes in suits who could
only have been Oldham Secret Security troops. (That's
the OSS. We didn't know it existed before, either, but
everything is falling into place.) Since neither Craigs nor
goons were wearing anything worthy of comment, our
sisters at FashionLobby.com didn't get pictures. Rumor
has it that the Chihuahuaaahhhhh met with a mysterious
untimely end (i.e., someone at *Tasty* tore its throat out
and drank its blood). Anyone who knows which staffer
did the dirty and which one disposed of the body, drop
us a line. . . .

TAGS: OLDHAM INC., LILLIAN HALL, UNEXPLAINED DEATH,
CHIHUAHUAS, MARC JACOBS

Clicking around, I learn that StakeOut has a running joke
that Lillian and other *Tasty* editors are vampires. I'm surprised

it's legal to say the stuff they say about them. And I'm uneasy that the site got this information. Who talked? Well, I did, for one. . . .

"Are you scared now, Kate?" Nin asks, one bendy-straw thin leg draped over the arm of her office chair. She's swiveled to face me. She's wearing a daisy-yellow blouse with black puffy sleeves like Mickey Mouse ears that make her arms look like twigs.

"Maybe we all should be scared."

She and Rachel exchange glances—*How much of a loser can she be?*—and move on to pointedly discuss an upcoming benefit *Tasty* is hosting at the media hot-spot restaurant Carnivoré. I'm tempted to tell them that I'll be going to a party myself tonight. Maybe I'll see them there.

Or maybe they're not invited.

7

A Finger on the Pulse

We're on a rooftop bar overlooking Gramercy Park. Black-and-white-clad caterers stand at the ready with trays of full wineglasses. In one corner, models wearing flare-legged jeans go through their paces. Scattered showers of flashbulbs announce the arrival of each celebrity. I've ID'd Milla Jovovich, Jonathan Rhys Meyers, and Luke Wilson.

Unfortunately, Annabel ditched me as soon as we walked in the door. Which leaves me standing by myself, nervously sipping my wine too fast and trying not to gawk, look out of place, or do anything else to draw attention to myself. My social anxiety isn't helped by the fact that I've spotted James Truax's tousled head through the crowd. He's working, adjusting the lights for a concurrent flare-legged-jeans photo shoot.

"Mwah-Mwah!" Two girls air-kiss in front of me.

"I love *your* look!" Both are wearing cropped leggings with ballet flats and elaborate blouses.

"I love *yours!*"

"Mwah-Mwah!" They air-kiss again and part ways.

A storm of flashbulbs at the door announces the arrival of Someone. I recognize Dolce and Gabbana.

A woman in a tall, elaborate hat and no pants swans by me, chatting on her mobile phone. A double take confirms that she's wearing thick, nude tights (I can see the waistband) under a bandeau halter in the new mini-muumuu style.

That reminds me: A telephone is a great accessory. I dial Sylvia. Perhaps I'll look in-demand instead of outcast. She picks up on the first ring.

"Guess where I am right now? A real, live celebrity-studded party for Saks Fifth Avenue department store." It should really be *her* on a rooftop overlooking New York City; she's always dreamed of living here. I run through the trends on display for her — ruffle-tanks, Victoriana, skinny shorts, trapeze tops, cropped leggings . . .

"Ugh," she says. "I'm on my way to Culver City for the second time today, and all because of shorty leggings. Nico is *obsessed*."

Sylvia's job entails driving all over L.A. buying clothes and then returning them a week later, sometimes after they've been worn on television (shopping bulimia!). The shows don't have the prestige that *Tasty* does, and so aren't able to borrow the clothes from the brands' PR departments. And the shops are naturally suspicious, so Sylvia's always stressed out, feeling like a criminal and trying to find stores she hasn't hit yet.

The silver lining is, she claims, the pressures of the job plus all the running around have made her lose weight. Since she was bookish and plump all through school, I can't quite imagine her as a size six.

"How are things going with Nico?" I ask, referring to her crazy cokehead boss.

"She made me put zit cream on her back this morning. And then she volunteered to set me up with her younger brother."

Nico has some boundary issues.

"Are you going to go out with him?"

"Oh . . ." Sylvia trails off. I can hear horns blare in the background. "I'm going to put it off and hope she forgets." She *hates* dating.

I spot Annabel talking to a group of people including Kristen Drane, the fashion director, whom I have previously only seen asleep. I reluctantly sign off with Sylvia and approach the group.

"You are working for Lexa, right?" the woman with curly brown hair and painted freckles—now that I see her up close, I can tell they definitely *are* painted on—asks me. "I heard her yelling at you this morning."

"Is that why you were crying as you walked into the bathroom?" Annabel asks.

"We haven't met," I say, attempting to change the subject. "Kate McGraw."

"I'm Noë Childs, the beauty director."

"Nice to meet you, Noë." I'll bet that when Lexa forbade me to talk to anyone on staff for the rest of the summer, that included at parties. "Lexa's not going to be here tonight, is she?"

"Oh, probably," Kristen says. "Lexa doesn't miss the opening of a shoe box."

Kristen has slanty, feral blue eyes, a slash nose, and perfect posture. She's smoking. I'm shocked that she would say something so disrespectful about a coworker in front of me, an intern. Backbiting, it seems, is de rigueur.

Kristen continues, "Even Lillian will show up eventually. They're giving out Crème de la Mer cellulite cream to go with the jeans."

"Lillian has cellulite?" Noë gasps, obviously enjoying herself.

"I haven't inspected it personally, darling," Kristen says. "But you must have noticed she's simply *obsessed* with product. She keeps expanding your section at the expense of mine."

"So why were you crying? What set Lexa off?" Noë persists, perhaps trying to change the subject herself.

"Lillian wants me to answer her phone during her assistant's lunch break," I say, unwillingly. "And Lexa thought I'd mess it up and get her in trouble."

Everyone gapes at me.

"Lillian talked to you?"

"And she didn't fire you?"

"What did you say to her?"

"Nothing. I don't know. She said she felt old."

They exchange meaningful glances.

"Kate's mom is Eva McGraw, from Eva 4 Eva," Annabel says, apropos of nothing.

Kristen snorts and puffs on her cigarette. "Is that an Eva McGraw slip dress?" she asks. "I thought it looked familiar."

"Oh my God. I loved Eva 4 Eva," Noë cries. "I wore one of her dresses every day my first summer in New York!" She gazes at me fondly.

My brain is whirling. I grab another glass of white wine off a passing tray and take a deep gulp. I had no idea that Eva was this popular. The only reason that's ever been given to me for her depression was that her last collection *failed*. If she had this many fans, surely she could have bounced back from one lousy fall.

"Did you know Gene Gantor loved your mom's designs?" Annabel asks.

"I don't know who Gene Gantor is," I admit, and wait for her to heap scorn on me.

"I wrote a paper on him. He was the editor-in-chief of British *Vogue* for thirty-five years—notoriously, the only straight man in fashion. He was a total diva, and famously a nightmare, but he had one of the world's greatest eyes." Annabel tells me that Eva was one of Gene Gantor's favorite rising stars during the last years of his rule. Apparently, my mom used to hang out with Le Gantor, as Annabel calls him, when he was "Stateside."

"After you told me that she was your mom, I Googled her and found a picture of them together at the Bowery Bar. I'll send you the link."

I don't want to be here. I don't want to be talking about this. I just want them to shut up. It hits me like a boot in the stomach to hear about Eva's glamorous secret life in New York hanging out with some diva-guy instead of being at home with my dad. I'm surprised by how painful it is. Eva's been gone for so long that I must have healed a bit without noticing. Hearing news about her—even if it's just about a photo I've never seen—rips open all the old wounds.

My back bumps against the glass wall separating the terrace from the indoor bar space. My coworkers have been closing in on me and, unconsciously, I've been edging away. I'm glad that they're being nice all of a sudden, but I can't talk about my mom for another minute. I slug the rest of my glass and excuse myself.

Making my way through the now-thick crowd, I notice a flurry by the door, followed by an explosion of flashbulbs.

Poised on the threshold is a thin, elegant woman in an off-the-shoulder black taffeta dress that's both Victorian-ruffly and Victorian-dominatrix-y. I'm sure it cost more than my dad's car. Her glossy black hair frames a perfect face: Lillian Hall. And behind her, Lexa, basking in reflected glory.

When Lexa finds out I'm at this party she's going to kill me.

I duck in the other direction.

And run into Rico.

"Kitten!" he cries, air-kissing me on both cheeks.

"Hi, Rico." Rico doesn't look nearly as fabulous as he did the night before. I know sportswear is hip at the moment, but he looks like he's wearing gym clothes.

"Don't eye my situation like that, Miss Mac."

"Sorry. Is that Stella for Men?" I name the trendiest gym wear I can think of.

"No. This is 'Rico was at Equinox when he'"—he glances at something over my shoulder—"'remembered about the Saks party and decided to come!'"

"Hey."

James has walked up to us, carrying a beer and a flute of champagne. There's a camera around his neck. "Hi, Kate," he says. "Your highness." He hands the flute to Rico. "Champers isn't included in the open bar, so I had to pay good money for that."

"Oh. Why do I not feel sorry for you?" Rico gulps down the glass and hands it back to James. "I'm a little dehydrated, darling, since I was *working out* and all. Why don't you get me another one?"

James, strangely obedient, goes back to the bar. Annoyingly, I notice a couple of girls checking him out. Rico surveys the scene. "Well, Kate, this party has it all. The coke. The girls. The boys. The tiny skirts. The oversized handbags. And you're right on trend."

My World Wildlife Federation canvas tote *is* rather large.

"What do you think?" Rico asks.

"People are rocking the trends, having fun," I say, using *Tasty*-speak. It's easy to talk to Rico. "It's counterintuitive for a season with so many dark points of reference, but I think fashion this summer is *playful*."

"Exactly! Brilliant, darling! Your finger is on the pulse," Rico cries.

A very un-playful-looking girl in nosebleed-high black platform heels and a cobwebby black lace dress that covers her ass by millimeters drifts by us. Her black feathered handbag incorporates a stuffed owl. Reese Malapin.

"Except for her. She's not so playful."

"Do you know her?" Rico sounds concerned.

"Not really. She's the assistant of someone I met tonight."

"Well, stay away, sweetie. She's certifiably clinical. That girl is known for taking the *Tasty* aesthetic way too far. I mean, everyone has an eating disorder, but she's been hospitalized, which is *not* chic. And her Goth statement is well executed but . . . I'm sorry, is today Halloween? I don't think so."

"I think she's pretty," I volunteer. She wasn't nice to me, but

I remember those broken blood vessels on her fingers and the way she told me about her senior thesis at Harvard, and feel sorry for her.

"Oh, Lord save me from *pretty*," Rico wails. "Anyone can be *pretty*, but only *Kate* can choose a tattered frock, pair it with what look like scuba shoes, and wind up looking like a breath of fresh air."

I've never thought of myself as stylish. I blush.

James reappears with a glass of champagne in each hand and gives them both to Rico. For a second, his questioning hazel eyes search my flaming face and my blush deepens. He quickly looks away.

"There's no more where that came from," he says.

"I'm going to powder my nose, if you know what I mean," says Rico, and suddenly, James and I are alone together.

"I like Rico. He's so funny he reminds me of a friend of mine from work—I mean from my old job. How did you meet him?" Uh-oh. I'm babbling.

"Craigslist. I landed in New York a few years ago with a thousand dollars, a couple of cartons of cigarettes, fifty-seven rolls of film, and a tropical disease. Rico was the only prospective roommate who wasn't scared off."

"How charming," I say, sarcastically, though of course it is charming to imagine him loose in the world, skinny and down on his luck. I can't look at him directly for too long without getting light-headed and having to look away. "What kind of infection?"

"Malaria."

"Weren't you taking drugs?"

"Not the right ones."

"That's crazy they didn't give you mefloquine, chloroquine, proguanil, Daraprim . . ." The words are hopping out of my mouth against my volition. He didn't bother to take anti-malarials in the first place. He doesn't care about the names of the medications.

There's a pause that's uncomfortable for me. Think of something more meaningful to say, I tell myself.

"So the crazy thing is that I haven't seen my mom since I was sixteen," I blurt. "And she was a fashion designer, and everyone here knows her. I haven't talked about her with any-one for years either, and all of a sudden everyone's asking." And now I'm bringing it up voluntarily. Have I lost my mind?

He inclines slightly toward me, eyes intense. "Why haven't you seen her?" he asks. Maybe he is interested. And now that I've begun, my crazy nerves prod me onward.

"She just left home. She didn't tell us why. It had to do with her career. Fashion consumed the nice, normal, down-to-earth woman that my mother used to be." I hope my voice isn't too bitter.

James seems nonjudgmental. "What's that mean?"

"She got into designing because she liked to sew. It was a creative pursuit, not about glamour and getting your picture in the paper. When I was little she made us the mother-daughter McCall's patterns."

"Go on," James says. A dark-tan girl passing by in an attrac-tively clinging white tank top does a double take, but he doesn't notice.

"Anyway, my mom loved to design, and she wanted to

make real clothes, with appliqués and silks and expensive linings. To see her dreams realized, she needed Manhattan. This was before my aunt Victoria could help her out with connections."

"Aunt Victoria?"

Oh, right, he doesn't know about Victoria. "My aunt's the one I'm living with this summer and who got me the internship. She married well and is now a prominent art dealer. But this was years ago. Eva was on her own."

He nods. I keep on overexplaining, something I tend to do when nervous.

"She sewed the first sample dresses herself in our living room. I'd try them for size—a ten-year-old girl and the typical fashion model have about the same figure. Then we'd drive together into New York to show to editors and buyers.

"The early successes were great. My dad was thrilled for her. We celebrated at the local ice-cream parlor when the first store placed an order." I glance at James to see if he finds this dorky, but he doesn't react. He's from Ohio, I remember; he should be able to handle it. "Later on Eva accused my dad of wanting to hold her back, but I don't think he did. He didn't *care* that we weren't invited to her parties. He didn't *mind* that she spent nights in the city. But she decided that there was a conflict, and if he denied it, he was being 'passive-aggressive' or 'guilting' her."

"When did she change?" James asks me softly.

"I don't know. It was gradual. She started showing at Fashion Week in New York. And of course then she had to go to the parties. And then she had to go to parties even when it wasn't Fashion Week. By the time I was in my teens, it was *her* in trouble for coming home late smelling like cigarette smoke. Or for missing the last train and having to take an expensive yellow cab all the way to our house."

"That's terrible. I'm so sorry, Kate. And this is inconvenient but . . . Lillian alert. She's heading straight for us."

I look over and see her, gliding in our direction like a shark fin. The crowd seems to part for her. Her ice-cold, thousand-yard stare gives no indication that she's looking at us, person-ally, but she's definitely looking in our direction. James and I simultaneously step further apart.

"She's got to have better people than us to talk to," I whisper.

But she doesn't. She floats up, severe and inhumanly gor-geous.

"Miss McGraw. Mr. Truax." Her voice is deadpan and thrilling. Again I find myself transfixed. I shiver and fold my arms over my chest.

"Hey, Lillian," he says. "I didn't know you were fond of the flare-legged jean."

I'm amazed that he jokes with her.

"I'm friendly with many types of trouser, *cherie*," she says silkily.

If it weren't impossible, I'd think she was flirting with him.

Lillian's gimlet gaze rakes over me. "I see you've found the party circuit," she says. "I'm impressed."

I'm not sure I should credit Annabel with my presence or keep her name out of it.

"Kate's one to watch," Lillian tells James. "I discovered her myself in Bryant Park last month and I knew she'd turn out to be one of us."

James turns to me, as if saying, *Med school, riiight.*

"Lillian, I'm only a summer intern. I'm going to med school in the fall."

"I think you might change your mind about that, dear." She smiles. Her dainty little fangs—I can think of no other term for her super-long incisors—wink out at us.

"Well, *Tasty* is a very interesting place to work." I don't want to be impolite and contradict her. And she's way too terrifying to argue with.

"Of course it is. Now run along, dear, and show these very original shoes you're wearing to Kristen. You've met her, I assume."

Lillian Hall noticed my shoes. I'm honored. "They're made from recycled tires," I tell her.

"Incredible. Go tell Kristen all about it. I need to talk to James about a little issue we're having with the party pages."

And though I really don't want to leave James with her—or leave him at all—what choice do I have?

"Good-bye, Kate," she says.

FINDING KRISTEN, unfortunately, means finding Lexa, since the two of them are standing together. I lurk behind a woman talking to a man in a pink velveteen blazer, wondering what to do.

"Breathtaking, darling," the woman says to him. "You are *owning* that color."

"You don't think it's too predictable?"

"No. You're *killing* it. And the bag is stunning."

He's carrying an oversized leather mail sack, embossed with the Prada label.

"They only made six hundred and sixty-six of them, and more than half were promised to celebrities. Wilmer wanted one but he wasn't on the list."

My dilemma is as follows: If I go talk to Kristen, Lexa is going to see me and be really, really pissed off. But if I don't, I'm disobeying a direct command from Lillian. I duck around the guy with the rare Prada bag and approach the group.

Lexa's beady eyes bore into me. She looks like she swallowed a hairball.

"Kristen?" Every time I have to address a coworker, I feel uncouth. This never used to happen at my old job.

Kristen raises her eyebrow. "Yes, Eva's daughter?" she asks, rubbing her nose inelegantly with the back of her hand. Either she's just snorted some coke or she wants people to think she has. Her I'm-too-cool-to-act-corporate demeanor should put me at ease, but it doesn't.

"Lillian thought you might be interested in my shoes."

"She what? *Your* shoes? I'm offended by that."

I freeze. Offended how? Why? But then Kristen laughs. "Kidding," she says. "Produce this fabulous footwear and I will opine."

"The shoes I'm wearing."

Kristen looks down, frowning. "Are they . . . ?"

"They're not scuba shoes. They're leather-free, cruelty-free slip-ons made from recycled tire rubber."

"I like it," she says. "I think green fashion is here to stay."

"So I've heard." I'm ridiculously grateful that she likes my shoes.

"Darling, we need to talk," Lexa interrupts, drawing me away from the group.

"I don't have much time," she says. "Have you seen if Patrick McMullen is here yet? I have to be uptown at the Conflict-Free Diamonds dinner in twenty minutes, and then back downtown for Molecular Biology by ten."

"I'm sorry. Who is Patrick McMullen?"

She scowls. "Only the king of New York society photography. You can't miss him."

"I haven't seen him." I try to be helpful. "But James Truax is here taking pictures for *Tasty*. He's behind that Modernist sculpture talking to Lillian. He can shoot you till Patrick shows up."

Lexa processes this statement for a few seconds. "Well, he's not A-list but he'll do in a pinch," she says. Then she makes an obvious effort to school her face into a concerned look. "I hope you feel we can be open with each other, Kate."

Is this how a boss about to fire her employee would start a conversation? With Lexa, I can't be sure. But she can't be happy I'm at this party. And I probably shouldn't get Annabel in trouble by admitting that she invited me.

"Please, say whatever you need to say."

"A person's family is a very important part of her social persona. You should have confided in me immediately about who your mother was. A blood tie to even a very minor Somebody is something to be proud of," she says breathily. "And it doesn't hurt *me* to have an intern whose mother was—and this is how I'll put it to the tabloids—'a cult figure who went insane and dropped out of the fashion world in the late nineties.'"

"I really wish you wouldn't."

Long pause. Then she says encouragingly, "And your name

will be in the paper, too." Her eyes flicker over my shoulder. "Oh. *There's* Patrick."

"Lexa," I ask her as she walks away, "does this mean I'm reinvited to the Tasty Girl meeting tomorrow?"

"Don't be silly, darling," she replies. "Of course you should be there!"

I walk back to where Lillian found us and look for James, hoping to pick up where we left off. I wonder if he was truly interested in my sob story, or just being polite. In hindsight, I didn't give him much room to talk. I spot him talking to Rico and Matilda, the designer. "Hey!" I bravely insinuate myself into their group.

"I want to know who it is," Matilda is saying. "It's like the Inquisition all over again." Rico looks amused. James looks nervous.

"Why do you think we know who StakeOut is, darling?" Rico asks.

"I refuse to be interested in that drivel," James adds.

"It's a witch hunt," Matilda replies bitterly. "And it's asking for trouble."

"I wish I could help you." Rico shrugs, but his demeanor strikes me as a bit too blasé. He knows more than he's saying.

James says, "Excuse me," and stalks off. I'm wounded. Doesn't he want to continue our conversation? I thought we were connecting. At least I was connecting.

"We've got to go!" Annabel suddenly appears beside me and grabs my arm. She's followed by Kristen Drane, Noë, and Reese, who is smiling mysteriously. "This party is about to become a major buzz kill," Kristen adds.

"Okay," I say. "Where are we going?"

Kristen makes eye contact with Matilda. "Two girls were just found murdered and stuffed into a catering van outside."

She says it so casually I think she must be joking, but Rico's stories about the fashion murders clue me in that this is not the case.

Matilda looks shocked but not too upset. "Somebody's getting greedy," she says, her mouth sour. "I'd like to know who it is."

"Me too," Kristen replies. "I'd like to have a little talk with them."

"I think that we would *all* like that," Noë interjects.

All I can think is, Two people were murdered? My hands start to shake.

Rico, for once, is silent, pressing a hand to his chest, looking stricken.

"We want to get out of here before the police come," Annabel says. They turn to go. My feet won't move. My chest feels buzzy with fear and adrenaline. Annabel pulls me toward the exit. "Come on! They'll shut off the music and close the bar and take statements until we've missed the rest of the night's parties."

"Been there, done that," I joke weakly, but she doesn't smile.

"Annabel, how can you think about going to another party right now?" I say. I look around for Rico, whom I consider a friend and someone I'd want nearby in a time of crisis, even if it is possible he's the StakeOut blogger. But we've lost him in the crowd. "Wait. I need to find someone."

"Come *on*, there's no time!" Annabel tugs. "We're going to lose Kristen and those guys."

The police—dozens of them—are just pouring into Gramercy Park as our glamour-clique hits the sidewalk. We hurry past the catering van, which is surrounded by black-clad spectators, the funeral-look for once grimly appropriate. Through the open doors I see a spill of strawberry-blonde hair, a ruffled blouse, and a foot in a sparkly Repetto ballet flat streaked with vivid scarlet blood.

I'm trembling. There are tears in my eyes. I feel as if my body is going to break down. Those are the same girls I saw air-kissing and complimenting each other's outfits earlier. And now they're dead.

Kristen notices my distress and snorts in either sympathy or exasperation, I'm not sure which. "Do you want some Xanax?"

"No. I think it's *natural* that I'm upset right now." The fact that the rest of them *aren't* is surreal.

Kristen shrugs, pops a pill, swallows it dry, and then lights up a cigarette. "Two great tastes that go great together," she says.

"Where are we going next?" Noë asks. She's taken a compact out and is touching up the gloss on her puffy, possibly collagen-injected lips.

I can't believe that they want to go to another party. I want to go home. But I also don't want to be alone. A brief discussion has us hailing cabs on Park Avenue South. I hang back. On some level I'm aware that this is my chance to hang out with senior editors, but really, people have *died*. Reese Malapin tucks her arm into mine.

"What are you thinking about?" The girl has a truly morbid curiosity. I wonder if she'll change her personality when fashion decrees that sweetness and light are back in.

"The girls who just died," I tell her. "Aren't you?"

"I didn't know them."

"I didn't, either! But a serial killer is out there stalking people in our industry."

"Fashion has always been a target," Reese says. "We're blamed for all of society's ills. Every disenfranchised guy in the world, when he goes off his meds, wants to kill a model. Or sometimes an actress."

"And that means you don't care?" My voice sounds shaky, even to me.

"Of course I care, but I'm not going to act like it," Reese says calmly. "I wouldn't give the murderer the satisfaction. You should look at how the senior staffers act and emulate them."

I should? I'm still processing this piece of information when Annabel snaps her fingers in front of my face (a lovely habit she's picked up from Lexa). "This is our cab," she says. "And look"—from within her fashionably huge shoulder bag she pulls out a square of folded denim—"Cheer up. I got you a pair of jeans."

We do a "walk-through" of the opening party for the restaurant Molecular Biology, which Lexa mentioned earlier. I knock back a drink, trying to calm my nerves, and am immediately unpleasantly tipsy. I keep seeing the splatter of blood, turning black in the girl's spun-silk hair, and imagining various scenarios. Were the two friends killed inside the van? How did they get in there? They must have left the party willingly, with the killer. Did I see them talking to anyone else?

The way everyone from *Tasty* is ignoring what just happened is making me feel even sicker. I find myself trailing the hors d'oeuvres guys, trying in vain to consume enough foam balls (since when is foam food?) to settle my stomach. The room is packed, thunderously loud, and filled with clouds of chili-pepper smoke from the open kitchen. Some of the conversations I overhear are about the murders—news travels fast—but mostly I hear self-absorbed chitchat uttered by people with dazzling, plastic smiles.

Lexa shows up at the peak of the festivities and clings to the celebrities like a stick-on bra at the Academy Awards. She's changed into a black dress that shows every bone in her pelvis. People wince when they look at her. She accosts the white hip-hop star Trey, with whom, as I learned in the meeting, we want to do a feature. It's Lexa's job to make it happen. Trey cranes his head desperately, searching for an excuse to escape.

Lexa doesn't look like she's giving a second thought to the dead girls in the catering van.

Mainly to get away from Lexa, I agree to go to a private club that I'm told is for the rich and successful in the media and film industries. Middle-aged people plastered with brand-name clothing throng the sidewalks outside. We've lost Noë but have picked up two ravishing French girls (market editors) whom everyone calls "the twins," though I don't think they're related. Our group of six cuts straight through the crowd.

"I have invitations here for all of us," Annabel says, pausing at the velvet rope to dig in her bag.

"Come on in." The bouncer waves us through without looking at the stiff squares of glossy paper. The jam-packed fifth-floor bar is James Bond swanky, gleaming, its darkness punctuated by pools of golden light. My coworkers head to the dance floor. I've had enough.

"I'm going to go," I shout at Annabel.

"I'm a terrible dancer, too!" she confides.

Instead of letting me leave, she finds us one vacant seat to share at the bar.

As I get drunker, I'm getting more overtly upset. "What the hell is going on?" I ask her.

"What do you mean?" she asks. Her face is suddenly immobile, her eyes flat and hard.

"Oh, I don't know. The deaths. The dogicide. It's my first week of work and there's a body count."

Her eyes narrow. My heart goes dry and constricts in my chest, as if a cold, ghostly hand has wrapped around it and squeezed.

Annabel smiles. She must go to the same dentist as Lillian, because her china-white teeth and long incisors are similar. She wraps a hard, thin arm around my shoulders and squeezes closer to me on the chair. "You really shouldn't talk like that."

I'm steeling myself to ask her why, when she goes pale— paler—and sways on the chair, pupils hugely dilated. Her nostrils flare and she breathes in deeply, as if smelling a delicious aroma.

"Are you okay?"

"I'm fine. I'm just hungry. I need something to eat. It's been too long," she whispers weakly. "I'll see you tomorrow."

She slips off the stool and pushes her way through the crowd with robotic determination. I'm concerned but uncertain what to do. If she needs to eat and then throw up, or binge on some particular thing that can only be consumed shamefully in the middle of the night, I don't want to get in her way.

8

Like Death
Warmed Over

WAKE UP Thursday morning on top of the red velvet spread in my room at Victoria's, still wearing my dress. My head throbs. Events from the evening before start filtering back to me ... though I can hardly call it evening, since I was rolled out of a speeding black Town Car by Kristen Drane this morning just before sunrise.

"Darling, are you still in there?" My aunt's voice penetrates my thoughts. What is Victoria doing up? She usually sleeps in. "What time is it?" I call weakly.

She flings open the door, dressed and looking perfect. "Darling, it's eleven-thirty! I had no idea you were here until I heard a moan. Are you okay?"

I lurch off the bed. "I'm late!"

Fortunately, Lexa usually doesn't show up until after eleven herself. Another memory slides into place. "Oh, no. I have to be at a meeting in half an hour."

I'm already shimmying into my new pair of free jeans (carried from club to club last night in my trusty World Wildlife

Federation canvas tote) and grabbing the first top my hand touches.

"Heels and lipstick!" Vic cries, dashing from the room. Seconds later she's back with a pair of Jane Mayle stack-heel loafers and a tube of brick-red M.A.C. She brandishes the lipstick at me as I'm brushing my hair. "A girl your age makes any outfit fashionable by adding heels and red lipstick," she proclaims. Vic's eye is right-on as usual. The color flatters my hair and my pallor.

I air-kiss her on both cheeks, snatch my bag, and run.

Fifteen minutes later I'm in the Oldham elevator. I check the reflective door to make sure that my fly is zipped and my clothes are on right side out. I am hungry, thirsty, and my hair smells like cigarette smoke.

I'm still not wearing a bra.

Please, oh please, let Lexa not be here yet.

"Good morning, Miss McGraw. You *do* know how to make an entrance," Felix needles. I catch him eyeing my Mayle loafers as if he knows how much they cost. He probably does. Me, I don't *want* to know.

"Has Lexa come in?" I gasp.

Felix gives me a weird look. "I assume so," he says. "She gets here before I do."

"Oh." I stop walking. "You don't see her come in every day?"

He looks like he's about to say something, then shakes his head. "*I* don't keep track of people."

Somehow I really doubt that. But there's not much I can say.

To my incredible relief, the only people in the conference

room when I walk in are Annabel—spiral notebook open and turned to a fresh page before her on the table—Rachel, and Nin. I take a seat next to Annabel, earning incredulous looks from the other two interns.

"Good morning," Annabel says. "Do you feel like death warmed over?"

"I don't feel bad," I lie.

She doesn't look like she's suffering at all. Her hair is salon-blow-out smooth. She looks fresh and well-rested. Her midnight binge, whatever it was, has left no traces.

"Is Lexa here?" I ask.

"Not yet," she tells me. "She's probably just awakening." If she notices my confused look, she pretends that she doesn't.

"Kate, was that you at the Molecular Biology party last night?" Nin asks.

How in the world do they know already what I was doing last night?

"We thought we saw you in the background of a shot of Trey on PerezHilton this morning," Rachel says. "But we couldn't believe it. How did *you* get invited?"

Both of them are so jealous, they can hardly fake civility.

I can't say I notice a difference.

"Were you at the party where the murders took place, too?" Nin asks.

Annabel glares at them, putting an abrupt end to the conversation.

James walks in, accompanied by Matilda. He's wearing army pants and his hair appears to be damp—it seems I'm not the only one late for work today. I catch his eye for a brief, unreadable second and am struck with an almost uncontrollable urge to giggle. He winks at me and my stomach flip-flops.

Lexa follows shortly on James's heels, smiling as if to a private joke. She takes out her BlackBerry, checks something, *tsk-tsks* theatrically, and sits down.

"Lexa, have you seen the tabloids yet?" Annabel asks her.

Finally, we're going to discuss the murders.

Lexa smirks. "Patrick is so naughty," she says. "I'm furious with him, simply furious. From that photo *anyone* could conclude that Luke and I are more than friends!"

Or maybe not. I guess two girls dying is less important to Lexa than getting her name in the paper. Her BlackBerry beeps again. She checks it, simpers some more, and then turns a threatening eye on us. "Of course, none of you would *dare* tip off the gossips that I'm checking my messages this morning."

Nin nods, wide-eyed. Rachel looks hesitant. Annabel, on the other hand, has been scribbling notes. She raises her hand. "Which gossips should we *not* be tipping off, Lexa?"

Our boss chortles with satisfaction.

After a little more of this, we get down to business. "It's time to pick the semifinalists," Lexa tells us. "Annabel, I want you and the interns to do the first cull. That means weed out the cows. Only thin girls are Tasty Girls. So make a special pile for attractive, thin . . ." She eyes me as if I might try to slip a fat one by her. "I mean *very* thin, girls."

"This contest is going to *make* the careers of the next crop of young models," Annabel gushes. "And they'll have you to thank."

Lexa pats her perfect roll of white-blonde hair with a limp hand. "I think so."

"I'm honored to be part of the selection process," I add quickly. I'm catching on. Sorting young women by weight is a big step up from fighting with Rachel and Nin over cigarette-fetching privileges.

"Once you've kicked the fatties to the curb, I want you to read the 'What Makes Me Tasty' essays. I'm looking for people with inspiring personal stories. Find models who have emanci-pated themselves from their parents, or grown up in foster homes. Refugees from Third World countries. We're looking for anyone who has shown that she's overcome hardship."

Since when did Lexa become a humanitarian? She must have the mother of all PR campaigns cooked up for this.

James clears his throat. "Shane is still worried about this," he says. "Even with a great photographer, the girls need to look like models. Are you sure you want to be judging them based on criteria like personal history?"

Lexa gives him an evil, icy smile. "Very sure. Please tell Shane that I appreciate his concern, but that PR and Market-ing have already signed off on this strategy."

James shrugs. "He'll do what you want, but he's not respon-sible for the photos."

"We have Giedra Dylan-Hall taking the pictures," Lexa reminds him. "I assure you they'll be a scream." She turns to Matilda. "You're doing the layout?"

"Yes," the girl says, nervously.

"Wonderful. If it doesn't do the pictures justice, I'll know just who to talk to." Her phone rings. She checks the display, murmuring, "Oh Luke, you naughty boy." Then she turns to us. "I have to take this. Girls, I want a list of candidates on my desk by Monday morning. Dismissed."

Lexa swans out of the room. James and Matilda, looking shell-shocked, follow her. On the way out, James's eyes pass over mine impersonally, but nonetheless I feel that strange, magnetic tug of attraction.

The rest of us stare around the table at one another in disbelief.

"By Monday?" I ask Annabel.

"Most of the contestants are pretty good-looking," Rachel says. "They're aspiring models. I don't think it's going to be so easy to weed them out."

"You have to know what to look for," Nin says to her, condescendingly. "Think from the camera's perspective."

"I'm a writer! I don't think from the camera's perspective!"

"You guys," I say, for once feeling as if we're all on the same team. "The final application tally was two thousand four hundred and seventy-five. If half of them are disqualified on grounds of looks, we'll still have more than three hundred essays each to read."

Annabel is already doing figures on her pad. "Four hundred twelve each," she says. "That's assuming that we eliminate half of them today based on head shots and then divide the rest of it up for everyone to take home over the weekend."

"How is that four hundred?" I ask. "There are four of us."

Annabel smiles. "It is a *huge* honor for you guys to skim the applications first, pulling out the ones with the appropriate personal stories. I want each of you to pick twenty semifinalists and then I'll narrow down the list for Lexa on Monday morning before the features meeting." She sighs in a theatrical fashion. "I just do *not* get enough sleep."

My stomach growls audibly and I clamp my hand over it, embarrassed. I still haven't eaten anything today and I'm always extra hungry with a hangover.

"I'll be back in ten minutes," I excuse myself and dash for the elevator banks without sparing a glance for Felix in reception, who I'm sure would love to make a comment about me leaving the building a mere hour after arriving.

For the last three days, I've been getting my lunch at a nearby deli, the Plaza Gourmet III. It's got a huge salad bar, a pizza station, and a depressing, fluorescent-lit windowless seating area in the back where I shovel in my lonely meal. I chose this deli specifically because I didn't want to run into anyone from work while eating. *She eats! How déclassé!* As I head in that direction, I call my dad on my cell. I'd planned to go back to Monticello for the weekend, and I want to let him know that it's off. Instead, I'll be reading essays written by wannabe models. I'm not going to mention the murders or any of the other weird stuff so as not to worry him.

"Dad. Did you know that green is the new black?" I ask him, jokingly.

"Hi, kiddo!" he says. "What did you say?"

"Green is the new black."

"What? What's that mean?"

"Environmentally responsible clothes are in. Or so they tell me around here."

"I'm glad to hear it. How's the new job going?"

"Sorry I haven't called you." I don't know why. We're usually so close. Actually, I do know why. Once we have time to talk, I have some hard questions about my mother. Questions I may not want to hear the answers to. "It's going not-so-bad," I tell him. "The editor-in-chief likes me for some reason."

"*I* can imagine why she likes you," Dan says. "You're *you*. You're smart. You're a hard worker. Why shouldn't she like you?"

"It's not that simple in the fashion industry."

But he knows that. He watched Eva go through it. Quickly I continue, "And my direct boss doesn't like me but she's growing to tolerate me."

That is, she's warmed up after she found out who my mother is. And there's going to be some kind of item about it in the newspaper. I don't want to mention that one to Dan, either.

"She's assigned me to work on this big-deal contest, which is why I'm calling. I won't be able to make it home this weekend."

"Oh, honey, that's great! I'm so proud of you. I knew you'd do well." His enthusiasm is infectious. And despite my gloom, I can't help but feel a little pleased.

"So DO you think that Lexa really hooked up with Luke Wilson?" Nin asks late Friday evening. The three of us are still flipping through photos of hot teenaged hopefuls, figuring out which files to take home and read over the weekend—we've been at it for two days now. Annabel left the office long ago for a perfume launch party, and we interns are so tired and slap-happy that Rachel and Nin have started being friendly to me. I welcome it, since left to my own devices, I keep thinking about those two slain girls. Every strawberry-blonde candidate reminds me of them.

I check to make sure no one is in the hallway outside our closet before replying: "Doesn't seem plausible to me. Luke Wilson went out with Gwyneth Paltrow. Why would he want Lexa?"

"She's an heiress," Rachel says.

"*I'm* an heiress," Nin scoffs.

I venture to offer more detail. "I saw her accosting Trey the other night. She's very . . . affectionate. A picture taken at just the right moment could have made it look like they were groping."

"Even if Luke had been gropin' her," Nin adds, "he wouldn't be texting first thing the next day. She was sending those messages to herself."

I laugh reluctantly. "I think you're right."

"There's something wrong with her," Rachel interjects.

My heart flutters. I agree with her.

"Did you know that she spends whole afternoons reading gossip sites? And while she's reading she mutters to herself and her hands clutch at the air. Like this." She mimes scary clutching motions.

"Stop that. You're freakin' me out," Nin says, laughing.

I feel dissatisfied. This doesn't cut to the heart of my fears. There *is* something wrong with Lexa, but it goes deeper than an addiction to Internet gossip. I consider bringing up the murders, but don't. It's been made abundantly clear to me that people around here don't talk about such things. And I don't trust Nin and Rachel enough to break the rules with them.

"This girl is interesting-looking." I lift up the head shot of a sixteen-year-old from Waco, Texas. "She's not *thin* thin but, like they say in the movies, I think the camera would love her."

I have no idea what that means. I just happen to like her face.

"You heard what Lexa said," Rachel cautions me. "Only super-skinny. Let's not make her mad."

She's such a kiss-ass. I toss the Waco girl on the yes pile. "Maybe she'll realize that we need some variety."

Nin looks over. "I like her, too." She smiles at me. "I like people with unusual faces. My agent always said I was too pretty for edgy editorial work."

Rachel rolls her eyes. "Oh, poor you."

Nin spreads out her hands. "It's true. It's a disability being this perfect." Her tone makes it clear that she's laughing at herself. I can't help but laugh, too.

"Why didn't you keep modeling?" I ask her.

Nin winks at me. "Power," she replies. "Models don't have enough power. And the photographers are all perverts."

It's at this inopportune moment that James Truax shows up in our doorway, slurping on a straw stuck into a plastic cup full of red liquid. I've been waiting for him all day. Waiting and hoping that our conversation at the Saks party meant something to him, too, and that he'd want to continue it.

"Are you maligning photographers?" he asks. He addresses the question to the room, but his honey-gold eyes rake over me and my body pulses.

How does he do that?

"Just tellin' the truth," Nin says. "What are you doing here so late?"

To my dismay, she's not insensible to his charm, either.

"We're closing September," he tells her. "Unlike your show-pony boss, some people in this office work."

"*We're* working," I say.

"You three ought to be working," he agrees. "That Tasty Girl shoot should have been scheduled weeks ago, and Shane has made me responsible for tracking the project in-house. He's been on my ass about it all week. You're excused, McGraw. You didn't work here weeks ago."

Now would be the time for some flirtatious banter. Too bad I'm no good at that. Instead, I turn back to the contest entries, feeling like an idiot.

Nin has no such inhibitions. "Why are you drinking that? Are you on a diet?" she asks, teasingly.

He shrugs. "Matilda just made a run to Jamba Juice. Shane drinks these and now everyone imitates him."

"Shane's assistant brings Lexa her beet drink every afternoon," Rachel says. "It seems like she distributes them for the whole office."

That explains what the juice was doing on Lillian's desk on Sari's first (and last) morning.

"I didn't think Lexa and Shane got along," I say. Everyone laughs at the understatement.

"The two of them have a history," James says. "They worked together a long time ago in Europe and hated each other then, too."

He finishes his drink and tosses the cup into our trash can. Rachel and Nin are hanging on his every move.

"Have a good weekend," he says. "Good luck reading those essays." He pushes off from the door frame and wanders away.

I know he can't make any personal comment to me in front of our coworkers, but I'm still disappointed. Waiting two days to see him again is going to be torture. When, I'm wondering, will our next drinks-date be?

"Yum, yum," Nin says after he leaves.

"I thought you only dated bankers," Rachel snipes. "He's not your type."

"I know," she replies. "But there's just something about him. . . ."

THE NEXT morning, I set up in my aunt's living room with a giant stack of essays to read. I've opened the floor-to-ceiling wooden-slat blinds that wrap around the glass-walled penthouse and I am enjoying the view. I hope I'm not allowing rays of sunlight to touch a piece of priceless art, but the sky is blue, the towers of Midtown sparkle in the distance, and on Vic's terrace there is an incredible profusion of plants. She calls it her night garden, because she focuses on night-bloomers and succulents, but it looks pretty during the day as well.

I have the terrace and the huge, black-painted living room, with its German transcendentalist landscapes and box-framed fangs, all to myself. Victoria is, as usual, sleeping in. In fact, I'm lying in wait for her, since the two of us have barely crossed paths since Monday and she's the main reason I'm in New York, working at *Tasty* in the first place.

At noon she drifts in, blinking, swathed in a pretty tulip-sleeved black robe. A thick layer of white cream covers her face.

"Bright in here," she says.

"Do you want me to close the blinds?"

"No." She gracefully sinks down next to me on the low, charcoal-colored sectional sofa. "Sterling is like a vampire. He's terrified of sunlight, but not me."

"Do you miss him?"

"I do. It's unusual to stay madly in love with the person you marry, but my feelings for Sterling haven't changed. He's still a mystery to me, I suppose."

"He seems pretty mysterious," I agree. "And speaking of mysteries, Aunt Vic, the most horrible thing happened at this party I was at. Have you heard about the fashion murders?"

"Fashion murders?" she asks, smiling. "Have the fashion police been accused of brutality again?"

But her smile fades when I tell her what happened. I throw in the rumors Rico shared with me, and Marc Jacobs's mysterious death as well. And conclude with, "Doesn't all of this together strike you as strange? And ominous? I was probably two feet away from a killer at that party."

Victoria snuggles tighter into her black silk robe. "What frisson, darling," she says. "It's tragic that people are getting hurt. But it sounds like you've come to the city at an exciting time. Your industry will be talking about this summer forever. You should soak it all up like a sponge. Get close. See and hear everything you can."

Get close? She's not worried that I'm going to get hurt?

"Not too close, naturally," my aunt amends. "But you've always been intrepid. I'm sure you'll take care of yourself."

"I'm sure I'll be fine," I say. "But shouldn't there be an investigation into that dog's death at the very least? I'll bet there's a connection. I've been thinking I should call that contributing editor, Susan Craigs."

"No," Victoria says emphatically.

"No?"

"Getting directly involved would be most inappropriate in your position. Any investigating should be done by the company itself, not one of its newest employees."

"But that's the point! Nobody at the company is doing anything."

"That's corporations for you."

9
One of Them

IT'S TEN O'CLOCK Monday morning. I'm reading the gossip blogs when an ice-cold hand descends on my shoulder.

"Oh, hi, Annabel. That's a really cute dress." She's wearing a silky, body-hugging floral number with epaulettes, capped sleeves, and self-covered buttons up the front. A nightmare from a sewing standpoint, but chic.

"Thanks," she says. "It's Tuleh. I'm not sure if I like it."

I'm surprised to see her here so early. Annabel usually appears just before Lexa. She's the only assistant I've observed to cut things so close.

"Have you finished the first cut for those semifinalists?" she asks me.

"I've done mine!" says Nin, walking in the door. "And it's y'all's fault if I've lost my tan over it."

Annabel looks at her reproachfully. "I would think as interns you would appreciate this level of responsibility."

"Kidding!" Nin holds up her hands.

"I have Rachel's," I volunteer. "She just stepped away."

As I help Annabel bring the applications over to Lexa's, I say, "We can make a summary of the results really easily using Excel."

"Good idea, Kate," she says supportively. "Why don't you show me how to do it?" We sit down at her desk and I walk her through the steps.

Lexa's door is, as is usual at this time of day, closed. It will remain closed all morning and then at some point it will open and out she will glide, clothing unwrinkled, hair in its perfect soft-serve waves, lips coated with frosty peach lipstick.

"Is she in there?" I whisper to Annabel.

"She's not to be disturbed." Annabel smiles at me blandly. "Now, why don't you run up to Barneys for me and pick up Phoebe's latest? Lexa has reserved one in every color. She's going to switch bags at every event tonight and hope it gets into the gossips."

"Clever," I reply.

"Isn't she?" Annabel gushes. "Here. I'll give you petty cash for a taxi."

Can anyone be as much of a kiss-ass as Annabel is? I wonder while stuck in crosstown traffic. Is it possible to love a boss as much as Annabel seems to love Lexa? I really don't think so.

THE FEATURES meeting starts on a grim note.

"We need to have a little talk about expenses, ladies," Lauren says. "Since I've been on maternity leave things have gotten lax. Unlike most publishing companies, Oldham doesn't skimp on your office supplies. You're allowed to send messengers and you can take a car service home when you work late. But"—she glares at each of us in turn—"don't abuse it. No more ridiculous purchases. She who expensed a charge at a blood bank knows who she is. And I'm keeping my eye on her."

Blood bank? James and I exchange what-the-fuck? glances. We're once again (to my delight) sitting next to each other against the back wall.

Lauren continues with the announcements. The guest list for Wednesday's *Tasty*-sponsored benefit for the Low-Income Ladies' Plastic Surgery Fund (LILPSF) is restricted. Staff members are invited, but no significant others or guests. No freelancers. No interns.

We move on through various items on the agenda until the topic of the Tasty Girl Contest rears its pretty head.

"Everything is on track," Lexa assures the room. "Giedra is flying in June thirtieth, and we'll shoot over the Fourth of July."

"Not to rush you, honey, but do we have models yet?" Shane Lincoln-Shane asks with exaggerated politeness.

"I'll be making the final decision this week," Lexa coos.

"Can you share a little more with us about the candidates?" He's putting her on the spot, since he must have heard that just last Thursday she had more than two thousand essays and hadn't read any of them.

Annabel swoops to the rescue, heaving an impressive stack of paperwork onto the table. "We've narrowed things down to . . ." She checks a piece of paper, which I see is the summary I suggested we make. "Twenty-seven strong candidates."

"Do you have a good geographical range?" Lauren asks. "It's

important that we reflect that our readership isn't just on the two coasts."

"I can distribute this spreadsheet if you're interested," Annabel replies smugly. "We have a wide range, broken down by state."

Lauren looks surprised. "That's the first time anyone around here has ever voluntarily made a spreadsheet. Strong work."

"Thank you," Annabel says demurely.

I'm a little indignant. It would have been nice if she acknowledged that it was my idea.

"What about the location?" Shane asks. "I'll need Giedra's contact information so I can discuss it with her."

"How are we handling this shoot?" Lillian takes an interest. "Teen models. But what's the angle?"

"Lillian, you remember," Lexa says patiently, though I'm sure she's seething underneath. "We discussed this back in the spring. We're shooting them at an abandoned farm-house upstate under the headline 'Farm Fresh: A New Crop of Models.'"

"You already have a location?" Shane feigns surprise and alarm. "Why haven't I seen anything? Someone had better e-mail me pictures right after this meeting."

"We don't have pictures. The place is three hours north, in Jeffersonville. Giedra's seen it and she can vouch for it."

"That won't work," Shane says. "The ultimate responsibility for the look of this magazine is mine, and I'll need to vet it first." A grin breaks out across his handsome face. "It's short notice but I'll have my people get you a few farm-alternatives by the end of the week." He pauses to enjoy the outrage on

Lexa's face. "Or," he muses, "maybe we could shoot it in the studio with props. I'm seeing bales of hay—"

"Hay just *screams* fall," Lillian agrees.

An idea starts forming in my mind. I'm going to be at my dad's house this weekend. Heart beating madly, I raise my hand. "Lexa?"

Heads turn to look at me en masse. My throat goes dry.

"I'm going to be near Jeffersonville this weekend, if I can help out in any way."

Rachel, across the room from me, stares in disbelief.

Lexa, too, is momentarily taken aback, but she covers it well. "Why, thank you, Kate," she says. "That would be very helpful."

I've just begun mentally congratulating myself when Annabel chimes in, "I'll go with her!"

She's coming with me for the weekend to my dad's house? I can't believe it.

AFTER THE meeting I'm asked to cover for Lillian's assistant.

I enjoy answering the phone, "Lillian Hall's office," aiming for the perfect cheerful, bland anonymous assistant voice. The callers are generally wheedling and hopeless. I am meticulous with the spelling of their names and company affiliations. Every now and then I walk into Lillian's office to put the pile of pink "While You Were Out" slips on her desk. Because Lillian is never in, even when she is in.

When I'm working for Lillian, her luxurious, leather-covered date book stays with me. It is my job to "mirror" any changes I make in it in my plastic copy of the book. Hers is a beautiful item, heavier than it looks, covered with buttery-soft calf's-blood leather. Embossed on the front is a brand-stamp that vaguely resembles the molecule for hemoglobin.

I have it open in front of me, struggling with Lillian's crabbed, antiquey-looking, cursive writing, when the woman herself glides in carrying the parasol she uses on sunny days. I have a hard time believing this trend will catch on, but if anyone can make it happen, she can. She's followed by her latest assistant, Carol, who grabs the date book as soon as her hands—deeply scored with lines from the handles of the many shopping bags she was lugging—are free.

"I'll do that, Kate." Her politeness masks seething resentment. Carol—correctly—suspects Lillian favors me. Yesterday I saw her tear up one of the pink message slips I left for Lillian and eat it.

Lillian looks disdainfully at Carol and says, "Darling, why are you all wet?"

Carol is wet because it's so hot outside the pavement is melting and she was carrying fifty pounds of garment bags.

"I'm sweating. It's nothing," Carol says nervously.

Lillian, of course, never sweats. She looks as cool and coiffed as ever. She squinches her eyes shut, as if she's in pain. "I can't cope with your hygiene issues now. I'm having a terrible day. Please don't take your post until you're presentable." Then she opens her eyes, smiles at me, and says, "And you, Miss McGraw, come into my office."

I totter carefully toward her door, since I'm wearing another pair of Victoria's shoes and haven't, as promised, adjusted to them.

"Sit down," Lillian sighs. She takes a seat at her glass conference table and indicates that I should take the one next to her. I do, goose bumps rippling my flesh from the ice-cold air. Lillian rubs her temples, without speaking.

"Are you okay?" I ask her. It's not my place to question the editor-in-chief's moods, but she looks upset.

"I'm the same," she says. "Every day is exactly the same."

"Fashion is treading water? You aren't seeing any original ideas for next season?"

She smiles. "That's why I like you," she says. "You're quick-witted."

I smile hesitantly. I've been meaning to ask her if there might not be another reason she plucked me from obscurity. "Lillian," I say slowly, "you mentioned last week that you knew my mother."

"Yes. We were friends. It was a happier time for me." She perks up a bit.

They were friends? My mom never mentioned her. But then again, my mom never mentioned a lot of things.

"You're not still in touch with Eva, are you?"

"Eva dropped us all some years ago, when, as I now gather, she left home. We had no idea she had a family hidden away, or we would have extended the hand of friendship to her daughter."

She pats my knee. And Lillian is just *not* a knee-patter. "I've been wanting to talk to you about this. I hope you'll come to think of me in time not as a mother—never as a mother, of course, I'm too young-looking for that—but as a mentor."

"Lillian. I'm honored."

"You're one of us. You have a consistent style, you understand clothes on a deep level, and I thought your offer to help in the meeting today demonstrated presence of mind."

Wow. I'm incredibly flattered. There's no one in the world I'd rather hear compliment my style.

Acting on impulse, I stand halfway up in my chair and give her a hug. Her shoulders are hard as marble, and she, touchingly, resists for a second before pressing her cold cheek to mine.

"Thank you so much," I say, backing away from her. I don't know what came over me. "I won't let you down," I stammer.

Her eyes mist. "I know you won't."

IF NIN and Rachel didn't already hate me, Wednesday afternoon clinches it.

Despite the fact that interns aren't invited, Rachel and Nin have been particularly obsessed with all the details of the Carnivoré party. From StakeOut they know who is on the guest list, what's on the menu, and so on. The Richards sisters will be there, supposedly, and an R&B star's designer daughter, Little Star. Rosie O'Donnell is hosting. StakeOut promises (or threatens, depending on your perspective) to crash and provide full coverage, with "photos of the bloodsuckers." (That means us.)

Around six P.M. Reese stops by my desk with a garment bag. She looks prettier than usual. Her little black Alexander McQueen dress hugs her graceful, springy figure; the top quadrant of her thick, dark locks is done up in a pulled-back

French braid while the rest of her hair falls smoothly over her shoulders.

She sits on the edge of my desk and asks, "Does this braid look like I'm wearing an extra brain on top of my head?"

I'm not sure what the right answer is here. "Is it supposed to?"

"Of course not!"

"Reese, you look beautiful. It would be impossible for you to look anything but beautiful. And your hair does not look like an extra brain on top of your head."

She leans further toward me. "I feel insecure. I need a pick-me-up. Want to go do a bump in the ladies' room?"

"You're crazy." Maybe all the staffers do coke, but as far as I'm aware, they don't do it at *work*. Also, I don't do coke. "You have nothing to be insecure about," I dodge. "Your look is great."

"Thanks," she says. "I came by to tell you the good news. The PR girls were in the fashion closet picking out outfits for tonight and they mentioned that we needed some seat-fillers for the party. I suggested you. Here's your dress."

She pats the garment bag lovingly.

My first thought is that James will probably be there taking pictures. Maybe this will be an opportunity to talk with him. My second is that the garment bag is from Marni and it doesn't get any better than that. And the third is that Nin and Rachel are going to hate me with a white-hot passion forever.

When Reese leaves, the silence in our closet-slash-office is thicker than Pringle cashmere. I glance at my coworkers. Rachel is pink with anger. Nin looks depressed. They've both dressed up, in case a last-minute invitation came through.

"It's nespotism, pure and simple," Nin snaps.

I'll assume she means nepotism.

"Alrighty, then," I say. I look into the garment bag. The dress is made of light blue taffeta and has a jewel-encrusted burlap string wrapped around the waist. I love it. "I guess I'll just go put this on."

ANNABEL AND I rush through the great vaulted hall of Grand Central Station. Noticing my craning neck—the misty-blue, star-spangled ceiling in here is really incredible—she wraps a conspiratorial arm around my waist. "It's a nice place, isn't it?"

I'm over-awed. Most kids who grow up upstate start taking the train into the city in their teens, but Eva's growing fascination with Manhattan made me shun it.

"I never expected it to be so beautiful," I confide.

"The longer you live here, the better New York gets. Imagine flying along the tops of buildings. The gargoyle's-eye view of the Upper West Side is incredible."

She hadn't struck me as the fanciful type. To be polite I say, "That sounds amazing!"

Beaming, she squeezes my arm. "You'll see."

I'm both flattered and uneasy by her new-best-friend act. It will be interesting to see how we get along over the weekend at my dad's house. I've already tried to talk her out of coming with, to no avail.

We step into Carnivoré, Lillian's favorite steakhouse, which, I have just learned, is located off the main concourse. Big slabs of bloody sirloin seem like an odd choice for a plastic surgery fund-raiser. For the moment, the guests are crammed into the bar area for cocktail hour. The dining room—a sea of white-clothed tables with huge flower arrangements—is still roped off. The place is ear-splittingly loud and choked with the inter-mingled scents of perfume, product, and cigarette smoke. Annabel snuggles closer to me and whispers, "Smile." I man-age to get my mouth closed just in time for the barrage of flashbulbs that goes off.

"Why do they want my picture?"

Annabel rolls her eyes. "The junior paparazzi guys take pic-tures of everyone. They sort out who's famous later."

We thread through the crowd. Annabel whispers a litany of names to me. The magazine's newfound cachet since Lillian took over (and changed the name from *Shop Girl* to *Tasty*) has brought NYC society out in force, and Annabel has a keen eye for celeb spotting. She points out a pair of New York–based filmmakers, a supermarket magnate whose private jet is Amer-ica's premiere party scene, and Lindsay Lohan—though that one I would have gotten on my own. LiLo is leaner, smaller, and more lizardy-looking in person. I can't help but stop to stare. And then I see James, camera in hand, walk up to her and say something in her ear, one hand on her bare arm. Lind-say giggles and lets him take a couple of shots.

"Kate! Come on!" Annabel pulls me by the arm. "We have mingling to do."

Disturbed, I push after Annabel. Lillian is seated across the room in a deep circular banquette. "Why isn't *she* mingling?" I say directly into Annabel's ear. "She shouldn't be sitting in a corner."

"She's depressed." Annabel waves her hand dismissively. "Sometimes she tries to leave these things early, which is a disaster from a PR perspective. Anthea Ferrari called Lauren about it last time."

My heart goes out to Lillian. Maybe I should go talk to her.

I duck under an upraised catering tray, trying to get across the room. The party is packed, however, and I find myself separated from Annabel, stuck behind two women, one of whom is wearing shorty pajamas stamped with the Louis Vuitton logo.

"Over a decade in the public eye and she hasn't changed at all!" one is yelling to the other.

"She looks *exactly* like she did in the early nineties!" the other one agrees. "I always thought it was airbrushing but it isn't!"

I peer over their shoulders to discover that they are talking about Kate Moss, who is just a few feet away, scowling and puffing on a cigarette.

"Paris Hilton doesn't age, either," the shorty-pajamas girl observes. "And neither does Nicole Kidman. Celebrities are so lucky."

I use my elbows to squash by these two into an area of the bar that seems even more crowded than the first. A woman with elaborate medusa-like loops of black hair bellows to her male neighbor, "It wasn't just the atelier. There have been four suspicious deaths at Barneys this year—"

"Not four! Two! And they were suicides. Young women driven to despair by the price of shoes."

"I heard that someone went into the dressing room in Eveningwear, put on an Yves Saint Laurent ball gown, and slit her wrists. There was blood everywhere."

"That was a *shoot*, darling. Someone is pulling your leg. A maverick stylist did it for *W*—and Barneys got stuck with the bill."

A perspiring waiter forces his way through the crowd, holding a tray high above his head. I take my chance, following on his heels until at last I reach the table where Lillian is sitting, propped corpse-like in a corner with a blank expression.

Kristen, Shane, and several other editors whom I vaguely recognize cluster around her, trying to seem lively. Reese Malapin hovers nearby, watching the senior staff with the oddest expression on her face—half-loathing, half-longing.

Feeling nervous, I walk up to the table. I'm not sure how I'll create an invitation to sit down if everyone ignores me, but fortunately Lillian notices me. "Make room for Kate," she says, signaling the people on the end. "I have *big* plans for her. She's my latest." I squeeze in on the end of a booth, wondering what kind of plans, and latest what. (And feeling rather pleased that I've scored a seat at this table.)

"Kate," Lillian says, "you know Shane Lincoln-Shane, our art director."

Beside Shane is the hip-hop star Trey, who saves awkwardness by introducing himself, though of course I already know his name.

Lillian continues smoothly, "This is Noë Childs, the beauty editor."

I say hello and murmur that we've met to Noë, who isn't wearing her painted-on freckles tonight.

"Kate and I go way back," Kristen Drane says when it's her turn for the introduction. From the looks of her blonde mane, you'd think she hadn't bathed in days—very Marc Jacobs ad (the designer, not the dog, of course).

The French twins are named Josephine and Mary-Catherine (Marika). They nod in acknowledgment of me without doing something as egregiously friendly as actually speaking.

A waitress arrives to take our order.

"Another round of Bloody Marys for the table," Lillian commands.

The fabulosity index is so high I'm having a hard time breathing. Or maybe it's all the illegal cigarette smoke indoors.

I catch sight of James through the crowd once again. This time he's talking to a tall girl with thick, bright-red shoulder-length hair and what's known anatomically speaking as a great rack. I don't like the easy way she touches him as they talk.

The waitress returns, carrying a tray laden with pint glasses of red drink.

"Do you know what the secret ingredient in a Carnivoré Bloody Mary is, Kate?" Lillian asks. "Fresh blood."

The waitress puts one down in front of each of us.

"Blood. Ha-ha." Is she kidding?

My coworkers slam down their cocktails like hardened alcoholics. Seven pairs of kohl-rimmed eyes swing toward me. My untouched drink takes on new significance as a hot commodity.

"Try it, Kate," Lillian says. "I think you'll like it very, very much."

I seize my Bloody Mary and drink. It burns going down. "I can't even taste the blood," I announce.

My coworkers find this hilarious. With a drink inside me, I start to feel confident—or foolish—enough to leap into the conversation.

"People in the crowd are talking about the fashion mur-ders," I say to the table at large. "I guess there's been one at Barneys."

Dead silence falls at the table.

I'm regretting opening my mouth when Trey breaks the ice.

"I hear they found this girl backstage at Joe's Pub, and she was all bloody and shit." He nods, looking satisfied.

Shane speaks softly but nonetheless his voice cuts through the ambient noise. "It's all the violence in fashion shoots these days. We seem to be sending the message that it's chic to go on a rampant killing spree. Which, of course, will bring us unwel-come publicity." His tone is pointed.

"Don't you think you're blaming the victim?" one of the twins—I've already forgotten which is which—asks. "Fashion people are the ones being *murdered*."

"I didn't think there was such a thing as unwelcome public-ity," Kristen Drane jokes.

"These murders *bring suspicion on everyone*," Shane says, looking at Lillian. "I've worked hard to get where I am. I do not want it all destroyed by the actions of a disturbed individual."

Lillian scans the crowd, not seeming to pay attention. "Peo-ple are murdered in New York every day," she says. "There aren't any 'fashion murders.' Just simple murders. It's nothing for us to worry about."

Noë jumps in quickly to agree with Lillian. "Fashion can be somewhat self-centered. Maybe it's not even about us."

Lillian sighs, as if the conversation is infinitely boring. "Kate," she says. "Go tell that young man from Photo to come over here and get a few pictures of us."

"Who do you mean?"

I know perfectly well who she means.

"James, of course," Lillian says. "Handsome young man. Brown hair. Lavender button-down."

Lillian thinks James is handsome? She knows what he's wearing?

I find him without difficulty. He's aiming a camera the size of Manhattan at some girls sporting the "robot" look. His cheek is dark-stubbly and the lightweight, lavender cotton shirt covering his just-right, wide-but-not-too-wide shoulders is creased and untucked. He looks insanely hot.

"Hi," I say. "Lillian wants you to come over and take our pictures."

"Kate!" he says warmly. "How did you get in here? Let me see this dress!"

"They borrowed it from Marni for me," I say. "I'm a seat-filler."

"Let me get a photograph." He stands back from me a few feet and shoots from the chest, without lifting the camera. "One more." From a pocket, he unearths a digital camera and takes a few snaps from different angles, never looking through the viewfinder. "The digital ones are for me."

Why does he want a picture of me?

"Can I see?" I ask.

"Nope."

"Why not?"

"Girls want their photos to be pretty. But I'm not trying to take glamour shots."

"Trust me," I say, "I don't expect to look pretty." And then I regret it, because he probably thinks I'm fishing for a compliment.

I take the camera. Every shot is a super-close-up. Half of my face. My arm and part of my torso. The hem of my blue taffeta dress, thighs, and knees. The random framing captures equally random parts of other people in the crowd, including, in one, a slice of the redhead I saw him talking to earlier. "I love how you get the feeling of the crowd," I tell him.

"Thanks," he says. "It's something I've been working on."

I smile. He smiles back at me and there's the sense of both of us wanting to say something else. Then he slips past me toward Lillian's table, briefly resting his hand on my waist as he does so.

FOR THE sit-down dinner, Lillian is at a table with celebrities, as befits her rank, and I'm in social Siberia, as befits mine.

On one side of my place, marked by a card with a whimsical cartoon scalpel, is an empty chair. On the other is a down-to-earth-looking lone brunette wearing an Indian tunic-dress, almost definitely made by child slave labor, but I'm betting she didn't think about that when she bought it. Three empty martini glasses line the table in front of her.

I order another Bloody Mary from a passing waiter.

"Do you have a light?" the brunette asks me.

"Sorry," I say. "I'm probably the only person in here who *doesn't* smoke."

"I'm Beverly Grant. I'm a researcher. And you're Kate McGraw, the new chew toy."

Aunt Vic says a woman should never respond to anonymous correspondence, electronic winks, or insults from drunks. I turn my head to watch as a boisterous party of four, talking amongst themselves, takes seats on the other side of the table from us.

"I'll bet you can't wait to be made into one of them," Beverly says, and takes a big slug of her martini.

I shrug and smile. I wish that seat on my left weren't empty. The name card says Gary Elders. I wish Gary would turn up so I'd have someone else to talk to. But whoever he is, Gary must be at a better party than ours tonight because he hasn't shown by the time the waiters bring around the first course. Beverly and I sit uncomfortably side by side without talking to each other. Then she turns to me. "I saw you give me that fashion-bitch evil eye when you walked over here, but you know what? Whatever. I don't care about your standards."

My standards? Who am I, Diana Vreeland?

I should know better than to try to reason with a drunk and belligerent person—but I can't help myself.

"I was looking at your top and wondering who made it because Indian tunics like the one you're wearing are usually made in sweatshops. I always wonder if people know that when they buy them. I'm sorry I gave you a look. I didn't mean anything by it."

"You care about shwetshops," she slurs.

"Yes, I do."

"Me too. I care, too." She pushes her bleary-eyed face into mine. "You're okay. I like you." She wraps an arm around my neck and repeats, "I like her," to the table at large. No one pays any attention to us.

"Waiter!" She grabs a passing attendant and orders another martini.

"Are you sure you want that?" I ask.

"Never been more sure of anything. I'll tell you a she-cret. I'm scared shitless. That's where Mr. Martini comes in."

She focuses, with difficulty, on me. "Have you noticed," she asks, "that there is something very wrong with our coworkers? Something not right with the glamorous inner circle you're becoming a part of? They don't eat. They drink only crimson fluids. They're skinny, pale, nocturnal, glamorous, look great in black. What *are* they?"

"Models," I say, and laugh.

She doesn't look amused.

The penny drops. "Oh, are you talking about that StakeOut stuff?" I ask her. "I don't think that's funny."

"It's not meant to be funny. Itsh all true."

"You've got to be kidding," I say. Though she doesn't sound like she's kidding.

She's leaning in close to me now, and her voice has dropped.

"You seem nice, even if you are their new best friend. So I'm going to tell you something I shouldn't."

I wait. It worries me that Beverly is starting to sound more sober.

"Lillian Hall is a vampire. She came over from Europe, and she brought most of the staff with her. They are all dead. They are all hundreds of years old. They kill people to remain eternally youthful. And when they meet somebody new who they want in their club, they kill her by sucking the blood out of her body, and then they do some kind of presto-chango and turn her into a vampire, too."

She takes a slug of her drink. "Think about it. Have you ever seen them eat? Or drink anything that's not blood-based?

Or use the toilet? I can promise you, no one has ever taken a piss in the executive bathroom."

I don't know what to say to her. She has access to the executive bathroom?

"I've been doing research. I've discovered a string of unexplained deaths plaguing people in the fashion industry. People get sick and pale. Their hair and skin become fragile. Sometimes they develop strange cravings for inedible objects like clay and paper—"

"It's called *pica*," I say absently. "It's a sign of acute anemia. And also spoon nails, when the person's nails invert and turn into tiny spoons."

She keeps talking without indicating that she has heard me. "The other stuff all makes sense now, because these sick people are the vampires' prey."

I feel light-headed. A slug of the Bloody Mary only increases my disorientation. I don't believe in the vampire theory for a second. Beverly Grant, unfortunately, is cracked. It's amazing to me that even in modern times people come up with quasi-sensible mythologies to explain medical mysteries.

"How incredible," I say aloud.

"You don't believe me?" she asks.

"Well, no," I admit.

"Okay, look." Beverly lifts up her long dark hair to expose her neck and collarbone area. "When those bloodsuckers you think are your new friends bite you, they get you here"—she indicates her neck. "And sometimes here, here, or here." She taps her wrists, the spot where the deep blood-bearing veins run across the stomach, and the great saphenous vein in the groin. "The reason that I'm drinking all these martinis—the reason I'm so scared—is because I think someone on staff knows I'm onto her. I am in perfect health. And you saw that I don't have any marks on me. But if I turn up like that little dog—yes, I know all about it—you'll know what's happened."

Beverly is swaying in her chair and we haven't even reached the dessert course.

"Nothing is going to happen to you." I put my arm around her shoulder and try to be reassuring. "Besides a hangover, that is."

"You don't think so?" she asks. "I'm scared. I think they've been monitoring my e-mails. And sometimes, at night, I feel like someone is following me."

"I definitely don't think so. And tonight I'll put you in a taxi."

I definitely *do* think it's time for Beverly to leave while she can still walk.

Twenty air-kisses and one annoyed taxi driver later and I'm back at the party.

I run into James at the door, which expels all thoughts of vampires from my mind. He's done for the night, the big camera stashed in a bulky black shoulder bag.

"I thought you left," he says.

"Nope." He was looking for me? "Are you leaving?"

"I could get another drink," he says. His cheeks are flushed and he has the dark line of a wine stain on his cherubic red lips. I wonder how many drinks he's already had. I follow him into the bar area, which, since dinner is still happening, is mainly deserted.

He orders wine. I order another Bloody Mary and vow not to drink it, since I'm already way over my limit.

We talk about the party, work, nonsense. Dinner ends. From the other room comes the sound of the band starting up. He says, "You know those photos of you I took? The ones I said weren't going to be pretty?"

"Yeah?"

"They're pretty."

His dark-golden eyes are guileless. We're sitting on bar stools facing each other, so that my knees are between his knees, our feet on each other's rungs.

"Thanks."

"Look," he says, "I'm sorry if I've been weird with you."

"I haven't noticed you being weird with me," I lie.

"Yes you have. I have been. You're so young," he says. "And there's a lot you don't know. You're a lot younger than I am."

"I'm not. How old are you, twenty-seven? I'll be twenty-three in March." I've already calculated his age from the year he graduated college (which I know because I Googled him).

"I could tell you," he says sadly "reasons that make certain things a bad idea."

We're leaning so close together, our noses are almost touching. Up close, I can see the individual flecks of gold in his eyes.

"Oh, fuck it," he says. He wraps a hand around the back of my neck.

He kisses me. We kiss. He is a fantastic kisser. I am perfectly, gloriously happy. And then he reaches underneath my bar stool and drags it closer, with me on it, and kisses me some more and I'm even happier.

He holds my chin and looks into my eyes. I grab him by the shirt collar. "Do you realize that a lot of our coworkers are here?"

"Yes." He kisses me some more. "It's bad. I know it's bad."

Aching with reluctance, I pull away. "People are going to see," I tell him.

"Do you want to go somewhere else? You can come back to Brooklyn with me. I promise I'll be a gentleman."

I'm about to say yes, I swear I am, when some vestige of Kate-ness reasserts itself in my lust-soaked brain. I don't just go home with guys. I *never* just go home with guys. Especially not with a guy I really like. If a guy likes you, he's going to call you, so you'll get a second chance. And if he doesn't really like you and this is your only chance, you don't want to sleep with him, anyway. Right?

"I don't think so," I whisper.

He's still holding my face in his hands, and he stares at me for a long time when I say this, opening his mouth a few times as if to argue and then shutting it. Then he lets go of me, leans back, and sighs. "You're right," he says. "I've gone insane."

It's at this extremely inopportune moment that Annabel chooses to interrupt. "We have an emergency." She looks genuinely upset.

James stands up, sliding off his bar stool and picking up the black camera bag. "I should go. I was just leaving," he says. The way he gets to his feet tells me that he's drunker than I realized.

Annabel and I both watch him stagger away. Then she leans forward and hisses. "Lillian wants him!"

"For what? I already sent him over there once."

Annabel gives me a withering look.

"You mean *wants*-him wants him? Doesn't she have better people to want than the photo boy?" Mentally, I apologize to James for the characterization.

"That's complicated. She likes them *because* they're young. Before James, she was after an intern in Ad Sales."

"What happened to *him*? Why doesn't she still like *him*?"

"He's gone. . . ." Annabel looks evasive. "It doesn't matter. You have to stay away from James. I don't think anyone but me saw you, but if they did, you're dead. Lillian will kill you. Literally, she'll kill you, if you make her jealous."

I hate the way people misuse the word *literally*.

10

Relative Notoriety

PERVERSELY, BY THE time the subway gets me home, I'm wide awake. I dawdle along Broadway and when my cell phone beeps, my heart lurches with the wildly improbable hope that it's a text message from James. Never mind that he doesn't have my number. The more rational part of me expects that it's Sylvia, who could easily be up at this time on the West Coast, but the number on my display is a 917, a mobile phone code for New York City. I open the message.

Congratulations Baby Mac, you're famous. -SO

I stare at it and type back:

Who is this? -KM

There is no reply. I quicken my pace toward home and call Sylvia, whose last name does not begin with O.

"This crazy researcher," she asks me after I fill her in on my dinner companion, "do you think she's onto something?"

"I think she might be *on* something. . . ."

"But the world of fashion would be the perfect hideout for vampires!" Sylvia says, having fun. She's very smart, but she loves this stuff—Anne Rice, Anita Blake, *Buffy*. Vampire novels were her secret vice at school. "You told me yourself they sleep all day. And didn't you mention something about them having cold hands and fangs?"

"They don't sleep all day every day. Sometimes they go to fashion shoots, or to spas, or to sample sales."

"So they've adapted to the modern world," she concludes, as if she weren't talking total nonsense. "You need a protective necklace or amulet and— Oh."

"*Oh* what?"

"Oh, never mind."

"No, what were you going to say?"

"What about James? Could he be one, too? He works at *Tasty*. Did you notice if his hands or lips were cold?"

"They definitely weren't cold."

"That's good but not conclusive. He might have just fed."

"Sylvia!" I screech.

I hang up with Sylvia before getting into the elevator of Vic's building. The apartment, as usual, is still and empty, populated only by nodding orchids and priceless art. I head into the kitchen and rustle up ingredients for a grilled cheese. Thanks to drunk Beverly Grant and her disturbing convictions, I didn't get enough to eat during dinner.

My aunt walks into the kitchen wrapped in a fuchsia silk robe with a contrast-band of brilliant blue around the waist and blue bias-tape trim. "What's this very unusual smell?" she asks.

I take my grilled cheese out of the pan and divide it between two plates. There is nothing more delicious than a midnight grilled cheese, though in this case it's a two A.M. grilled cheese.

"So tell me, darling, what was your evening like?"

Chatting with Vic about her party and my party, I realize this is what I hoped that staying with her would be like. I'm about to suggest we do it more often when she drops the bombshell.

"I'm flying to Italy tomorrow evening and I'm not sure when I'll be back."

My heart plummets. If she hadn't been lured by the smell of food cooking, would she have just left? No note? Nothing?

"I'm sure you'll be fine here by yourself. The maid will come. She waters the orchids." Victoria waves a hand airily, as if my only concern would be taxing myself with the house-work.

"Why are you going?" I try to cover my distress.

"A collector I've been working on for ages has decided to sell a Schiele. I have to hold his hand to make sure he doesn't change his mind. It's utterly vexing, but the painting will be the sensation of the fall auctions."

"Oh. Congratulations."

"Thank you. It is a coup de grâce, if I do say so myself. So go ahead, do whatever it is you've been dying to do except for the presence of the old bat."

I haven't been dying to do anything except spend some quality time with my aunt.

"Have a nice trip." I air-kiss her good night.

• • •

I DRESS myself with extra care in the morning. Blue velvet wedges. A stark, super-short black sheath dress with tulip sleeves of my own design, very punk princess. I tie a white velvet ribbon around my wrist. Not bad.

But when I get to the office, I begin to feel paranoid.

Is it me, or am I sensing a pregnant hush? Felix eyes me with more interest than usual. A couple of girls who I think are in the face creams department fall silent and stare at me when I walk past. By the time I get to my area, I'm actually relieved to see Nin and Rachel. At least I know why they hate me and aren't speaking to me.

But, ominously, they are speaking to me.

"Hi, Kate!" Nin says. "Did you have fun at the party last night?"

I don't like the way she cackles after she says this.

"Did you talk to anyone interesting?" she asks coyly.

"Why do you ask?"

"Just trying to live vicariously. Enjoying my proximity to the new It girl."

I wonder what new form of mockery this is.

"What are you talking about?" I ask her. "I was a seat-filler."

"Why don't you read StakeOut, and then you tell us," Rachel suggests.

SOON-TO-BE-FATAL ATTRACTION

Looks like someone is getting long in the tooth. Among her many other charming attributes—sleeping in a

coffin, drinking blood, and having a "signature style," to
name just a few—*Tasty* EIC Lillian Hall is known to enjoy
flirtations with her younger (and we're talking centuries,
folks!) male colleagues. At last night's party at Carnivoré,
Hall's flavor of the month was seen deep in conversation
with an attractive young junior staffer while the Queen
of the Damned Fashionable was a bored stiff in the dining room. Heads are going to roll if Hall finds out. Oh,
oops, she just did.

TAGS: TASTY, VAMPIRES, OLDHAM INC., LILLIAN HALL, THE DAMNED

Deep in conversation. That's not so bad. That's not
"engaged in ravenous kissing," which would be closer to the
truth. Who the hell is writing this stuff? I've suspected Rico,
but Rico wasn't at the party. Unless, I realize with horror,
James told him when he got home. But why would he do
that? James may be maddeningly elusive, as is the way of
cute guys, but he wouldn't want to get me in trouble. And he
told me he tries to stay out of the gossips. Unless that was a
front.

I click the browser window shut and stare at my screen,
brain churning, afraid to turn around and face my fellow
interns' questioning gazes. Since we're at a temporary lull in
Tasty Girl work—Lexa is deciding on winners from the list of
semifinalists Annabel gave her—I'm free to freak out, and wait
to be fired.

Around eleven-thirty a message comes in from Annabel.
It says:

Don't panic. No one but *me* knows it was you.

I e-mail back:

> People are acting weird. Rachel and Nin all but accused me.
> Are you sure?

Her reply:

> Yes. They are gossiping about everyone, and your name is
> on the list as a junior staffer at the party, but there's
> nothing specific.

Me:

> Thank you, thank you, thank you.

Her:

> Don't thank me yet. You're toast if Lillian suspects you.

I try not to despair. But if StakeOut is right—and evidence suggests that it is—then I'm in serious trouble. Because one other person has seen me tucked into a corner with James, deep in conversation. And that's Lillian herself at the Saks party last week. Even if no one else is especially suspicious of me, she will be.

THE DAY drags on.

For once, Lexa isn't bombarding us with requests. I want to walk by the photo department and catch a glimpse of James, but I can't muster the courage. All I can do is check my e-mail every thirty seconds, hoping that he'll send me a greeting or acknowledgment after last night.

Just as I'm starting to think about lunch, a brisk rap sounds on our door. I don't turn around until I hear Rachel in tones of scandalized awe say, "Hello, Lillian! Hello, Lexa!"

I whirl in my chair, palms sweating. Lillian looks fantastic in a black pencil skirt (they're calling them "skinny skirts" this season), black blazer, and patent-leather shoes like alien architecture. She catches my eye. Her matte red lips grimace. I think it's a smile. But it can't be a smile. Lillian *can't* continue being friendly to me after reading on the Internet that I, a lowly intern, am her rival. Especially because StakeOut committed the unforgivable sin of making fun of her age.

Lexa looks grouchy. Belatedly, I realize that my morning's perusal of the tabloids didn't turn up a single mention of her. No wonder she's pissed.

"Kate," Lillian says. "We have a special surprise for you."

Oh, God.

"Now that Reese is no longer with us, we have a column opening up. She wrote a page in the 'GirlTalk' section that was supposed to be youthful and casual."

Wait a minute. What happened to Reese?

"So someone with no writing experience should be able to handle it," Lexa adds.

Lillian continues, "Lauren told me that you had spoken to her about wanting to write something. She said you'd been working on some ideas for us."

I came up with them only last week but it seems like much longer than that.

"I have," I say hesitantly, acutely aware of Rachel and Nin listening. "I've been exploring good fashion. *Morally* good fashion. If I wrote a page on that, we could show clothes that are sweatshop free. Environmentally responsible fabrics for people who sew. Accessories with small carbon footprints. The theme could be different every month. . . ."

The room is silent.

"Sounds PETA to me," Lexa says coldly.

At the word *PETA*, there's a nervous rustle. Nin glances surreptitiously at Lillian, as if awaiting her wrath. It's well known that our fearless leader and PETA have a personal enmity.

"Would the clothes be cute?" Lillian asks.

Around here, "cute" is the highest form of praise. The opposite of cute is "enh." And believe me, you don't want to be "enh."

"Of course." Sweating, I stumble forward with my explanation. "They are great for our demographic. A store in Los Angeles just hosted an Eco Fashion Week. And that brand Stewart + Brown uses all organic cotton and donates part of their profits to save the environment." I've done my research.

Lillian's look is unreadable.

"*Tsch!*" Lexa leaps into the breach. I take it that's even worse than "enh." "Fashion is supposed to be *fun.*"

"It can be fun to wear environmentally clean clothes."

"Clean clothes," Lillian pronounces. "I like it. Have something for us by Wednesday."

Lillian is famous for her relentless awareness of current media. The only possible explanation for her continued favoritism is that she hasn't read StakeOut today.

Why hasn't she read StakeOut?

Lillian and Lexa sweep off, leaving us in stunned silence.

Then Rachel collapses onto her desk and starts wailing. "I should have gotten that assignment! I'm the writer! I blog thanklessly, day in and day out." She bangs her head on the desk. "I've begged them—Lillian, Lauren, Lexa, Kristen, Alessandra, Reese, all of them!"—Bang—"to give me a byline. Just one tiny byline so I can get a real fucking job!"

"You've asked people for writing assignments?" Nin squeals. "You lied to me!"

"Of course I've asked, you idiot!" Rachel cries.

Nin's ordinarily happy face goes dark. "I may not be a genius," she says, "but at least I didn't go into magazines for the *writing*."

"I think I should close the door," I say, hopping to my feet.

Rachel keeps sobbing and banging her head. "What's the *point* of publishing if you don't do it while you're young and hot?"

"You guys," I say, hovering anxiously between the two of them. "We should try working together. Maybe if we *supported* each other we'd all get what we want."

They both glare at me. They're so myopic, it's frustrating.

"I could help you both," I tell them. "I could help you get into parties. I could put in a good word with you for the writing. But the way you've acted, why should I bother?"

"Why would you do that?" Nin asks. "What would you get out of it?"

"I'd do it because I'm nice."

Rachel lifts her head off the desk. Her face is red and her hair is sticking to her lip gloss. "Nice?" she asks. "I want to be a magazine editor! Being mean and not doing any work is the industry standard!" She balls up her fists and folds over in her chair.

"Try *ujjayi* breathing," Nin suggests. "It's a yoga thing."

"Look," I say, slowly and patiently, "let's just give it a try. Right now. I've always wanted to go to the cafeteria. Do you want to come?"

•　•　•

THE OLDHAM cafeteria is disorienting like the first floor of a department store—crowded, confusing layout, too much choice, danger of asphyxiation by secondhand perfume—but it's much, much more fabulous. I'm way too overstimulated to choose my food properly, and end up with the odd combination of a beet-and-goat-cheese salad and a plate of sautéed broccoli rabe.

"Look at that girl," I say to my fellow interns after we've found a seat in the undulating-glass-walled room. I subtly indicate a Nicole Kidman look-alike wearing a giant corset belt. "Cute or enh?"

"Enh," Rachel says. She's got her notebook out and is madly scribbling notes.

She and Nin have seen it all before, and today they don't want to talk about clothes. They want to talk about Lillian.

"So what do you think?" Nin asks me. "Is Lillian losing it?"

"She clearly hasn't read StakeOut," Rachel says. "She doesn't know that there's an ugly item up there about her. The old Lillian would *never* have missed something like that. And she would have fired the entire junior staff rather than let it go unpunished."

"Speaking of firings, what happened to Reese?" I ask them.

"We were going to ask you! You were at the party."

"That doesn't mean I know everything that went on there."

"It was during the sit-down dinner," Rachel says. "You couldn't miss it. We heard there was screaming."

"One of the women at my table got really drunk. I had to take her out and put her in a cab."

"Well, you know how Reese has gone Goth lately?" Nin says. "It's because of that ridiculous vampire rumor. *She believed it.*"

Lauren's comment about someone trying to expense a purchase at a blood bank clicks into place. "She's not the only one," I mutter. "But still, I can't believe she got fired for that."

"She tried to bite someone at the party!"

"And then," Nin adds, "she went insane. She started crying and begging and saying she wanted to 'fit in.' They took her straight to the mental ward at Bellevue."

"That's really sad," I say.

"Please," Rachel says. "You benefited. You got her column. Don't pretend you aren't psyched about it."

I don't want a column at the expense of someone's mental breakdown. But Nin and Rachel would never believe that.

"Worst of all, Lillian ignored the whole thing," Rachel says. "She sat there talking to a male model. What happened to ruling with an iron fist in a velvet glove?"

"Gloves are in," Nin contributes.

Rachel continues: "She's distracted. She barely edits anymore. She lets Lauren, of all people, do the heavy lifting. Mind you, Lauren dresses from Banana Republic and has spit-up on her clothes."

"Lauren just gave birth to twins. And she works full time," I interject.

"Whatever. She's not a *qualified* trendsetter."

I feel uncomfortable criticizing Lillian, who has been so nice to me, but this line of thought gives me an opportunity to bring up something I'm dying to discuss.

"I mentioned the fashion murders last night and Lillian ignored that, too," I say.

Nin's eyes widen. Rachel's hand makes a reflexive dive toward her notebook, before she quells the motion.

"You were at that Saks party, weren't you?" Nin whispers.

I nod. *Finally* someone is taking the situation seriously.

"Did you see the bodies? What did they look like? What were they wearing?" Rachel asks.

Of course I remember in vivid detail, but I don't feel right gossiping about it. "We left before the police showed up. I was with Kristen, Noë, and Matilda when we found out, and none of them acted like they cared at all. Don't you think that's weird?"

"I'm not surprised," Rachel says. "Nin cried when she heard about that double murder at the Jean Saint-Pierre atelier—"

"My *mom* reads *Yarn Daily*," Nin explains.

"—and Annabel came in all huffy and told her to get ahold of herself," Rachel finishes. "We're supposed to be glamorous and poised at all times."

"Doesn't that strike you as excessively cold?" I ask. "Don't you two get the sense that people here are weirder than can be explained by the industry? Like, have you noticed that they sleep in their offices all morning?"

"I have," Rachel says. "I saw Kristen Drane lying on her floor. And I've seen those French girls sleeping, too. Together."

"What do you make of it?" I ask cautiously. I'm not sure I want to bring up the vampire rumor, especially because she's been so scathing about it in the past.

"I think they party too much, so they have to sleep in. They're addicted to the limelight. And probably drugs," Rachel says disapprovingly.

"You don't think they're actually . . . kind of evil?" I press.

"Oh, come on, darlin'," Nin says. "They're no different from you and me when you get down to it." Her gaze is drawn by a passing figure. "Ooooh," she says. "Ruching!"

JAMES DOESN'T call me after lunch. He doesn't stop by my office to chat or even walk by to secretly signal that he's thinking of me. I don't dare go talk to him, so I send him an e-mail that says, "Hey. How are you feeling this morning?" It's lame but it's the least lame thing I can come up with.

And then I wait for a response. And wait. And wait.

At six P.M. I walk by his desk, but his computer is off and he's gone for the day.

11

The Queen of Suck-up

" CAN'T BELIEVE she still wants to come upstate with me,"
I'm telling Sylvia via phone Saturday morning. "People
like her vaporize if they leave Manhattan."

But of course, I can believe it. Annabel is the queen of
suck-up and our location-scouting mission is of the utmost
importance to Lexa, a high-profile assignment. Annabel
wouldn't miss it for a brand-new pair of Chanel wedge heels.

"And she's really going to sleep over at your dad's house?"
Sylvia is scandalized.

"Yes!" I wail. "She wants to. She says it's too far for a day
trip."

Moreover, it's Saturday morning, and now I have to wait for
her to wake up and call me. I'm eager to be on the bus, leaving
behind the island of Manhattan and all its bloody rumors.
With my aunt in Italy, the too-big apartment feels even emp-
tier than before.

"You know, in *Dracula,* the count had difficulty crossing
bodies of water."

"Blood-sucking is the least of my problems right now."

"I wish I was there," Sylvia says.

"I wish you were here, too," I tell her. "Believe me."

MONTICELLO HAS never struck me as particularly green, but two weeks in New York City has put my native town in perspective. The grassy median strips look positively bucolic. I roll down the window of my dad's car for a deep breath of the fresh country air.

"Kate, that's pitiful," my dad says, laughing. He's just picked Annabel and me up from the Greyhound bus stop.

"Dad, you're numb to the beauty of your natural surroundings. Look at all that grass. Those trees. The wildflowers by the side of the road."

"Sounds like you're turning into a New Yorker! God forbid," he says, still laughing.

"Dad!" I say. "Be polite. Annabel is a New Yorker."

Annabel, wrapped up in a black Indian-cotton shawl, and wearing oversized sunglasses, is perched eagerly in the backseat of our tiny lime-green Prius.

"I don't mind New Yorker jokes," she says, jumping to Dan's defense.

I'm glad to see she's fully recovered. Leaving New York by bus sent her into shock—the emotional kind, not the medical kind, which in fact is a state of inadequate tissue perfusion. She was quiet and jumpy for the whole ride, but is now gawking at the countryside as if she's never seen it before.

"Born and raised in the Big Apple, huh?" my dad asks her cheesily.

"I've lived on Park Avenue for my entire life," she says. "Was that a wolf?"

"Might have been. But it was probably somebody's dog," Dan replies tactfully.

It's going to be a long weekend.

Dan McGraw learns more about Annabel in one car ride than I have in two weeks.

"How do you like your job?" he asks her.

"I hate it," she promptly replies.

"You do?" I turn around in my seat. "I thought you adored it."

"Do *you* adore working for Lexa?" she asks me. Then she addresses Dan. "Our boss is a nightmare, an *incompetent* nightmare. It reflects badly on me. I'm worried she's jeopardizing my chances for promotion."

"That's what you're after?" Dan asks. "A promotion?"

"Yes. I've been at *Tasty* for a year already."

"I see." Dan nods thoughtfully, though he's the least ambitious person in the world and would probably work ten years before starting to simmer about a promotion. "What's the next step? Can you change jobs?"

"If I do that, I'll have to start at the bottom again," she says.

Dan mulls this over. "Can you get the boss fired?"

He's joking, but Annabel doesn't realize this.

"Kate," she says, "I love your dad!"

Basking in the attention, Dan insists we go out for ice cream. Privately, I don't think Annabel will eat any, but it turns out to be the right call. Our local White Horse Farm Stand has a blood-orange sorbet that's her favorite.

We sit at a shady picnic table in a grove of river birch and lick our cones, Annabel still mummied up in her shawl and glasses like a celebrity gone grocery shopping. She and my father totally hit it off.

"Let me ask you something," Dan says, leaning across the table toward her. "Do you like fashion? Do you truly thrive on it?"

Again, I'm surprised by her answer. "I'm not sure," she says. "I know I love the magazine business. And I know I want to be an editor-in-chief. But . . ." She shrugs. "I never like what I'm wearing. It's kind of agony and ecstasy all at once."

"Have you explored your options? Considered working at a different magazine? At this point, it's so important that you get on the right track. Now is the time for you to find out who you are and what you want, before you get stuck on a career path."

A crease forms between her blonde eyebrows. "Thanks, Mr. McGraw, but it's too late," she says. "I'm already stuck."

"Sweetie, you're what, twenty-four? You can still move around. I know it seems old to you now, but take it from a guy who's pushing fifty—you ain't old."

"I can't leave the fashion industry," she tells him, an edge creeping into her voice. "It's impossible."

He acquiesces gracefully. "Well, what do I know? I'm just a guy who makes hemp shirts for a living."

"Now, that's *cool!*" she says, gushy again.

They are *so* annoying me.

ONCE WE'VE dropped off our bags at my dad's house, Annabel wants to scout the Tasty Girl location while we still have light. We borrow the car, leaving Dan, who is looking a little wistful, behind. I drive. The directions take us out of the village on Route 97 and then right on 52, deep into Sullivan County. It's not an area I'm very familiar with.

"What are we looking for?" Annabel asks as the car glides along.

"Turn left at the rusty bridge five miles outside of Jefferson-ville. After the first three miles, the pavement ends. Keep going straight. Cross the creek, cross the dry creek-bed, and then turn right at the fork." I hand her my notepad so she can see for herself. "These directions came from Lexa. I hope we find it," I add.

"We'll find it," she says. "We won't leave till we find it."

Eventually we do find the rusty bridge—or at least *a* rusty bridge—and I pull the car off the road and into the woods. We hum along through thick foliage. I'm thinking about Lillian, and how she doesn't know I'm the one responsible for that mean StakeOut item. She gave me Reese's column. I know it's not my fault, not really, but I feel guilty.

"Your dad is so nice," Annabel says, her head tilted back on the headrest.

The pavement ends with a jolt. The underbrush, pierced only by a narrow lane, swells up around us. Branches scrape along the sides of the car as we nose forward.

"Do you think this is right?" I ask Annabel dubiously.

"They said it was isolated," she replies, sounding pleased.

I turn on the headlights and we crawl forward.

"I don't have parents," she says, making me regret my uncharitable thoughts about her and Dan.

"What happened to them?"

"Oh, they're alive. But it's too unhealthy for me to expose

myself to them. I took over a maid's apartment in our building and haven't spoken to them in ages."

"That's awful. Why?"

"Lecherous stepfather. Controlling ex-model mother who just *can't* get over losing her looks. You know the drill."

I don't, and I'm not sure what to say about it, either. "That's awful," I repeat. Annabel doesn't seem inclined to add any more.

"You might want to close the window," I suggest as some leafy greens are ripped off and swirl into her lap.

She smiles at me. "You're so thoughtful. It's no wonder everybody loves you at work."

"No one loves me at work! Lillian is going to discover that StakeOut item about me and James sooner or later, and then she's going to kill me. Lexa already wants to kill me. And Rachel and Nin are only putting up with me because I might be useful to them."

Annabel shrugs. "Internet items are fleeting. If Lillian hasn't seen it yet, you might get away with it. And for now she loves you. Lexa, I agree, needs some work. And Rachel and Nin don't matter. They don't have what it takes."

"How is that possible? They're rich and connected. Rachel's smart, Nin's beautiful and stylish."

"You'll understand eventually. Trust me, okay?"

"Maybe they just need more experience. . . ." I trail off. "Holy shit."

We have arrived at the location.

Two hundred years ago it was probably a nice clapboard farmhouse in the New England saltbox style. Now it's a ruin of broken windows and collapsed foundations. Queen Anne's lace has overtaken what once were fields. I turn off the engine. Sticky air and the drone of insects flood the car.

"Is *this* what Lexa had in mind?" I ask.

"It's perfect!" Annabel jumps out of the car, beating a path through the tall grass toward the house.

I follow more slowly, dutifully taking pictures with my digital camera. My bare legs are immediately aflame with the phantom itchies caused by walking through underbrush on a hot day, and I scratch absentmindedly. The place is definitely on the creepier side of beautiful, if not downright creepy. But I suppose I can see it as a backdrop for girls in luxurious clothing. It makes fashion-shoot sense. And Giedra Dylan-Hall is known for her lush, unusual work. I wonder what Shane is going to think of it.

Closer to the house, the ground becomes hummocky and uneven. I stumble over it, thinking of burial mounds and shallow graves.

"Annabel?" My voice sounds forlorn. She's gone around back. I pick my way after her, following the trail of crushed grass and scratching my prickly skin.

She's standing at the edge of a dark hole in the ground, head bowed.

"Annabel!" I yell, freaked out. She looks up at me and smiles radiantly. "This is some kind of cellar," she says. "Isn't it great? Take my picture."

"Why don't you stand away from the edge?" I ask her nervously. "I don't want to have to come down there after you."

"Kate," she says, "you're bleeding."

"What?" I look down to see that my nails have dug shallow grooves in my legs.

"Oh. It's the humidity. Did you know scrapes bleed more easily when it's sultry like this outside?"

She gives me a very weird look. Her face falters. Then she says, "Give me the camera. We won't have useable light for much longer."

BECAUSE OF the tight deadline for my first "Clean Clothes" column, I have the perfect excuse not to socialize after dinner (Dan cooked, he and I ate, Annabel moved the food around on her plate without taking a bite). Even though she's being perfectly nice, and has even confided in me about her creepy rich-girl family life, something about her makes me edgy.

Dan, with an aura of gentle reproach for my sulkiness, has gone over to his friend Phil's house for poker night. I try to work while Annabel flops around on the sofa in our den, reads a competitor's magazine, stares at herself in the mirrored panels on our TV cabinet. Finally she gives up on the quiet night at home and starts texting with our coworkers. "They're at Death & Co."—a hip underground nightclub in Manhattan. "They want to know what we're doing. What should I tell them?"

"How about working?"

"Nah," she says. "Boring. I'll say we're going through your closets."

"Okay," I reply, distracted. An e-mail from Sylvia has just come in, supplying me with a list of vampire qualities. She's been research-mad since I told her what Beverly said. The qualities are:

1. Nocturnal, sunlight intolerant, sleep in a box or coffin, or don't sleep at all
2. Cold fleshed, drink fresh blood
3. Endowed with eternal life
4. Driven away by garlic, holy water
5. Can be killed by a silver bullet, a stake through the heart, sawing off the head, fire
6. Don't like to eat but can, if need be
7. Superhuman strength, extrasensory powers, transformations into bats or dogs
8. Glamorous, materialistic, well-dressed

Besides for the bit about turning into a bat or a dog, that sounds like my coworkers to me. And garlic, according to Rico, is banned in the Oldham cafeteria. Ten minutes later Annabel says, "Hey, let's really go look at your closets," and I give up on my research for the night. I can't concentrate, anyway.

As we're getting ready for bed—after unearthing and trying on every stitch of my perfectly preserved collection of Eva 4 Eva originals—I hear a beep come from my bag.

"Who's that?" Annabel asks.

The number on the display looks familiar, but I can't place it until I open the body of the message. It reads:

Somebody's about to blow . . . again. Who's going to get hit next? Hope it won't be you, kittyKat -SO

I slam the clamshell receiver shut. My hand is shaking.

What the hell? It's the same person who called me "Baby Mac" before, and claimed I was going to be famous. The night *before* the first piece ran about me on StakeOut.

SO . . . *oh, no*. "It was my best friend, Sylvia, from L.A."

"What did she say?"

It might be my imagination, but Annabel sounds suspicious.

"She's at a good party."

Annabel has produced a long white cotton nightgown from the depths of her Gucci carryall. It wouldn't have looked out of place in the Victorian era. She looks like a ghost.

"That's very spring 1882, isn't it?" I joke, trying to change the subject.

"I haven't been around that long. It's a reproduction." She smiles a hard, cold smile at me, showing her fangy teeth.

I dive into my twin bed and pull the covers up to my chin.

She gets into the other one and turns off the light.

No surprise that I don't drift off right away. *Baby Mac. KittyKat*. StakeOut is texting me. And he/she/it knows my real name. I can't see Rico outing James to all of Oldham, or sending me anonymous, threatening messages, unless I've really misjudged him. But still, it has to be someone who knows me and who is connected to work.

The only thing I can be sure about is that it isn't Annabel, since she's lying right here. Equally worrisome is the message content. Who is about to blow her top? There are so many crazy people at work, it could be anyone. Lillian. Lexa. Beverly Grant.

Even Annabel.

Please let them not mean Annabel.

A slow half hour later, I'm still wide awake. Worse, I have the feeling that Annabel, lying next to me in a twin bed in the dark, is awake, too. She hasn't moved so much as a twitch, and I can't hear her breathing. Nonetheless, I sense her unblinking gray eyes staring at me. It's making my skin crawl.

The communiqués from StakeOut, spreader of vampire rumors, and from Sylvia, aficionado of vampire pop culture, are having a bad effect on me. I know how unhinged it is to be considering this. And I wouldn't be if the light were on. But I'm remembering that night when, overcome by hunger pangs, Annabel ditched me. What was she hungry for? And didn't she look really weird when she saw those bleeding scrapes on my legs today? *Please let her not get hungry while I'm lying here sleeping next to her.*

I tell myself I'm just worried about Beverly. For a person in the grips of a paranoid delusion, she seemed nice. I hate to think of her at home in New York feeling much more scared than I do right now. I should check up on her on Monday, find out how her weekend was and make sure she's okay.

The minutes click by slowly. After an hour, afraid to look in Annabel's direction—because what if she really is lying there staring at me?—I quietly slip out of bed and creep from the room.

I think I'll research the "Clean Clothes" story after all.

I'm in the thick of it, trying to understand what Bamboo's claim that its cashmere "comes from sustainable forests" means, when a breeze brushes the back of my neck. With a muffled shriek, I leap in my chair.

"Tense much?" Dan asks.

"Dad! I'm so glad you're home!" I whisper-cry.

"Thanks, kiddo. Had a late-night winning streak." He holds up a bag of wrapper candy, which is what they use instead of cash.

"Looks like Halloween came early this year."

"So it's two A.M." Dan pulls up a chair. "What is my daughter doing up and working at the computer?"

"I got a writing assignment for the magazine," I say. "It's about environmentally responsible fashion choices."

"That's fantastic!"

"Shh!" I roll my eyes toward the ceiling, reminding him of Annabel's putatively sleeping presence. "It's cool, I guess."

"I'll bet they don't let many interns write," he says, beaming. "I'm proud of you."

"I'm well aware that one article isn't going to change the world."

"Who said that it's your job to change the whole world? If only everyone who wore cotton would switch to hemp, that polar ice cap would stop melting. Individuals *can* make a difference."

"The purpose of go-green articles in magazines isn't to change people's behavior," I explain. "It's to make them *feel* like they've changed their behavior. Twenty minutes of being concerned while reading about the environment and a person can, guilt-free, hop in their SUV and drive to the mall."

"So you hate what you're doing? You're having a bad time? You're sitting here at two A.M. working on your story. Looks to me like you're interested."

"That's true," I admit. I have been enjoying myself.

My father sighs. "You might want to listen to those feelings," he says. "Sometimes I worry that this med school business is a reaction to what happened with your mother. I'd hate to see you play it safe that way."

I open my mouth to protest, but he forestalls me. "If med school is what you really want, I support you one hundred percent. But I've always felt that you might need a more creative outlet. Since—and please don't get mad at me for saying this—I see so much of your mother in you, I think she'd be happy to see you exploring your options."

"Well, you saw where being creative got her," I retort childishly.

"That shouldn't matter. You can't let that hold you back. You can't let an *idea fixay*, pardon my French, determine your future." He lowers his voice even further. "That's what your friend up there is doing. And she seems like a very troubled girl."

Dan sits down with me and provides a list of his contacts in the sustainable-clothing industry, then goes to bed. I stay up until dawn working on the story. I'll just need to make a couple of phone calls during business hours on Monday and it will be finished. Since I still don't relish getting into a bed next to Annabel, I curl up on our sofa under a knitted throw rug and fall asleep wondering what Eva would think if she could see me now. Would she be really be happy? That would be nice. . . .

12

Fashion Victim

MONDAY PASSES IN a blur. During the features meeting, Lexa announces that she's chosen the contest finalists, and not a moment too soon: Giedra is set to shoot the following Monday. Shane approves of the location. Lauren comments that since it's not a working farm, we may need a headline other than "Farm Fresh." Lillian suggests "Babes in the Woods: Winners of Our Tasty Girl Contest," to general acclaim.

After the meeting, Rachel, Nin, Annabel, and I convene in Lexa's office. We're told to call all the Tasty Girls finalists and brief them on the where and when.

"But Lexa, what if they have jobs and they have to work? Or they already have plans?" I ask, feeling that it's unreasonable to give the girls six days to pick up and fly to New York City. I've known when the date of the shoot was, but hadn't thought through what that would mean for the girls.

"People will do anything to be in the magazine," Lexa tells me dismissively.

Annabel raises her hand. "Is Oldham Corporate going to buy their plane tickets?"

"And where are the girls going to stay?" I add. In my hazy imaginings of the process, they were all going to sleep on the farm. But clearly that's out.

Lexa stares at us, her face frozen in outrage and disbelief. "You haven't made the bloody arrangements?"

"I asked you last month. You told me not to worry about it," Annabel says faintly.

"And you didn't think to follow up? Are you daft? Are you trying to sabotage me?" She picks up the daily folder of Internet-gossip printouts and throws it in our direction. Rachel and Nin remain quiet.

"I'm sorry," Annabel says, looking traumatized. "We'll sort it out."

"Obviously I can't trust you," Lexa says. "I want to see backup materials for all the logistics on my desk by the end of the day. Plane tickets. Hotel reservations. What else do we need?"

"Maybe a charter bus to take everyone from the city upstate?" I suggest.

"Order a car service for me and Giedra. A bus is fine for the girls."

"What about us?" Annabel asks. "Are we going along to help out?"

This is not the best time to ask. Lexa looks at her scathingly. "I think I've had quite enough of your help," she snaps.

"Is there a budget we should be sticking to?"

"Don't bother me with petty details. Just get it sorted!"

We retreat to Annabel's half-walled cubicle. I take two

Coach bags, a hair dryer, and a box of Chocolates from the Bald Guy off of her guest chair and sit down, stress buzzing in the back of my neck. Giedra needs to shoot on Monday, July 2, and Tuesday, July 3. We agree that the girls will fly into New York, spend Sunday night in the city, and then take a charter bus upstate early Monday morning. For the night of July 2, I agree to get them accommodations at a motel in Jeffersonville.

"Everyone's going to have to stay at the motel on Monday night. There's nothing else up there," I say to Annabel. She's on hold with the Oldham travel office, working on plane tickets.

"You can't find a nice B&B for Lexa and Giedra?"

"I'm trying, but I'm not having any luck."

"Try harder," Annabel says. "This is Lexa we're dealing with."

BETWEEN ORGANIZING the contest and making phone calls for the "Clean Clothes" story, it's Tuesday before I have a chance to go check on Beverly Grant the way I promised myself I would. And on the way over to her side of the office — Research, Copy, and Production are all on the opposite side of the floor, closer to Shane Lincoln-Shane — I stop by Lauren's office to thank her for suggesting to Lillian and Lexa that I write something.

Our managing editor barely looks up when I come in. "Can I help you?" Lauren's tone is tense. Looking at her, I see that her eyes are bloodshot and weary. Lauren is usually the nicest person on the thirty-seventh floor. I add her to my list of people "SO" might have meant when she (or he) said someone is cracking up.

"You sound stressed out," I say.

"I've just had a shock, but I'm fine."

I wait for a second. If she doesn't volunteer anything else, I'll have to leave.

Lauren drops the galley she was reading. "I don't even know what I'm looking at here." She's blinking back tears. "One of our researchers died this weekend."

My stomach plummets through the floor. "Who?" I whisper. The free-form anxiety I felt over the weekend returns with a vengeance.

"Her name was Beverly Grant. You wouldn't have known her."

I sink into Lauren's guest chair, tears filling my own eyes. "I talked to her at the Carnivoré party. How did she die?"

"She was found in a Nolita dressing room on Sunday morning. Her sister just called to say she'd be picking up her things later on today."

Nolita is a fancy shopping neighborhood in downtown Manhattan. It doesn't seem very Beverly to me.

"But how did she die? Was there a suggestion of foul play?" I ask, hearing how TV-show-cheesy I sound.

"Not that I know of. Why would you think that?"

"You know, the fashion murders . . ."

Lauren sighs wearily. "You're too new to this business to have seen much of the real dark side. The drugs. Beverly probably OD'd."

"Would she be getting high by herself in a dressing room on a Sunday morning?"

"You would be surprised. That particular neighborhood is

notorious. Some stores have one-person-per-room policies because of it."

Beverly knew. She *knew* she was going to die.

One of my professors liked to say that the biggest mistake in medicine is not listening to the patient. This professor claimed that the patient often knows what's wrong with him and his intuitions should be our guide.

So to follow *that* logic . . . Beverly Grant was killed by a vampire.

I offer my condolences and stumble back to my desk without ever thanking Lauren for her help with the column. What if my coworkers actually are vampires? Their movements are inhumanly swift and silent (*Oh, hello, Lexa, I didn't see you standing there*), they're fiendishly strong (Annabel pinning Bambi to the wall by the throat). It would explain the sharp teeth, the cold hands, the blinds always being shut, the not eating, and even, I realize with a shudder, the beet juice. What if those drinks are actually blood? And then: Oh my God, whose blood is it and why is Shane's assistant the one distributing it?

I've had such a strong sense of things not being right around here. . . .

I slouch down in my chair and cradle my head in my hands.

"Are you okay?" Rachel asks me. Maybe she really does have an instinct for news.

"PMS," I say.

Calm down, I tell myself. People here go outside during the day. Vampires can't do that. *But Lillian carries a parasol. And when Annabel came home with me she was all wrapped up in that shawl.* Maybe they can tolerate sunlight it if they have to?

And working in Midtown, with its tall buildings, shady streets, and plentiful awning coverage, would be ideal. My coworkers fit the profile in other ways as well. They stay out all night with ease. They like to sleep during the day. And what about those Bloody Marys with the "real blood" at Carnivoré? I drank some of those! I don't know if they can turn into wolves or bats, or if they have any of the powers of mind control Sylvia mentioned, but then it occurs to me:

Perhaps fashion *is* mind control.

Nin walks in and Rachel asks, "Do you have an Advil for Kate? She has PMS."

"I don't take that," I say automatically. "It's much worse for your liver than the pharmaceutical industry would have you believe."

"My liver's got more serious concerns," Nin drawls.

I take a deep breath. Not everyone in this office is a vampire. Nin isn't and neither is Rachel. They don't drink the Kool-Aid. They get here early. Usually. And Lauren probably isn't. Vampires can't procreate, right? And Beverly wasn't. And the non-fashion people like James . . .

James. At the party he said there were things I didn't want to know. And he made a big deal about being older. What if he meant *really* older?

At this moment, I do not care that being seen talking to him will spark rumors. I head down the hall to the photo department.

JAMES IS at his desk with headphones on and doesn't hear me when I approach. I poke him in the shoulder. He looks up, unsmiling, and takes the headphones off.

"Hi," I say quietly. "I need to talk to you. I have questions about some things you said on Wednesday night."

He looks transparently nervous. It's obvious that he doesn't want his coworkers to overhear this exchange.

"There's a deli around the corner on Fifty-ninth Street," he says. "It's on the northwest corner. There's seating in the back. Meet me there in fifteen minutes. Just buy something and sit down."

Ah, the Plaza Gourmet III. I know it well. It's where people go to hide.

I SIT down in back, bathed in greenish glow. Crazy-quilt mirrors reflect my own moon-faced image. James walks back a few minutes later. He doesn't sit down.

"Did you hear about Beverly Grant?" I ask him.

"It's so sad what people do to themselves," he says.

If he were a vampire, of course that's what he would say.

"You think she did it to herself?"

"That's what I heard."

"But, you know, a lot of mysterious things have been happening lately. What happened to Beverly might not be as simple as it appears."

He looks irritated. "I came down here because you said you had something to say to me about Wednesday night. If you just want to talk about Beverly, I have to go back to work."

I wish he would sit down.

"You . . . said that there were some things I don't know," I say, hating how tentative my voice sounds. "What if I *do* know them?"

"What? I have no idea what you're talking about."

"You said there was a serious age difference between us. I get that now. *I get it.*"

I feel like an idiot.

James gives me a very weird look. "Listen, Kate," he says stiffly. "Let's forget about the other night. I'd had a lot to drink and . . ." He trails off and then finishes with, "I'm sorry if I misled you."

Shouldn't he be jumping at the chance to confess? That's where this conversation went in my imagination. But he's being stone-faced and uncooperative. He can sure turn off the charm when he wants to. I try one last time. "So there's *nothing* you want to tell me? Like perhaps you know a bit more about what's going on in this office than I do? Fashion murders? Mysterious deaths?"

"If you're accusing me of something, I really don't appreciate it."

"No! I'm not. I just . . . Forget it. I'm sorry."

He softens, slightly. "You're taking what Rico said and what you've read on the Internet too seriously," he says. "StakeOut is a joke. The whole idea of fashion murders is intended to get people excited. It doesn't mean anything. Half of it is made up."

Someone we know has died, I want to yell at him. But I don't want this encounter to get ugly. I'm already embarrassed by how far I've gone.

"Okay," I say. "Sorry to bother you."

He looks piqued but then shrugs. He stares at me for a long moment, as if he's about to say something else. I stare right back at him and then his face clouds over, he mumbles, "See you around, Kate," and walks off.

I slump over the table on my elbows.

James Truax may or may not be a vampire, but he's definitely a player and an asshole. I leave the Plaza Gourmet III and immediately call Sylvia.

"You remember that researcher I told you about? She's *dead.*"

"Are you serious? Because I'm taking you seriously. If this is a joke it's not funny."

"Would it be like me to joke about something like this?"

"Wow. No. You're serious?"

"Beverly Grant was found dead in a shop in Nolita on Sunday morning. They say it looked like an overdose, which could mean she had a heart attack, which is something that happens when the blood is suddenly sucked out of your veins and the poor heart tries pumping and pumping but there's nothing left to pump."

"You're freaking me out. Stop it. Take a deep breath."

"Sorry. I'm freaking myself out."

As we've been speaking I've been practically running away from Oldham toward the Hudson River. Now I'm on what looks to be a more residential street with some four- and five-story tenement houses. Hot summer sun bakes down on the top of my head. I'm sweating. "And I'm pretty sure the vampires who killed her work at *Tasty,*" I continue. "That's why she was killed. She was onto them!"

"Real vampires?" Sylvia whispers. "Which of your coworkers are vampires?"

"I don't know." All of them? "Definitely Lexa. I've seen the fashion director Kristen Drane sleeping in her office. A fellow intern saw our market editors, who we call 'the twins,' sleeping in theirs. Shane Lincoln-Shane the art director gives off scary vibes." Felix the receptionist? "And I have a bad feeling about Matilda from Art."

I don't want to say it, because she's been so nice to me, but of course Lillian is also a strong candidate. Her body felt weird that time when I hugged her. And it would certainly explain the parasol.

"Well," Sylvia says, "not all vampires are bad. Angel was good. And Anita Blake's Jean-Claude is good-ish."

"I never expected 'fashionably late' could have a double meaning!" My voice rises hysterically.

"Calm down," Sylvia says. I picture her channeling Buffy. "You'll need proof that your suspicions are correct before we confront the vampires."

"*Confront* them? Forget it. I'm already halfway to Victoria's."

"You're just going to bail?" Sylvia asks. "You're about to get published."

My steps slow. "I'm not ready to *die* for a byline," I tell her.

"Right now you have suspicions. You aren't one hundred percent sure. Before you quit the job for a crazy reason, you need real proof."

"How am I going to get proof?"

"Test one of them. Expose her to sunlight. Or brandish some garlic. Or sneak up behind her while she's looking in the mirror and check for a reflection—"

"They're always looking in the mirror. They have reflections."

"Well how about the garlic?"

Why do I get the feeling that Little Miss Goth is enjoying this?

ON THE way back to the office I stop at a deli to buy that head of garlic, which I dismember, stuffing the cloves in the pockets of my skirt. Feeling ridiculous, I break one clove in half and dab it on my pulse points. We'll see if anyone notices.

In the elevator two ice-pick blondes give me a wider berth than usual, but they don't work at *Tasty*. Felix sniffs when I walk in. "Have you been eating Italian food?" he asks me. "I smell garlic."

I knew it! He's a vampire.

"Holistic spa treatment," I tell him, feeling nervous.

He raises an eyebrow. "I have a degree in aromatherapy. I've never heard of any such treatment," he says, sniffing again. "What is garlic supposed to do?"

Okay, maybe he's not a vampire. "Unblocks your energy?" Maybe he just has a sensitive nose.

"Garlic, huh?" he says. And he changes the subject. "I heard that you knew Beverly. Such a shame about her, isn't it?"

"Yes. She was nice." I force myself to walk over to the reception desk and lean on it, smiling. He doesn't flinch from my reek.

"You know"—his tone becomes confidential—"the problem with Beverly was she thought she had this place all figured out. That's a big mistake for a junior staffer. I've been here since before Lillian showed up—I've survived three regime changes, actually—and my advice is: Know nothing. Just stick

your head in the sand and do your job. Don't get too clever."
He winks at me. "And don't apply unusual scents."

A red-eyed, dark-haired woman carrying a banker's box
comes through the glass doors leading from the main part of
the office to the reception area. Her outfit—running shoes,
ponytail held with a scrunchy—says she doesn't belong here.
And from her wan, shell-shocked face, I suspect I know who
she is.

"Excuse me, are you Beverly Grant's sister?" Lauren mentioned she'd be coming in.

Her puffy eyes widen with what looks like fright. "Yes. Who
are you?"

"I work here. I'd just started to get to know Beverly. I'm so,
so sorry."

The down elevator dings.

"Thank you," she says automatically, stepping inside the
elevator, away from me.

I follow her.

"That's *not* what I was talking about, Kate," Felix's voice
floats after me.

Once the doors close, I whisper, "Beverly told me some
things last week that maybe you should know about."

Though I doubt knowing about it will do her much good.
It's not as if she can go to the police and say that her sister pre-
dicted that she would be killed by vampires.

The woman seizes my hand. Tears well up in her eyes.
"Walk me to my car," she says in a trembling voice. "I don't
feel comfortable talking in here."

I plunge back out onto the sweltering street, nervous in case
anyone sees me walking with Beverly's sister. Fortunately, she

is parked in a garage not far from Oldham. I follow her down the ramp.

"So you were friends with Beverly?" she says. "I didn't get the impression that she had many friends in the office."

"I can understand that," I sympathize. "It's not the easiest place to work. Beverly and I bonded over just that topic at a party last week. I'm Kate, by the way."

She extends a meek hand. "Linda. You aren't some socialite like the rest of them?" she asks.

"Not at all. My dad sells hemp T-shirts for a living."

"Do you think they're as evil as Beverly did?" she asks.

"I haven't worked there as long," I dodge. "And Beverly had some . . . theories about our coworkers. Did she mention them to you?"

"Yes."

I don't want to be the first person to use the V-word.

Linda seems to understand my hesitation. "She thought some of her coworkers, and especially the editor-in-chief, were vampires. Real vampires, not just publishing bloodsuckers." Linda smiles bitterly. "She was always the imaginative one in our family. A little flaky. Sweet." Tears well in her eyes again.

She probably *was* sweet when she wasn't drunk and bitter, and afraid for her life. "She told me the same thing, about the vampires. Did you believe her?"

"Of course not," Linda says. "But now . . ."

"I feel the same way," I assure her. "Especially because— I'm sorry if this is too much but—Beverly was worrying that something like this might happen the night I met her."

Linda takes a couple of deep breaths. I wonder how her parents and the rest of Beverly's family are holding up.

"I didn't believe her," I whisper.

"No one did," Linda says. "Beverly had been saying outlandish things for months. She thought 'they' were onto her. She thought someone was following her. But we all thought she was being facetious. I'd still think she was joking if I hadn't found this." She fumbles in her bag, pulling out a cell phone. Dread spikes through my veins when I see it. "She'd been getting these text messages."

My hand shakes as I take the phone and click open the first message.

> **Better straighten up. You've got company downstairs. -SO**

Trembling, I page through the other messages.

> **Congratulations, you're on the list! This is one party you'll give your life to attend. -SO**

And another just says:

> **Good night. Sleep tight. Don't let the bitches bite. -SO**

"I came to clean out her desk," Linda says. "To see if I could find anything else."

"Was there anything?"

"A *Chicago Manual of Style*, a dictionary, and a box of red pencils. But I know Beverly and there's no way she kept her cubicle that clean. At home, her drawers were stuffed with garlic. Her cache was full of occult Web pages. And we're Jewish but she had a crucifix hanging on her bedroom door."

Note to self: Buy crucifix.

"Have you seen the Web site StakeOut?" Linda asks. "Beverly was addicted to it. Don't tell anyone, but she was one of their tipsters. I was thinking, Stake Out, SO. It might be them."

She's figured it out faster than I did.

"Was she out alone on Sunday?"

"Yes. She had a date on Sunday night. She wanted to buy a new top. Maybe she thought she'd be safe in broad daylight."

We're standing beside her car, a Honda with Pennsylvania plates and a city of Philadelphia parking tag on the back window. Linda glances at the keys in her hand.

"She mentioned one other thing," I tell Linda. "She told me that if anything happened to her, we should look for bites. On the neck, wrists, or other places where the veins carry blood close to the surface. They might look like dry white sores."

Linda blanches.

"My God," I whisper. "Did she really have them?"

"On her neck and wrist."

"What did the doctor . . . or medical examiner say?"

"They brought her to the hospital even though she was already dead." The word comes out as a whisper. "The doctor said she'd had heart failure."

"Did you point out the marks to the doctor?"

"If those marks were important, wouldn't the doctor have brought them up herself?"

"Sometimes doctors miss something if it doesn't fit their picture of what happened. You need to request an autopsy. You'll have to go to the police."

"I wouldn't know what to tell them," Linda says.

"I can write down for you what the doctors should be looking for. You'll have to raise hell, but you can do it."

Linda shakes her head. "I'm not sure that's a good idea. I have two kids and a husband back in Philadelphia. I don't want to get mixed up in whatever Beverly got herself mixed up in."

"But you have to do it. Only you can!"

She presses the button on her keychain and her car bleeps to life, flashing its lights and popping open the door locks.

"It was very nice to meet you, Kate," she says. "I'm glad you were friendly with Bevvie. But I don't think we should continue this conversation. I can't jeopardize my family this way."

"But wait. What if they strike again?"

"You see my point," she says, slamming her car door in my face.

I flatten myself against the car in the adjacent space as she revs out past me and tears off. In my pocket, my phone beeps. I pull it out.

> what did sissy say? -SO

Jesus Christ. Do these bloggers keep tabs on my every move? Who knows that I'm out here with Beverly, besides Felix? *Felix.* He may not be a vampire but he could be a blogger. Whoever SO is, though, they didn't do Beverly any good. I text back, angrily.

> u knew. why didn't u help?

The reply comes immediately.

> not my mandate, kk.

Me:

> some1 died!!! u could have stopped that.

SO:

> Oh K, I don't make the news, I just report on it

Me:

> You're not a real journalist. you work for a BLOG.

SO:

> u wanna get rough, do you?

Me:

> I want YOU to do the right thing.

Typing this naive sentiment, I'm expecting snark from SO. Strangely enough, though, she/he/it falls silent.

"YOU'VE BEEN gone for ages," Rachel says when I return to my desk, badly shaken. "How's your PMS? And why do you smell like garlic?"

"Natural headache remedy," I reply. "Try it. Put a clove in your desk drawer."

"No thanks, darlin'," Nin says.

"Is this a trend?" Rachel asks, taking a clove.

I'm tempted to confide in them. Our conversation at the cafeteria indicated to me that they're suspicious, too. But I don't want them to be in danger. Biting my tongue, I open my "Clean Clothes" file and try to calm my frazzled nerves by focusing on the story.

My very first phone call, to My No-Chemical Romance, a lingerie company, gets the owner (it must be a small company). Before I know it, the receiver is jammed between my shoulder and ear and I'm typing as fast as I can. The guy is a font of information. He suggests a few more calls. Ignoring the unease tickling my nerves and the smell of bruschetta around me, I dig in.

At seven-thirty, Rachel blinks the lights on and off. "Earth to Kate," she says. "We can't get in to the Louis Vuitton shoe awards gala, but there's a couple of lesser events tonight. Don't you want to come?" Her tone is cross.

I don't want to stay in the office alone. Nor am I in the mood to party with a bunch of vampires. "Thanks, but I don't think so," I say. "I'm going to finish this up and leave it on Lillian's desk for tomorrow."

"How'd your story turn out, then?" She asks this with ill-concealed jealousy. I've been tactless. My other problems have temporarily eclipsed our rivalry.

"I can ask Lillian if we can turn Reese's column into an intern *page*," I suggest. "'Voice of the Young Generation' or something like that."

Rachel's eyes widen. "Kate, you'd do that?"

I am a sucker, but yes, I would.

She and Nin depart happy. I even convince them both to carry a clove of garlic—to ward off hangovers.

Once they're gone, I gather up my things, turn off the computer, and head down the hall toward the printer. Since the falling-out with James, I've switched to using the one near the features department, not the one near Photo. The hallway is deserted, but just as I'm approaching Lillian's office, I run into Kristen Drane, looking gorgeous in a floor-length silk charmeuse dress. She must be going to the Louis Vuitton event.

She bursts into a fit of coughing when she sees me. Garlic? Or disapproval of my outfit?

I need a better vampire test.

I leave the printout of my story on Lillian's assistant's desk—her name is Charlotte, she replaced Carol last week—and my eye falls on the mail bucket of swag sitting outside Lillian's doorway. There's one surefire way to deliver an anti-vamp substance to a vampire: product. They *love* product. I glance in both directions to make sure the coast is clear before digging through the bucket looking for something easy to mix with something . . . like *holy water*. My hand lands on a Crème de la Mer lavender-Provençal facial mister. Lillian won't be able to resist it. And besides, whatever kind of reaction she has, she'll blame the product and not me. I look around again, then tuck the tiny bottle into my purse and hurry away, feeling like a swag-stealing criminal.

MY AUNT'S apartment is not the haven I'd hoped it would be. As soon as I'm back within its charcoal walls, surrounded by ancient teeth and realm-of-the-sublime art, I wish that I'd gone out with Rachel and Nin. It's creepy in here. I pass the study with its family photos and trespass into the master bedroom. A few minutes' struggle with a bank of switches gets the Fuseli painting illuminated.

A monkey-like demon incubus crouches on the chest of a sleeping woman. The piece is called *The Nightmare*, and it was painted in 1781. Sterling has owned it ever since Victoria's known him. This is his apartment, actually. She moved in without changing anything but the plants on the terrace. I know I'm jumpy, and probably seeing monsters where they don't exist, but I'd like to talk to my aunt about Sterling's taste. And I wish I'd paid more attention to when he's due back from Japan. I glance at the painting a last time. I wouldn't want to wake up and find *Sterling* standing over me.

I flee to my room, close my door, and prop a chair against it. It's scary to feel the dark apartment lurking out there; being in an enclosed space is slightly better than being out in the open.

A few hours on the computer and I'm more educated about vampires than I ever thought I'd be. The lore is at its most con-tradictory on the topic of how to ward off or kill a vampire. Some are repelled by garlic, some aren't. Some turn black when doused with holy water, some don't. Chopping off the head of a vampire-bitten corpse should prevent a corpse from rising. A shot with a silver bullet should kill an active vampire, as will pounding a pointed stake through its heart.

Of course, a silver bullet or a stake through the heart will kill most things.

The weirdest thing I discover is that some are allergic to peanuts.

The biggest mystery to me is how a nest of vampires survives in the era of hidden cameras and forensic evidence. There have been some deaths since Lillian came to town, but not nearly as many as there should have been if these girls are getting a full meal every day. They must be able to feed off of people without killing them — otherwise the body count would be too high. And even so, it seems odd.

Very late in the evening, once I've stopped jumping at every shadow, I pour out five hundred dollars' worth of Crème de la Mer scented water (after misting myself with it a few times — I too like expensive product) and run through a couple of scenarios that would enable me to give it to Lillian. In all likelihood, the swag bucket will still be outside her door when I go to relieve Charlotte for her lunch break. I'll be able to put the doctored water back. And suggesting to Lillian that she might want to see the contents of the bucket will be a piece of bloody red-velvet cake.

There's a Roman Catholic church around the corner on Seventy-first Street.

I hope this basin-of-holy-water-thing isn't just something you see in the movies.

13

Special Delivery

THE DIVINE HOUSE of the Blessed Sacrament on Seventy-first Street looks like something out of *Rosemary's Baby*. I'm still dazzled by the architecture on the Upper West Side—great modern wealth next to looming Gothic strangeness. Gazing at the church's rose window and soaring clerestory, I shiver.

The water turns out to be right inside the door frame in small, arc-shaped stone basins, but I'm too flustered to immediately take out my heathen jar and plunge it in. I scuttle into the nave, slowly becoming aware that the pews on either side of me are scattered with dozing homeless men. I find an empty row and sit until the shock of my entry has subsided. Then I walk back to the doorway and dip my little vial in the font, so quietly and quickly I'm sure nobody notices.

THE ILL-GOTTEN bottle rests, repackaged, in my WWF tote when the time comes for me to take over for Charlotte. Just carrying it around makes me feel guilty. And there's a nervous burble in my stomach. What if the product has no effect on Lillian? It won't mean she's definitely human, it could just mean that holy water doesn't bother her. Or what if she has extrasensory perceptions and knows that the Crème de la Mer bottle has been tampered with?

I'm so out of my league.

Happily—or unhappily, I'm not yet sure—Lillian is in. In fact, she's lying on her back on the heavy, black-glass table in her office while an Asian woman in spa whites stands over her, swooshing her hands through the air, frowning intently.

"Hi, it's Kate." I knock on the partially opened door. "I'm taking over for Charlotte."

"Grab my appointments book and *entrez!*" Lillian calls.

Charlotte, not yet departed, gives me an evil look, as if reading Lillian's appointments to her while she receives Reiki is the world's greatest privilege. I stare back at her until she picks up her Balenciaga knockoff bag and goes. Then I drop the Crème de la Mer product from my bag into the mail bucket of swag, scoop the heavy leather appointments book off Lillian's desk, stack them on top of each other, and *entrez*, staggering under the weight.

"How are you doing, Lillian? Are you feeling better?"

"Do you ever feel," she asks, "that you've got nothing to look forward to?"

I think of the holy-water spritz and answer truthfully, "I have lots of things to look forward to."

"You're young yet," she says. "You haven't had time to grow bored with everything, the way I have. The advertisers eternally clamoring for better coverage. The assistants eternally writing personal missives. The celebrities eternally plucking their mustaches and walking around topless at photo shoots. And I vow to you, Kate, if I have to see the eighties come back one more time, I'll put out my own eyes."

"Do you want to see what came in today?" I soothe her.

"Is there anything that warrants a look?"

"Some Taschen hotel books, a La Perla camisole, a new Provençal line from Crème de la Mer."

Lillian sighs. "Oh, I suppose so. Later."

I read the calendar out loud to her, going over Thursday, Friday, and Monday at her request, looking for slots to schedule more Reiki appointments. Penciled in during the features meeting in Lillian's elegant, old-fashioned script is a note that says "tOdeliv." *Tode liv? To deliver?*

"I can't read one," I tell her. "It looks like t-o-deliv. And it looks like it's scheduled for the middle of the features meeting on Monday."

"Don't worry about that one," she says.

Something about her tone of voice gives me pause. "Are you sure you don't want me to reschedule it?"

"Quite."

T-O-deliv? Could t-O stand for type O blood, the universal donor? A fluid known at *Tasty* as beet juice? It's possible that I've even witnessed the type O delivery. On my very first day, while I sat with Felix filling out paperwork, a man came in pushing a handcart stacked with coolers. It would make so much sense if the vampires have found alternative methods of sustenance rather than killing humans right and left. But one drink a day . . . that must be the worst diet on earth for all eternity. No wonder fashion people are so bitchy all the time— they're *starving*.

"Kate?" Lillian asks.

"Oh, sorry. What?"

"I have your "Clean Clothes" edit here."

Nervousness of a different kind twists my guts. She's read it already?

Lillian gropes on the table beside her, then hands over a stapled printout of my article, drenched in red pen.

"I'm so sorry," I tell her. "I tried . . ."

She laughs, earning an extra hand-flourish from the Reiki master. "You can't expect to get it perfect overnight," she says. "You've done fabulously well for a first effort."

"You've changed almost everything!" I protest.

"That's what editors *do*, my dear. You didn't think someone just writes it and we publish it in the magazine, did you?"

Well, yeah, that is what I thought.

"If you look closely, you'll see that you had all the correct ideas, which I must tell you is phenomenally promising. I've just moved them around a little. You're very talented, Kate. Most first drafts from so-called professional writers look worse than this."

"Really?" I want to believe her.

Lillian sighs. "I wish it weren't so, but yes. If only the people who make their living by writing could actually *write*, darling, my job would be so much easier. *You* can write. It's apparent already."

Warmed by her praise, I look more closely at the comments,

quickly realizing that Lillian has honed and clarified what I was trying to say without changing it too dramatically.

"You've really improved this," I admit.

"I learned from one of fashion's greatest editors, Gene Gantor. I'm sure you've heard about him from your mother."

"Yes, of course," I murmur, heart thumping. "Annabel told me that Gene Gantor doted on Eva."

"What did Eva herself tell you?"

Lillian's voice is light, but I sense a subtext. I wish she wasn't staring up at the ceiling; from this angle I can't see her expression.

"I was young, I don't remember," I dodge.

"It's true that Gene took Eva under his wing. By that time, I was practically his equal — we'd been partners for simply centuries, darling. Eva must have mentioned me."

"She didn't talk to me about her career. I'd never heard of Gene Gantor until I started working here." And I don't like to think about him now. The last thing my family portrait needs is infidelity.

Lillian rolls her head, turning toward me for the first time during this conversation. She looks pleased, or maybe it's just the Reiki taking effect.

"Ah, well. Eva dropped Gene when she dropped the rest of us."

Good. I'm glad.

"The poor darling was heartbroken. Shortly thereafter he went back to the Continent. He said the colonies are no more civilized today than they were three hundred years ago. He *did* love to amusingly condemn things; it was one of the many traits that made him such good company." She sighs.

Her crystal-blue gaze probes me. "I hope Eva gave you and your father more warning than she gave us," she says.

"Not really," I reply. "I didn't realize she was unhappy until one of her fall collections bombed. She fell into a deep depression. After a few weeks of lying in her bedroom with the lights off, only to sneak out of the house to God knows where at night, she announced that she was leaving us to 'save her career.'"

I was sixteen years old and my mother threw some cosmetics and a trademark slip dress or two into a Vivienne Westwood rolly suitcase and walked out, never to return.

"What happened after that?" Lillian's voice is soothing. The Reiki woman pretends not to listen and at the moment I don't care whether she is or not.

"At first she sent cards on my birthday and at Christmas, but it's been years since she made even that effort."

"Do you know what she's doing now?"

I sigh. "We hired a private detective. Eva wasn't in New York. She wasn't working in the industry. The apartment on Seventh Avenue that she'd rented the year before, when her weekends in the city became weeks in the city, turned out never to have existed. We don't know where she was living all that time. We tracked her to Milan, but she wasn't working there, either. And after that the trail vanished. Then, a couple years ago, an old friend of hers gave my dad a page torn out of an Italian fashion magazine. Eva—at least it sure looked like a very skinny version of her—was on the arm of someone identified as Prince Dimitri of Moldova, attending a film opening at Cannes. She was listed as 'friend,' so I guess that career isn't going so well."

Lillian nods sympathetically. "It must have been very hard

for you," she says. "Your mother leaving like that must have felt
like a vote of no-confidence in *you*, though I'm sure it wasn't."
She gets it. That *is* how it feels. I smile tremulously.

"She was a fool not to understand how promising you are,"
she says. "I'm so proud of how you turned out. Seeing you
makes me wonder what it would have been like to have a
daughter."

The Reiki woman does a last flourish, then stands back.
"Finished!" she says.

We three pause awkwardly. This is a pretty intense conversation to be having with a boss.

"Okay." Lillian sits up, looking girlish. "Let's see what you
have in the bucket."

Obviously, after how we've just connected, it's now impossible for me to spray Lillian with holy water.

I start laying the loot out on her table, trying to avoid setting
out the mister. But Lillian sees it and pounces on it.

"I'm not sure about that one!" I say, trying to take it away
from her. "The packaging was damaged."

She ignores me and starts taking it out of the box.

"No, no!" the Reiki lady intervenes. "No product! Block
energy! Energy very weak."

Thank the Lord! I take custody of the bottles. "I'll pack this
up for you to take home."

Time for Plan B.

Plan B involves asking Lexa if she'd like to try a refreshing
lavender facial mist—"The press release said it makes your
skin look luminous and photogenic," I add, so she'll bite.

Lexa takes off her black-frame glasses and tilts her face
back.

I hold my breath.

She opens her eyes again. "Can it go on over makeup?" she asks me.

Annabel has been looking at the packaging. "The box says it can."

Lexa closes her eyes and I pump the nozzle several times, releasing the mist.

And nothing happens.

Then Lexa opens her eyes, looking straight at me. "This stings," she says. Her expression twists in pain. "This really sodding *burns*, Kate!"

"I'll get a washcloth!" Annabel hurries out of the office.

Spectral white hands waving, Lexa leans back in her chair. A pained hiss emits from her blanched lips. Redness seeps into her skin. Tears well and pour from her eyes. I'm horrified to see that tiny blisters are appearing on the delicate skin around her mouth. It's difficult to think I've harmed anyone. Even, as it turns out, a vampire.

Oh my God, she's really a vampire.

"This isn't a Crème de la Mer product. What is this?"

"I don't know," I stammer.

Lexa's eyes bore into me, and I think I see the gleam of red behind their feline green. "I think you do," she growls. "I think you know quite a bit, don't you?"

"Let me go find Annabel." I turn and flee the room. My brain tries to contradict what it's learned, telling me maybe it's a coincidence, an allergic reaction to something left in the bottle. But it was only scented water. Nothing more. I spritzed my own face last night to no ill effect at all.

On instinct I return to the intern room, forcing myself to walk, not run. Despite the fact that it's only three-thirty, I shut down my computer, gather my things, and leave the building.

I don't plan on coming back.

14

Death Is the Most Fabulous Makeover

WAKE UP from disturbing dreams.

Slowly the living room coalesces around me. I'm curled up on the extra-wide L-segment of Victoria's slate gray sectional sofa, sleeping underneath my sweater. Muted, the flatscreen shows Fashion TV. A trend piece on the vampire look, ironically. The models have been made up to look ghoulish, with dark circles under their eyes and hollow white faces. Designers are showing black satin capes, shirts appliquéd with funeral wreaths, and plunging, tantalizing necklines. Coffin chic. The clock reads 8:05 A.M. My necklace of garlic bulbs rustles when I move.

I conclusively demonstrated yesterday that at least one of my coworkers belongs to the legions of the undead.

I leave messages on both Lauren's voice mail and Lexa's. To Lauren, I apologize and say simply that a matter of a personal nature has come up and I won't be able to return to work. To Lexa, I apologize profusely, hope that she's recovered from her reaction to the product, and wish her all the best with the Tasty Girl photo shoot. I'm trying to imply that she has nothing to worry about from me. I'll just go on my way (med school, only two months away) and she can go hers (fashion shows, until the end of time). Neither one of us needs to worry about the other.

Seconds after I hang up, the phone rings.

The caller ID shows an Oldham exchange. I don't answer it, imagining Lexa, enraged, swathed in bandages from the neck up. After an excruciatingly long twenty rings, the phone falls silent. The caller dials again after only a few seconds. I rush to unplug the phone from the wall, but I can still hear it ringing, faintly, from the extension in Victoria's bedroom. And then my cell phone starts ringing, too. With trembling hands I silence it.

The calls continue every twenty minutes. The pacing and duration seems deliberately intended to intimidate and harass. And it's working.

I hope Sylvia is up early. I dial her West Coast number.

Sleepily, she asks, "Has anything happened?"

"They're calling me every twenty minutes. Do you think I should make a run for the bus station and go to my dad's?"

"I still think you'll be safer at Victoria's."

Her rationale is that a vampire can't enter a dwelling or privately owned building unless invited. But once they've *been* invited, they can come back anytime. Annabel, Sylvia rightly pointed out, would be able to walk right in to my dad's house. If she's one of them.

"Did you get more garlic?"

After work yesterday, I cleaned out all three delis close to

Victoria's, staying on the sunny part of the sidewalk and look-ing around like a crazy person for any sign of a woman in designer duds.

"I did. And I've scattered it on all the windowsills and by the doors and I'm wearing a big wreath of it."

"That's what they did in *Dracula*. So don't worry, you should be fine."

"I don't like the sound of that 'should be.'"

"Well," she says, "they could use mind control to force you to invite them in. So avoid direct eye contact. That's usually how they assert their will on people."

"I'd like to avoid laying eyes on them in general. But what am I supposed to do, never leave this apartment again?"

Sylvia sighs. "I haven't figured that out yet. But Kate, you can't face this alone. You should tell your dad what's go-ing on."

"Out of the question. He'll think I've lost my mind. Or started taking drugs."

"Then call Victoria. She's cosmopolitan. She'll believe you. Or at least she'll humor you."

She has a point.

"I'll call her right now." I don't tell Sylvia my suspicions about Sterling. It feels disloyal to my aunt.

"Okay, honey," Sylvia says, signing off. "Don't worry. Every-thing is going to be fine!"

Victoria's phone goes straight to voice mail. I'm not sure how to explain my situation. "Hi, Aunt Vic, it's Kate. I'm sorry to bother you, but I'm having a little problem. Don't worry, the apartment is fine. It's the job." I'm about halfway through—mentioning the word *vampire*, actually—when the line goes dead.

I dial again only to be met with a blare of static.

I WAIT for a long time in the living room, too wound up even to watch TV. Until, paradoxically, I start to feel sleepy. Around twilight, I find it impossible to keep my eyes open, yet every time I close them, I see horrors. A bat's wing flaps behind my eyelids. A red eye opens in the dark. Blood pools in an empty stiletto. I smell earth. And jolt awake again, revived by the pungent stench of garlic all around me.

Suddenly I'm roused by loud tapping on the glass of the terrace door.

Standing outside swathed in ruffled party dresses are Annabel and Lexa. White skin glows in the dark. And their eyes are inhuman red.

I shriek and dive behind the sofa.

They have materialized outside my window on the eleventh floor. They can fly.

Attempting to control my hyperventilating, I peek back over the sofa. They're still there. And even though I was expecting something like this, seeing two *Tasty* staffers where no staffers should be is terrifying.

"Go away! You are not invited!" I yell.

Lexa digs in her handbag, pulls out her mobile phone, and dials. I notice, to my great relief, that the ill effects of holy water were fleeting. Her skin looks normal—except for the fact that it glows in the dark. My mobile, tucked in the pocket of my skirt for easy access to 911, begins to ring.

This time I answer it.

"Invite us into the flat, darling, we need to talk."

"I don't think so," I say.

"Kate, this is really unprofessional."

Annabel taps Lexa on the shoulder and takes the phone from her. I'm watching from my position behind the sofa, peering through my fingers like you do when you see something scary on TV.

"Hi, you," she says. "I know you're freaked out right now, but I want to tell you that it's all going to be good. We're friends, right?" She smiles, revealing her chic, wicked-looking little incisors.

"You're one of them."

"I am," she preens. "They transformed me in the spring and I've never been happier. Plus, you know, stopping the aging process is great for your skin."

"Congratulations. I'm happy for you. Why bother with Botox when you can be one of the living dead?"

"Don't be that way. Death is the most fabulous makeover ever."

Lexa grabs the phone back. "If you were in any danger, darling, you would have been dead on your first day at the office. There are very strict rules on how to get along without attracting attention in First World societies."

I clamber out from behind the sofa.

"So what about the fashion murders? What about Beverly, what about—"

"Oh, *that*." She rolls her eyes and dismissively flaps a hand. "Rogue vampire. Happens every now and then when a girl can't control her hunger."

I really don't like the way she says *hunger*.

"I quit," I say to her.

"How can you quit? You haven't even been to a Fashion Week yet."

"Fashion Week is the highlight of the year!" Annabel yells into the receiver. "You'll come in September. It's parties all night and back-to-back shows all day. And you get goodie bags."

"I have four Alice Roi tote bags from four consecutive seasons," Lexa wheedles.

"Lexa, thanks for coming by," I tell her, moving forward. "I'm sorry, but I'm not coming back to work. That's final. I'm going to hang up now."

"I'd think about your aunt first, before I did that," Lexa says. She fixes her red glare upon me. Evilness wafts through the apartment like Tom Ford Black Orchid.

I don't hang up.

"Victoria is a perfect candidate for a bite," she muses. "Classy. Well-dressed. Spends a fortune on accessories."

Annabel spreads her hands out in a What-can-you-do? gesture.

"We don't like to—what shall we call it?—*take sustenance* from just anyone. We're more discriminating than that. And the more you shop, the *Tastier* you are."

Our magazine's last ad campaign takes on a whole new meaning. I hang up the phone and open the door to the terrace. "So what are you saying?" I ask, nervous but trying to sound strong.

Lexa's expression goes dreamy. "I'm saying that not all bites are fatal. We have a relationship with a donor for months or even years. But sometimes one is all it takes."

Scratch that. Lexa's expression is hungry.

"I wouldn't want that to happen to your aunt," she says.

"Okay, what do you want?"

"I just want my faxes sorted, like the next girl," she says. "Sodding cow, I want you to come back to work."

"Why? You don't even like me that much."

"I don't like you *at all*," Lexa says, smiling. Now I can see that the holy water did some damage. She's wearing much heavier makeup than usual, and though her skin glows like Annabel's, it looks rough.

She sees where I'm looking and shudders. With rage.

"Lillian wants you to return. And I do Lillian's bidding. Lillian says she has big plans for you. She doesn't care what you've done to me."

I don't like the sound of *plans*. Even a friendship with my mom shouldn't carry this much weight.

"If I come back, do you promise I'll be safe and my aunt will be safe?"

"She'll be safe from me," Lexa sniffs.

"How can I know you'll keep your word?"

"You can't, darling. But you can be *sure* we'll pay Victoria a little visit if you don't come back to *Tasty*. It would be my pleasure to take care of both of you," she hisses. Then she gets ahold of herself, amending, "But in this situation that wouldn't be professional. And I'm *always* professional."

"I'll be in tomorrow," I say. I don't like it, but I don't know what else I can do.

The strange drowsy feeling is again lapping at me. I clutch the door frame.

"Sorry!" Annabel says apologetically. "See you tomorrow!"

My vision swims. Dark motes drift before my eyes. My editors fold into their glossy clothing like wings. My head lolls forward, sucked at by sleep. My knees weaken. I hear the beating of blood in my ears, and the sound of my pulse becomes the flapping of wings. Just when I'm about to lose consciousness, the pungent odor of garlic revives me, and I find myself alone. Annabel's voice drifts back to me on the wind.

"Steven Alan sample sale at two . . ."

WHEN THE house phone rings half an hour later, I'm still shaking, wrapped in a throw blanket in the living room, haunted by their terrible red eyes and needle-sharp teeth.

With dread, I pick up the receiver. They've already ensured my cooperation. What more do they want? My attendance at a perfume launch party?

"Miss McGraw, this is Miguel downstairs. A James Truax is here to see you."

"Send him up," I say dully.

I've got to assume that James is one of them. Why else would he be coming over? I'm just appreciative that he's arriving via the door.

I hurry into the kitchen, grab a steak knife (no time to make a real stake), and tuck it into the back pocket of my jean skirt. If Lillian has "plans" for me, I should be safe for now, but I believe in taking precautions.

James Truax stands on my threshold looking slightly aggressive or maybe slightly nervous. A digital camera hangs from its strap around his wrist.

"The buildings up here are amazing," he says. "I've been on the street for twenty minutes taking pictures of your gargoyles."

Gargoyles and then some. I wonder if he got snaps of Lexa and Annabel winging away. "I suppose you want to be *invited* in," I say.

"That would be customary."

"You are invited in." I step back nervously, braced for a transformation. But he easily crosses the garlic perimeter, looking around curiously.

"Nice place," he says.

"I have a rich aunt, remember? How did you get my address?"

"Rico knows a StakeOut tipster, and he called in a favor for me."

"How does StakeOut have my address?" They have my phone number. I shouldn't be surprised. But it's still creepy.

"They're like the 411 of the *Tasty* world. When it comes to Oldham, they've got more files than Human Resources."

"Why are you here?"

James puts a hand on my back. "Let's sit down." He points me into my living room as if it's *his* living room. I allow myself to be guided.

"They said you quit," he says as we sit down. "I cornered Annabel and she told me."

I nod. "So?"

"I don't think you should quit."

Members of the undead do career counseling? This is not what I wanted to hear. What I wanted to hear was "I'm sorry I was rude to you in the deli." Or "When I heard you quit, I realized I was in love with you." Or "I'm a good vampire, like Angel."

"Don't bother," I tell him. "Lexa and Annabel have already been here. You can go report back to Lillian that I have been persuaded."

He frowns at me. "I'm not reporting to anyone."

I don't believe him. "Then what are you doing here?"

"Look," he says. "It's hard to come clean with you acting mad at me."

With his every word I'm more convinced that he is here for some nefarious purpose. But at the same time I'm sliding closer to him on the sofa. "I'm not mad at you. I don't *think* about you enough to be mad at you."

"That's what I'm talking about. You're mad." He's grinning a sexy little grin. "You're pretty when you're mad. And that strange wreath-necklace you're wearing is very fetching."

Smoothly, somehow, he's come forward until he's on his hands and knees, leaning over me on the sofa. My heart hammers. The eyes, I remember. You aren't supposed to look into a vampire's eyes, but I'm doing it. That must be why my resistance to James has melted.

"I don't care," he says, wrapping an arm around my waist. "Mad. Suspicious. Strict-looking. I want to take pictures of all your expressions."

He leans forward. Obediently, I tilt my face up to be kissed.

It's like the last time. The minute our mouths touch, my blood turns to pink champagne and I'm drunk and helpless. I could kiss him until the end of the world.

I should be scared. I am in the presence of something magical, violent, and ancient, but his lips are so light, and he keeps stopping to stare into my eyes. He kisses my mouth and then rubs his thumbs over my lips and face until I'm not thinking about vampires or mind control or anything.

It's me who finally pulls him down on top of me. And then we're passionately entwined on the sofa. His knee is between my legs, the miniskirt is seriously riding up, and the wreath of garlic bulbs rustles and crackles between us.

Maybe, I think, he's willing my body to respond to him like this. Because I've never felt this way before. And if that's true, is it so evil? Shouldn't I wish all guys could do this?

"What is this thing?" he whispers into my ear, tugging on the wreath.

"Take it off," I reply heedlessly.

He smiles and I see the change come over him. His eyes are dark and wicked as he lowers his mouth to my neck. There is a searing bolt of heat. I convulse as if I've been defibrillated and shriek a long, loud, bloodcurdling scream the likes of which I never knew I had in me.

"What?! What's wrong?" He scrambles off of me.

I clap my hand to my neck and check my fingers for blood, which I'm surprised not to see. "You tried to bite me!"

"I didn't bite you. I kissed you!" He looks really freaked out.

"Don't pretend with me! I know what you were trying to do!"

"I wasn't trying to do anything!" He sits down on the far end of the sofa, holding a hand to his heart, looking stricken. "You scared the shit out of me!"

"You were trying to hurt me!" I'm blushing scarlet and am angry and just a tiny bit worried that maybe I'm wrong and he's not a vampire after all. He stands up, running a hand through his hair in confusion.

"What are you talking about? Kate, I'm sorry about the other day. I promised myself I'd never get involved with another *Tasty* chick. I did it once and it didn't end well."

"Right. Because you sucked her dry?"

"What the hell are you talking about?" He scrambles for his shoes, staying as far away from me as possible. "Maybe this was a bad idea."

Oh. My. God. "You're not a vampire."

It's not a question. He's either not a vampire or he's the world's best actor.

He looks at me in disgust. "You've been reading that blog again? You need medical help."

"James. Wait." Some perverse part of my character is starting to find this funny. "Please listen to me. I'm not crazy, although I know I will sound that way. Our coworkers *are* vampires. Lillian. Lexa. Annabel. Kristen Drane and I don't know who else. I thought you were one, too. I'm really, really sorry."

"You know what?" He's getting pissed now that he's less scared. "I came over here to tell you that I've been stupid, that I'd promised myself a long time ago that I would never date a girl I met at Oldham. So since you worked there, I thought nothing should happen between us." His voice cracks. "But then when I heard you weren't coming back to work, I realized . . ." He stops and shakes his head. "Whatever. I must have been wrong."

Ahhh! What did he realize? "You weren't wrong," I plead. "I can prove it. Please, will you at least consider some evidence?"

"What kind of evidence?"

Oh, hell. What kind of evidence? "Your camera! You were taking pictures of the building half an hour ago. I know this will seem insane, but Lexa and Annabel flew here, landed on the terrace, and basically threatened to kill my aunt if I don't come back to work. Did you see some huge, weird-looking . . . bats?"

I can tell from his face that he did. I'm getting somewhere.

"Do you think you got a picture of them?"

He retrieves his camera and starts clicking through the images, still seated as far away from me as possible.

"They looked great next to the gargoyles. I took a bunch."

"Well, can you tell that they're not normal bats?"

"I don't know what bats normally look like."

"Can I approach you and also look at the screen? I will not scream or make any sudden movements."

I think/hope that he had to repress a smile.

In his photographs the turrets and crenellations of Victoria's strange, Gothic building drip like dark lace from the rosy sunset clouds. In a few, he's caught the bats in mid-flap, tenebrous wings spread-eagled against the sky.

"These are gorgeous."

James maintains a resentful silence.

"Normal bats wait until it's dark to fly around," I say tentatively. I think that's true. I find the clearest picture and stare at it. There has to be evidence here, if only I can find it. "Can you zoom in?"

He takes the camera from me and fiddles with it before handing it back. Thank God for high resolution. I toggle back and forth, examining the creature's wizened black face, scrolling along its slender mink-like body and tiny clawed feet.

"I think this one is Lexa," I say.

"I gotta go," James says.

I click along the wingspan, hoping for a miracle.

"Look!" I tell him. "Her claws are tipped with Swarovski crystal." It's true; you can just barely see the transparent baubles against the blushing sky.

He looks at it. "That's a sun flare."

"Look more closely."

He takes the camera back, scrutinizes it for a long minute, then clicks it off and puts it in his pocket. "I can't believe I'm asking this," he says, "but do you have any *more* evidence?"

TWO HOURS later I've told him everything, and he's filled in a few things I didn't know. For example, it's his job to run invoices for the photo department, and he has a chronic problem finding and paying many of the models who have worked for us. "These are newbies, they only get a stipend and a chance to build their portfolios," he says, "so I figured they couldn't be bothered, but it's still weird. These are sixteen-year-old girls. You'd think they'd want their fifty bucks, but they do the shoot and then we never hear from them again."

It's not the details of the fashion murders that most interest him, though. It's Lillian's unnatural fascination with me. I've been mentally glossing over this point. The secret vain part of me wants to believe that she likes me because I'm smart and funny and she was friends with my mom. But while acknowledging that I am smart and funny, James worries that there's more to it. He doesn't think it's a good sign that I've been initiated into the mysteries of vampire life. He thinks it's too much like when a murderer lets you see their face: Then you know he's going to kill you.

"Not to freak you out or anything."

We're now sitting companionably together on the sofa. My bare feet are quite close to his leg.

I tell him it doesn't matter. I've got no choice. If I don't go back to work, they'll come for Vic, or Annabel will target my dad. I can't let that happen.

"Okay, but we aren't going to let anybody hurt you," he says. "You can go back to work, but you've got to promise to find me at the first sign of trouble."

Now he's all protective?

"I also don't like you staying alone here while your aunt is out of town." His dark eyes slide toward me, slyly. "I could stay with you until things calm down."

Twist my arm.

This makes him think of something. "Why the hell did you let me in your house if you thought I was a vampire? Maybe I hadn't gotten the memo about Lillian having *plans* for you."

I blush. This is embarrassing. "Just forget about it," I mumble.

"Seriously, Kate, that was crazy."

Crimson to the roots of my hair, I admit, "I like you. And I also thought you were using vampire mind control to make me feel unusually attracted to you."

He squeezes his eyes shut for a long time, an indescribable expression on his face.

Then he opens them and says, "Come here."

15

Tasty Girl

'M WAITING OUTSIDE Lexa's door when she opens it on Friday morning at eleven-thirty.

I make a mental note to ask Annabel why they all sleep in their offices—and if they have actual apartments. Lexa's filing cabinet is stuffed with shoes and leggings and accessories, so between that, the fashion closet, and spa body-scrubs, she may not need a separate place to live. Especially since she goes out every night.

"Good morning," I say in what I'm hoping is a cheerful but remorseful tone. "Here are the gossips." I hand her a folder of printouts I've prepared.

"Put it on my desk." She waves me into her office.

If the holy water damaged her, it doesn't show—that's another thing I read about on the Internet. Vampire injuries heal fast.

"What is this?" she asks, flapping a different folder in my face.

If she's going to pretend I didn't douse her with toxins two days ago, that works for me. "I don't know. Let me see."

I reach for the folder she has in her hand but she doesn't relinquish it.

"It's sheer carelessness is what it is!" She gesticulates angrily with the folder. I catch a glimpse of my writing on the tab. It's the Tasty Girl logistics information that Annabel and I prepared.

Another thought occurs to me. Where do vampires *without* offices sleep? I haven't seen Annabel yet today. I hope she's not a blonde bat, hanging in the fire stairs, breathing the air of illicit smokers.

"Who is going to greet the Tasty Girls at the airport? How are they getting from there to the hotel?" Lexa asks me. "Why haven't you made a call sheet for the shoot?"

"No one," I say, choosing to answer one question at a time. "I thought they'd take cabs."

"That's no excuse. What good are you? Now I have to straighten out your cock-up."

I guess it doesn't count that I arranged the charter bus and the hotels for the models. If she'd just told us Monday how she wanted things done—instead of telling us not to bother her with petty details—we could have carried out her instructions to the letter. But the boss is always right.

"I'm sorry, Lexa," I say. "I'll meet the Tasty Girls at the airport," I volunteer. "And if you will explain the call sheet, I'll make one."

"Being an airport greeter is a good job for interns," she says. "Too good for you. I'll ask your colleagues to do it."

"I'm sorry, Lexa." There's nothing else I can say.

"You may have Lillian fooled," she tells me, "but you don't have me fooled. You'll get what's coming to you."

I guess this is the part where we talk about what happened on Wednesday.

"I'm sorry," I repeat. "It was a mistake."

She snorts. "Do you see what you've done to my skin?"

"Your skin looks perfect."

This is the wrong thing to say. Her eyes narrow. "I've lost several degrees of luminosity. It will take *weeks* before I look lustrous in photos again."

This is probably the worst thing I could have done to her. Her turquoise cat's eyes are burning with rage.

A muscle jumps in her powder-white cheek, and her delicate hands tremble. I can feel that I'm in danger. She holds her hands up so I can see her nails—still manicured, though with arcs of dirt visible through the pale pink polish. Before my eyes the nails grow, turning into wicked, pale pink lacquered talons. She draws one along my cheek, and I feel my skin tearing. The garlic I've rubbed myself with this morning is not deterring her.

"Lexa!" Annabel has appeared in the doorway, a "juice" in each hand. I've never been so glad to see her. "Remember what Lillian said!"

Lexa takes a few steps back. "She damaged my skin," she says.

"But *Lillian* is going to take care of her," Annabel says brightly. "And then *you* are going to get a promotion. Remember?"

Annabel rolls her eyes at me. "Lexa's mad at you," she says sympathetically. "But what can you expect?" She shoves a juice—I'm going to keep calling it that—into Lexa's hand and puts the other one on the desk.

Lexa barks orders while slurping. "Get me a call sheet," she tells Annabel. "Arrange for those other two interns to greet the models at the airport. And get Giedra on the phone."

Then her eye falls upon me again. "Someday I'm going to torture you, slowly and for a long time, and then I'm going to kill you," she says pleasantly.

Annabel pats her on the shoulder. "Maybe we should go to yoga after work. And Kate, I just ran into Charlotte. Lillian wants to see you in her office."

THIS TIME, there's no Reiki healer. Lillian is at her desk wearing an off-the-shoulder crimson dress so tailored it reminds me of armor, or eighties Armani.

"Shut the door behind you."

Goose bumps prickle my flesh.

"I heard about the nasty little trick that you played, *cherie*," she says finally. "Have you no loyalty to me?"

"Lillian . . ." Despite everything I now know about her, I feel guilty.

"You show me no gratitude," she says bitterly. "You're just like your mother." She stares and I can feel her gaze slice through me. "I declared your ensembles *creative* when everyone else said they were *confused*."

Ouch. That hurts.

"And you repay me with holy water? It's *so* last century."

She gets up and walks around to the front of her desk,

revealing the fact that her shoes are off and she has twists of
paper between her toes. Somebody just got a pedicure.

"You know," she says, "I was willing to forgive you even this.
I thought, She's a young girl, of course she's curious."

A strange lassitude soaks into my limbs.

Lillian leans over me. "So I went to your house last night. I
wanted to talk to you after you'd seen Lexa. To help you come
to terms with what you had learned."

I'm perfectly alert but so weak I can hardly move my limbs.
And I have a terrible feeling that I know what is coming next.

"But somebody else had arrived before me."

James. She's finally found out about James.

"Please, Lillian," I croak. "I was as surprised as you were."

She shakes her head. Her movement is fast, brutal, inhuman.

"You took from me the one thing that could make this
boring parade of glamorous parties and expensive new outfits
bearable."

"No . . ."

"Nothing has been the same since Gene left," she says.
"Where did all the enjoyment in existence go?" I know what's
coming. She's going to bite me. She lifts my limp arm from my
lap. My tulip sleeve tumbles back, exposing my pale forearm
with its occasional dark freckles. Her eyes now glow red as
embers, her lips stretch back, her mouth distorts, and her
fangs are bared. Lillian turns the tender flesh on the inside of
my wrist skyward, then dips her dark head. Her sharp teeth
puncture my skin and sink into the meat of my wrist. The pain
is exquisite, but I can't cry out. I shudder with revulsion at the
feel of her cold lips, her dry mouth, and her burning, invasive

teeth. The life force pulses out of me with each spasm of my heart.

It seems to last an eternity but can only be a few seconds.

Lillian breaks the seal, licks the wound, and drops my arm like a dead thing.

My face is wet with tears. I grab my wrist and squeeze to staunch the flow of blood. And to prevent her from coming back for seconds.

"That wasn't enough to do you any serious harm," she says. Then she smiles. "Except you'll find your new boyfriend less eager. He liked you because you were different from the other girls. How will he feel when he knows you're one of us?"

I'm not one of you, my eyes say.

"Didn't you know, sweetheart?" Lillian mocks me. "We prefer to feed off of the people who are most like us. And you're one of us indeed. You'll be mine forever."

She claps her hands.

My volition returns. I get to my feet, shakily.

"Are we clear, darling?" she asks me.

I nod. And stagger out of her office.

"I'd put something on that if I were you," she calls after me. "I hear velvet ribbons are 'of the moment.'"

ANNABEL TAKES one look at my face and hustles me into the women's bathroom. I sink down onto the immaculate floor below the unused tampon machine and cradle my knees to my chest. Annabel hugs me. Her body is corpse-like cold, but the hug, perversely, is comforting. Then she starts rubbing her cold hand in short circles on my back. For some reason, being touched by her isn't repellent.

"Let me see it," she says, taking my wrist and examining the tacky puncture wounds. "This is nothing! This is just a sip. You'll want to shop a little bit more than usual, but that's it. And you'll look good. Anemia is chic!"

"Am I going to die?" I'm not sure I want to hear the answer.

"With just one bite? You'll live to a ripe old age. Though why you'd want to—"

"How many bites does it take to kill? Three bites to kill a person, is that right?"

"Unfounded rumor. There are so many of those . . . like we have no reflection. Not true. Those kinds of vampires went out of style a long time ago. Bram Stoker would hardly recognize what we've become. Stylish. Forward-thinking. We *are* garlic intolerant. You smell disgusting, by the way."

"Thanks."

"In the old days, once a vampire bit you, she would feed on you until you died. But now it's better to keep the body count down. That's one of our adaptations to modernity. We just bite and move on to the next thing."

She frowns. "Although once you've been bitten, you become more *attractive* to vampire-kind. So you're likely to get bitten over and over. You become what we call a 'blood donor.' Sometimes the donors die. But that's really frowned upon."

I can't turn off the clinical part of my brain. "When people die that way, it looks like they've had a heart attack or died from severe anemia, right?" I ask. "That's what happened to Beverly."

"That's correct," Annabel says. "Beverly had to be put down because she got suspicious. We tried to make it as natural-looking as possible."

"And what about the fashion murders? That has to be vampires, too, right?"

Annabel looks uncomfortable. "It's *a* vampire, we're sure about that. Someone drinks and then messes up the body like a human murderer would. That's what happened to the girls at the party. Whoever the fashion murderer is, she was at that party."

The conversation at the Carnivoré party, when Shane claimed that the murders brought suspicion on all of them, makes more sense now.

"Do you think whoever is doing this is on the *Tasty* staff?"

Annabel winces. "I'm afraid so. And worse, Lillian doesn't seem worried. It's her job to keep order but she's not doing it. Some of us even suspect that *she's* the rogue."

"So I've been bitten by a vampire who might also be a homicidal maniac?"

"Personally, I don't believe it's her," Annabel says. "She has too much to lose."

"So what happens to me now? Lillian can drink my blood whenever she wants?"

Annabel looks evasive. "It's more complicated than that. Most people can't become vampires; there's a genetic predisposition for it, and it's very rare. We call it the 'style gene.' But I think you've got it. The fact that you can remember your encounter with Lillian is strongly suggestive—most humans black out during a vampire attack. And Lillian thinks so, too—

that's why she's been so nice to you. If she keeps biting you, you won't die but you *could* become a vampire."

I'm weirdly happy to learn that there is a gene that predisposes a person to vampirism. If there's a biological basis, there is potentially a cure.

But the bad news is I've got the gene and I've already been bitten once.

"Lillian can only transform you if you consent," Annabel says. "And you would change a lot before it even became possible. You'd start to shop a lot. You'd fetishize objects out of your price range. Your own father's funeral wouldn't keep you from a sample sale. By the time immortality was offered to you, you'd be simply *desperate* to stop the aging process."

"What's it like to transform? Does it hurt?" I ask, unwillingly.

Annabel's gaze goes dark. "Oh, it hurts." Two red spots appear on her cheeks, burning with the memory. "But it's the most glorious pain you'll ever feel."

"Thanks, I'll pass."

"You might change your mind. I hope you do! It's nice to have you around the office. I'm the newest-made on staff by decades and sometimes I still feel like an outsider. You and I could go through our undead youth together."

Under different circumstances, this would be sweet.

She continues, "You should be proud. Vampirism is a sign of an aristocratic bloodline. Vampires were queens and countesses all the way through to the 1700s. But that got too . . ." She rolls her eyes at me. "Well, the revolutions."

"So that's when vampires made the leap into fashion?"

"Late nights. Beautiful clothing. It just made sense. Of

course, they had to single-handedly change the human aesthetic. Before vampires, attractive women were chunky. Rubenesque. You've seen the paintings. The undead brought thin in."

Vampires truly are evil.

I have a million more questions, but Annabel gives me a final pat and gets to her feet. "We've got work to do," she says cheerfully.

I WALK back to my desk, holding my wrist with my hand. My phone is ringing when I get there.

"*We're* greeting the models at the airport on Sunday," Nin announces.

"Congratulations," I say absently, picking up my phone.

"Hi, Kate, this is Tom at Green Arrow Motel in Jeffersonville. You made a reservation with us."

"Right."

"Someone from your office just called . . ." He hesitates. "She asked me to cancel the rooms. She said the girls wouldn't be needing them. And here's what I wasn't sure I understood: She said they'd be spending the night up at the old Turcotte place. But that's not a safe spot for camping. I just wanted to double-check with you before I unblocked the rooms."

I don't like the sound of this.

"I think she did want to cancel the rooms," I tell Tom slowly, "but I'll make sure they know they can't camp up there. Thanks for calling."

With dread I telephone the charter bus company I'd arranged to take the girls upstate. The woman on the phone confirms that my reservation is now "drop-off only."

The medical questionnaire. The focus on finding young women with hard-luck stories—i.e., girls without concerned family to search for them. Lexa's determination that only she and her hand-picked crew would be on location. It all makes sudden horrible sense.

The Tasty Girls aren't going to be the next Cecilia Mendez. They're going to be lunch.

Lexa is mentally unbalanced. She's obviously been strained to the breaking point by the pressure of achieving It girl status on this side of the Atlantic. And like any other woman, she's been *snacking* to relieve the stress. Lexa is the rogue vampire, I'm sure of it. And the Tasty girls will probably die in those woods. Those who don't will return to the city to be meals on wheels. Or rather, meals in flip-flops and skinny jeans, endlessly hanging around at cattle calls hoping an editor will bite. Sickened, I remember the girl I saved from the reject pile. She was one of the winners. And it will be my fault if she dies.

I never thought I would be saying this, but ten aspiring models are going to meet their doom, and it's up to me to save them.

16

A Blood Donor

Saw Lillian. Avoid at all costs. She knows about us and is angry.

I'm not sure sending this text message to James is the best idea, but he should be warned in case Lillian decides to punish him, too. We all know she thinks he's tasty. He shows up in the doorway to the intern closet minutes later, just as I'm finishing tying the ribbon I found in my desk drawer over my wrist. James looks stubbly and bed-headed, just like when I last saw him, but is wearing a change of clothes, and he's dark-eyed and angry.

"You didn't tell me you were going to talk to Lillian."

"There wasn't time. I'm fine, more or less." I roll my eyes toward Rachel and Nin, who are both looking at us curiously. "But you might want to steer clear of her."

"More or less?" He strides into the room, radiating concern, as if he's going to examine me then and there to make sure I'm uninjured. I need to get him out of here, fast, while I can still stop Rachel from tipping off the gossips.

"Let's talk about this later."

"I have to shoot a party downtown tonight after work. Why don't you come with me and we'll talk then?"

"Why don't I meet you there?" I counter. Lillian already knows about us, but I don't want to rub her face in it.

He restrains himself from saying something else, nods curtly, and stalks out.

"Woo-hoo!" hoots Nin.

"You guys . . ." I'm torn between pride and embarrassment.

"That StakeOut item *was* about you and him," Rachel puts it together. "And if you're avoiding Lillian, that means she's found out. And you've gone from It list to shit list!" She's already composing the piece in her head.

There doesn't seem to be any point in denying it.

Rachel continues, "So we missed our chance for you to ask her if we can turn Reese's column into an intern page."

"I guess so."

"That's okay," she says, though I didn't apologize. "It was nice of you to offer."

She's acted genuinely concerned for my health since I was out yesterday. Some of those calls I was ignoring were from her and Nin, I found out later; they were ready to messenger over some soothing aromatherapy they'd gotten in a beauty give-away. Their friendliness is confusing.

"You can't tell anyone about this," I say. "It will be the end of me."

"We won't!" Nin interrupts. "We agreed: Interns are sticking together from now on. So"—she grins—"get us on the list for that party. And tell us *all* about him."

Two HOURS later, Rachel, Nin, and I leave Oldham, heading downtown to a well-known garage-cum-hipster-party-space. The event is an opening for an artist who built a jetty in the shape of a Louis Vuitton logo and carved Karl Lagerfeld's face in the side of a mountain. Then he flew by in a small plane and took pictures. Fashion will be out in force. All I want to do is grab James, go back to my aunt's place, and . . . strategize. He's very good at it. I fell asleep last night pressed up against his chest, with our limbs entangled, and I've never slept so soundly with another person. How can I be scared out of my mind and falling in love, all at once?

But duty calls.

Hidden underneath its velvet ribbon, my bite throbs. I have to repress the urge to dash back to Barneys and *just look* at the handbags. My aunt would be so happy if I charged one to my dad's credit card. I am contaminated, and the poison is spreading. Luckily, a deep breath (redolent of garlic) breaks the spell. I've learned that the pungent plant isn't much use for warding off vampires, but the bad smell keeps their mind control from working so completely.

We arrive and push past the people waiting by the door. (Garlic doesn't hurt there, either.) Inside, it's difficult to see the photography through the crowd. I overhear a woman say, "It's the new anti-environmentalism." And her friend replies, "It's so un-PC. I love it!"

I want to smack them both. Instead, I try for the hundredth time to get in touch with Sylvia, but inexplicably her phone is switched off. The BlackBerry is her baby, so this is odd.

James materializes next to me. His hair is wet with sweat and he's carrying a big camera of the type that comes with a digital voice recorder for photo IDs. "I saw you come in. It's a madhouse." He looks around, then quickly kisses me.

Rachel and Nin stand there avidly watching us until I glare at them.

"Don't you guys want to go to the bar and get us drinks?" I ask. Once they've left, I peck James back quickly and say, "You really shouldn't do that."

"Are you okay?" he asks. "Your lips are cold as ice."

I want to tell him what's happened to me. I'm the furthest thing from okay—I've become a blood donor. I want to curl up and cry on his shoulder.

"Just anxious. No big deal."

"Your first day openly working among vampires was no big deal?"

Some of the dark ice that formed around my heart when Lillian bit me chips away. "Well, we *do* have a slaughter to prevent this weekend."

He raises an eyebrow. "We do?" He squeezes my hand. "Sounds like a date. I went home during lunch and packed a bag. Don't be freaked out or anything, but I'm going to be by your side until we know you're safe."

I love this protective streak he's displayed ever since he found out about the vampires. I wonder how he's going to react when he sees the teeth marks on my wrist.

He catches my expression. "You don't want me to stay over?"

"No! Of course I do!"

My enthusiasm is a tad too transparent. James grins. "I'll sleep on the sofa, if you want, but I'm not leaving you by yourself."

"My aunt's apartment is awfully huge," I point out to him. "You might need to stick a bit closer than that."

We agree to meet by the door in an hour, and I plunge into the crowd to find Annabel. I need to talk to her privately, before Rachel and Nin catch up to me.

I find her standing in the long line for the garage's single unisex bathroom. "Kate!" she squeezes my hand. "Hi, lady. I'm so glad to see you! What do you think of the photos?"

"Cynical, high gloss, morally bankrupt, from what I was able to see of them."

"They're brilliant, right?" She gives me a dazzling grin. "I shouldn't be telling you, but the photographer is one of *us*. Photographers almost always are."

I wonder if Giedra Dylan-Hall is a vampire. If she's in on this scheme with Lexa, she must also be a murderous rogue vampire as well as a high-profile photographer.

Speaking of high profile . . . the person standing directly in front of us in line is a famous downtown celebrity wearing the season's most coveted Chanel neck-ruffle and a faux-soiled Paul Smith tuxedo.

"Do you see his tux?" Annabel whispers to me. "It's dirtied with Prada Earth. I can smell it. It must have cost a fortune."

There is something strange here. "Why are you in line for the bathroom, anyway?" I ask her.

She smiles at me, showing her tiny fangs, and jerks her head toward the celeb. "He's a blood donor."

"What are you doing?" I have a bad feeling about this.

"Wait and see."

The bathroom door opens and three girls come out together.

I really don't want to wait and see. Also, if Nin and Rachel spot me this close to a celebrity, they're going to make a bee-line over here.

I cup my hand close to Annabel's ear and say, "I think Lexa has been the one doing the fashion murders."

"Why do you say that?" She looks cautious.

"The Tasty Girl shoot. Hasn't it occurred to you that Lexa's interest in the girls' backgrounds and medical histories is beyond the scope of a modeling contest? She's not picking models, she's picking victims. She's bringing them up to those woods to kill them."

"She wouldn't. That would be professional suicide." Annabel's lip quirks. Clearly, she wouldn't mind if Lexa *did* commit professional suicide. "Even *Lillian* would have to get mad if she brought suspicion on the magazine like that."

"But we both know Lexa's not the most rational decision-maker. She might think she can get away with it. Or she might be so sick of dieting that she doesn't care."

"How *sad* if she got caught, then," Annabel says facetiously. "Come on, he's moving!"

As the star opens the bathroom door, Annabel swarms up behind him. Her highlighted head leans close to his ear and she whispers something. I see him startle, then hear her laugh. She steps inside with him. I hesitate briefly on the threshold and then follow her, ignoring the chorus of protest from the people behind me in line. I'm not done talking with her yet.

Up close, the guy looks bad. He's pale, breathing heavily, and weaving unsteadily on his feet. Before he became the actor-auteur-director he is today, he was a model. He has that famished frame and a very pretty face. His bloodshot eyes are the deepest, brightest shade of cornflower blue I've ever seen on a human being.

"You have blow?" he asks in a faraway voice.

Annabel ignores him. "This is the hard part," she tells me. Her face assumes an expression of intense concentration. "The victim should get sleepy and go into a trance. The blood donors don't complain afterward because they don't remember. It's fuzzy, like a dream."

The guy leans against the sink, gazing passively at us through half-lidded eyes.

"The older a vampire is, the better she is at numbing the victim. And the more often someone has been bitten, the easier they are to numb. If this guy was untouched, I wouldn't have been able to do this."

Someone starts pounding on the bathroom door.

Right. To business. "Don't you think we should do something about Lexa and the Tasty Girls?" I blurt. "It's going to be a bloodbath up there. And even if that doesn't bother you, it's bad for the magazine." I try to speak in language she'll understand. "As her assistant, you might be implicated!"

Annabel pulls aside the neck ruffle, revealing two deepcrusted holes in the man's white neck. The edges of the wounds are bleached dry, their centers black with clotted blood.

"Annabel! Are you listening to me?"

She tenderly brushes strands of his limp red-gold hair away from his ear and then lowers her mouth to drink. He doesn't resist, but when her lips touch his skin, his body trembles violently.

I'm transfixed with horror. The back of my friend's ash-blonde head bobs slightly as she sucks. In the quiet bathroom I can hear her guttural swallows.

In my pocket, my cell phone beeps. Nervously, I pull it out to discover that I have a new text message.

Are you thirsty? -SO

My skin crawls. Someone out there—probably someone who has to pee—is SO. I'm being watched. My chest gets tight.

"Stop!" I yell at Annabel. "We have to talk. Now. You can't want this shoot to happen, you said your . . . kind is careful when it comes to humanity. You have to help!" I am really cracking up. I might cry.

Annabel releases the guy and snaps the neck ruffle back into place. She grimaces at me, revealing incisors tipped scarlet with blood.

"Kate," she says, "you have to let fashion police itself. If Lexa does what you say she's going to do, the consequences will be immediate and harsh. It will be a *good* thing in the long run. I won't interfere."

I lean back against the bathroom wall, fighting back tears. I'd really hoped that she would take my side.

She pats the blood donor on the cheek.

"He doesn't have much left," she says. "People must be hitting him every few minutes."

"Why does he come to places like this?" I mutter resentfully. "He must know on some level that it's dangerous."

Annabel pulls a tube of M.A.C. lipstick out of her purse and starts freshening up. "All the donors are slaves to fashion. We have a symbiotic relationship."

"And now he won't remember anything? Is he going to be okay?"

Annabel dips back into her clutch for a glassine Baggie full of white powder.

"He's gonna be feeling great in just a minute."

Quickly—because people are freaking out with the door-pounding at this point—she lays out lines on the edge of the sink. Eyes closed, the donor snorts a couple of times, breathes deeply, rubs his nose, then opens them, seeing us as if for the first time.

"Thanks. You ladies are the greatest," he slurs at us. "You want to dance?"

"We're huge fans of your work!" Annabel trills, unlocking the door.

"Hey, what's your names?" he calls after us. "I've got a suite at the Mercer!"

Annabel heads to the bar for a chaser. Trembling, I scan the bathroom line, looking for Felix or Rico or any of the other people I've suspected might write StakeOut. Suddenly all the New York City glitterati look alike to me. That Asian girl in the tent-sleeved top and shorty leggings—wasn't she at the other parties I went to? What about the gym-bodied guy with short dark hair and stubble? I've seen him before. And the tall, very braless red-head wearing a black-and-white-striped leotard? I saw her talking to James at Carnivoré. I glare at her and she glares back.

Someone grabs my arm.

"We saw you go into the bathroom," Rachel says. "Why did you bother to invite us if you were just going to go hide with your famous friends?"

"That's okay," Nin says with a touch of sarcasm. "She doesn't have to take us everywhere."

"He's not a friend of mine. I just followed Annabel," I protest.

Rachel shoves a highball glass of light green fluid into my hand. "Here's your drink," she says, and walks off.

I can't take it anymore. "I'm going to go home," I tell Nin, who's looking at me resentfully. "I've had enough of this horror show."

But of course it's impossible to find James in the dense crowd. I try calling him, but when he picks up all I can hear is a blast of noise. I fight my way toward the door, where most of the photographers are clustered, and don't see James but am in time to witness Lexa's arrival. I guess the damage from the holy water wasn't bad enough to keep her in for a night. While she's still poised by the door, bathing in flashbulb adoration, Annabel dashes up to her and starts whispering. And I have an uneasy feeling that this conversation might concern me. Maybe I shouldn't have mentioned my suspicions about the contest to Annabel. The two of them scan the crowd, as if they're looking for someone. I really, really hope it's not me.

"Hey," a thrilling male voice with a mild Midwestern twang whispers in my ear. "You want to get out of here?" He found me. His lips are hot against my ear and I smell something—wine?—on his breath.

• • •

JAMES AND I alight from a taxi in front of Victoria's. A speeding dark-haired apparition shoots from the lobby of Vic's building and hurtles toward me. I'm opening my mouth to scream when I recognize Sylvia and the shriek of horror turns to one of joy. We hug and yell "Oh my God!" and "Honey!" until I notice that James has put his fingers in his ears.

"Sylvia—James. James—Sylvia," I introduce them.

Sylvia's eyes widen.

"James is staying with me now," I tell her.

"I thought you were on the West Coast," James says.

"I flew out because I've been worried about Kate." Again, her glance asks me how much he knows about what's been going on.

"James is fully up to speed," I assure her.

And then I can't restrain myself anymore. "Sylvia, you look amazing!" She really has lost weight and she's wearing a cute, trendy outfit that still looks exactly like her style, but better. She seems more poised and confident than she used to.

"Thanks!" she says, and even this is more confident than I expect. I'm so happy for her.

WE SET up in Victoria's living room. Before she left L.A., my best friend was busy. On the coffee table is her archive of vampire-related material. She's also brought a rosary from Gucci with a huge, jewel-encrusted crucifix, stolen from her props closet, wooden doweling cut into ten-inch lengths, and an industrial-size bottle of Xanax. That last one's for her, since the real-life existence of the monsters from her beloved books is proving more stressful than she anticipated.

While we talk, James is whittling the ends of the stakes into points, as per Sylvia's instructions.

"... so I'm pretty sure that Lexa is planning to lure the Tasty Girls upstate to make fashion snuff. We have to go stop her."

"How are we going to stop her?" Sylvia asks. Despite the Xanax, she sounds nervous.

"Well, we're lucky that the only probable vampires on the call sheet are the photographer and the stylist."

"I noticed that Lexa didn't ask for a photo assistant for that shoot," James adds.

"She's keeping the numbers down so there will be more models to go around. This benefits us because there will be fewer opponents."

"Three vampires still sounds like a lot of vampires," Sylvia mentions.

"I know. We're going to have to trap them somewhere so they can't run or fly away from us. I told you how they move really fast, right?"

"You've mentioned it three times already," she says.

I must be nervous.

"I'm not sure *them* running away from *us* is what we need to be worried about," Sylvia adds.

I rub my temples with my fingertips. It's late, I'm upset, and I'm not thinking clearly. "There's a cellar at this place." I recall Annabel standing close to the edge of a yawning black hole in the ground. "Maybe we can find a way to trap them in there."

Blank stares greet this idea.

"Trap them how?" Sylvia asks, trying to be supportive.

"We're thinking about this the wrong way," James says. He puts down a finished stake and starts a new one. "Instead of confronting Lexa and her crew, why don't we deprive them of their victims? Is there a way to prevent the models from showing up?"

He's so good in a crisis.

"We could tell them the shoot is canceled!" I suggest. "By the time Lexa finds out they haven't flown to New York, it will be too late."

"What's to stop her from rescheduling?" Sylvia asks.

"Nothing. But at least it would buy us some time. And Lexa would definitely get in trouble at work." Anything that gets Lexa in trouble is a good idea in my book.

"Can it be done?" James asks me.

"They're flying in tomorrow, so we would need to call them first thing. That might work. I don't think anyone from *Tasty* is meeting them at the hotel," I muse. "And Lexa's traveling upstate separately from them, so she might not know anything is wrong until Sunday morning when the charter bus doesn't show up." I smile at him gratefully. I like this idea. "I wish we'd thought of this before I left work today. I could have brought contact info for all the contestants. As it is, we're going to have to go into the Dark Tower to get it."

"Then we'd better do it soon," James says. "The ones that sleep in their offices will be back at dawn."

"I don't know if they sleep there on the weekends."

He's focusing on carving the stake, and doesn't look at me. "I think we should play it safe and go now, not in the morning."

"How are we going to get into the building in the middle of the night?"

"Easy. Big corporations want their employees to work ungodly hours. We just sign in."

I don't love the idea of venturing out into the night with Lexa suspicious and Lillian on the warpath, but we don't have much choice.

"Oh, wow," Sylvia says. "Do I get to see the cafeteria?"

Now that we have a plan, there's just one more thing I need to share with them, but I feel reluctant, almost ashamed. I've been fiddling with the band of cloth around my wrist, uncertain of how to break the news, when James grabs my hand, turns my palm up, and kisses the inside of the wrist, looking up at me with intense, unreadable eyes. I try to pull my arm away. He turns and rests his cheek against the velvet band.

"Let me see it," he says.

"How did you know?" I ask, still reluctant and ashamed.

"See what? What's wrong?" Sylvia asks.

James sits up and unties the knot, his fingers working with delicate precision. The swathe of black silk falls to the floor, revealing the wound in all of its ugliness.

He licks his lips. Closes his eyes. Looks away. His hand tightens convulsively on my wrist.

"I'm going to kill her," James says. "No matter what else happens, she's dead."

At the moment, I'm not going to argue with him.

17

A Dead Zone

AWN WILL COME at 5:28 A.M. today. An hour before that we're crossing onto Fifty-seventh Street, the Dark Tower looming before us when my phone rings. Not beeps, but actually rings.

"Who is calling me at three A.M.?" I ask no one in particular.

"Maybe your aunt," Sylvia says hopefully. "It's weird she didn't call you back."

In addition to the usual mess inside my bag, I now have sharpened stakes and the giant Gucci crucifix. By the time I find my phone, it's stopped ringing. The number comes up *Private Caller*, a good sign that it may be my aunt.

I'm just slipping the receiver back into my purse when it starts to ring again.

"Hello?"

"May I speak to Kate, please?" It's a woman's voice, sounding hesitant.

"This is Kate," I answer suspiciously.

There's a long pause. "Kate, this is your mother."

Adrenaline slams through my veins.

"Very funny," I say. I don't recognize her voice.

"It's Eva. I realize you weren't expecting to hear from me."

I've imagined this conversation hundreds of times. I've prepared speeches. For a year or two I wrote letters even though I had no address to mail them to. Now I can't think of a word to say.

"Hello?" she says. "Kate? Are you there?"

She disappears for six years and thinks she can just pick up the phone?

"Kate?" Sylvia's face swims into my field of vision, looking concerned. I turn away from her. "I'm sorry, this is a bad time," I tell Eva, aiming for an impersonal voice, the one I use to answer Lillian's phone. "I have an urgent matter to deal with. Why don't you call back in another few years?"

"Kate, please give me a chance. It's important that I talk to you."

"Look, the weepy mother-daughter reunion is going to have to wait."

Behind me, Sylvia gasps.

"And we're about to get cut off. I'm heading into the office and the building is kind of a dead zone."

"Wait!" she says, and I hang up.

My hands are shaking.

"Was that your mom?" Sylvia asks.

"Are you okay?" James asks.

Sylvia steps forward to hug me and then James comes and puts his arms around both of us.

"What the hell was that about?" I ask, trapped between

Sylvia's hair and the soft cotton of James's T-shirt (another obscure photo-boy shirt, this one says BLACK TEAM on it).

"What did she want?" Sylvia asks.

"I don't care what she wants. It's too late for her to want anything."

"What did she say?" Sylvia asks.

"Nothing. Just that it was important that she talk to me." I don't feel anything. I must be in shock.

"She'll call back," James predicts, hugging me tighter.

"I'm *fine*, you guys." We break apart. "And ready to ransack an office. Let's go."

WE'RE STYMIED, though, in Oldham's obsidian lobby. The magazine shop is closed and shuttered. The high-speed elevators hang like sleeping bats. But the guard on duty at the central security desk—just one guy instead of the four they have during the day—won't let Sylvia up. After hours, access is employees-only.

"You two can go, but not her," the guard says after checking our IDs.

"I don't want to leave her by herself in the middle of the night," James protests.

Sylvia looks at me, wide-eyed. She doesn't want that, either.

"Can she wait in the lobby?" James asks.

"That's against company policy," the guy says.

"I'll be fine," Sylvia says bravely. "I'll wait right out there on the plaza. Don't forget that I've come prepared." She's referring to the stakes we've made, though I'm still not sure our stakes would kill anybody. Since we don't have much choice, I nod slowly.

"Call us if you have any trouble," I tell her.

"We'll be quick," James promises. Then we both sign the security log and the guard waves us toward the elevator banks.

As soon as we're on the floor at *Tasty*, we race toward the intern closet.

"Should we close the door?" James asks. "In case anyone is around?"

"Do you really think there's someone around?"

"What if someone didn't go out tonight?" James goes to the hallway and listens intently. "I don't hear anything." He turns around.

I've already stuffed the folder containing the winners' applications in my bag, but I want the flight info, too.

My computer has never booted up so slowly. But finally the progress daisy stops twirling and I'm able to call up the spreadsheet I've made of the Tasty Girl Contest winners' travel itineraries.

"Shit," I say, my hands shaking. "We'll need to warm up the printer, too."

I press Print and James and I hurry together down the hallway. We stand in front of the machine watching the row of yellow lights turn, achingly slowly, to green. My cell phone rings again. I check the display, hoping against hope that it won't be Sylvia, fleeing a woman in black. It's her. Her voice is high-pitched.

"Kate, someone blonde with an updo and glasses just cruised in there, fast. She looked pissed." She drops her voice. "And, oh my God, here's another person. A really fashionable-looking dark-haired woman."

Lillian. "Okay. Thanks." I hang up. To James I say, "Lexa and Lillian. We have about thirty seconds." The printer makes a preparatory grinding sound, then chirps a few times.

"I just heard the elevator ding," James whispers. My heart is pounding.

The sound of a machine taking paper from a tray has never been so welcome. Loudly, the printer disgorges first one, then two pages of Excel-formatted information.

Here it is! Tasty Girls! I stuff sheets of paper in my bag. "Let's go."

"Oh, shit," James says. "Look."

Lexa is stalking down the hallway toward us, teeth bared in a terrible grimace. Her eyes are shining with mad, unhinged hatred. Terrified, I dig in my bag, pulling out a sharpened stake and a rosary. James does the same. His cheap punk-store rosary looks puny next to my Gucci bling.

"You!" Lexa snaps.

I start to lie about why we are in the office, but she cuts me off.

"Don't bother. Annabel told me what you said. And if you're on her side, don't expect me to go easy on *you*," she tells James.

She continues to storms toward me.

This is it. I ready myself to strike. Though I don't really know how to strike. I've never even taken a boxing class at a gym. I don't even belong to a gym.

Lexa flinches away from the cross but still manages to easily rip my bag from my shoulder. Snorting, she rifles through it, pulling out the Tasty Girl folder.

"What were you going to do with this?" she shrieks. She throws the folder at me. It smacks me in the face and then falls to my feet, disgorging a jumble of head shots and medical questionnaires.

"The shoot isn't a good idea." Maybe I can talk my way out of this. "Overgrown farms are so . . . passé."

"Hah!" she screams, and stomps her foot. "That just shows you what you know. The shoot won't be just any old ultraviolent chic, it will be *dismemberment* chic! We're not going to feed on the girls, we're going to cut them into little pieces! In their designer clothes! It's all mapped out. The last shot will be of a severed arm in a perfect, sculptural Comme des Garçons sleeve. The tabs will all say how bold and witty I am!"

Lexa's ecstatic description is truly chilling.

"You can't kill people and run photos of it in *Tasty!*" I tell her. "You'll bring the law down on yourself!"

Lexa's expression turns sly. "I chose those girls carefully. No one will miss them. And the farm belongs to a friend."

"But *Lillian* will know, and *she'll* be furious." I keep expecting Lillian to appear before us, but she must be lurking in the shadows somewhere.

"Lillian. She's too depressed to lift a finger. Go ahead and tattle on me."

I try again. "*Lillian* must be on to you. You've killed a lot of people."

She looks momentarily confused, and then her expression clears. "You think I'm the fashion murderer? Well, I'm not, but she's my inspiration. If she can get away with it, so can I."

James finally speaks up. "Even if you could get away with it, you're not going to do it, because we're not going to let you."

Lexa puts down her Chloé satchel and shrugs out of her small, flared-white bolero tie-front top. Now she's just wearing an expensive-looking leopard-print camisole and shorty leggings. Is she trying to scare us to death with her gross emaciation?

"I think you're forgetting who your friends are," she tells him. She folds the top and drapes it over the back of a chair. "This top is Giambattista Valli," she says. "I don't want your tacky blood to ruin it."

James and I have time to exchange one quick glance before she lunges. Lexa leaps upon James in a storm of whirling limbs and blonde locks. I see her knobby spine through the camisole and then hear it rip as James gouges at her with the stake. The cami is ripped down the front.

Seeing the boss's breasts is an unspeakable abomination.

Indecent exposure doesn't bother her, though. Grinning, she does the nail-to-claw maneuver I saw earlier: The tips of her fingers sprout ten pink-polished talons.

Manfully, James strikes at her with the stake, but she's too fast for him. Her movement is a blur. And then she's behind him, on his back, stick-insect legs wrapped around his waist. With her claws, she rakes his neck and chest, shredding clothes and flesh. Screaming, I lunge at her with the cross and my stake. I'm so terrified and enraged that I really do have the strength of ten, because the stake breaks the skin before being stopped by Lexa's bones.

The cross—thank God for Gucci—has more of an impact. It hits Lexa's bare shoulder with a sizzle. The flesh seems to melt around it. Lexa's scissor-gripped legs loosen and I'm able to pull her off of James. He hits the ground. I think he fainted. I can't look because Lexa, with a terrible lithe power, is twisting away from the cross. Her deadly nails whistle through the air inches from my thigh.

I run, hoping she'll chase me and leave James alone.

Frantically, I pound through Beauty and Fashion, pushing chairs behind me into Lexa's path. She is right behind me, screaming the foulest obscenities I've ever heard. She has superior speed, but I take a sneaky turn at the kitchen (a room she likely isn't familiar with) and then manage to lose her in the maze of cubicles.

The cursing stops.

I dart and dodge and then sprint back to where I left James.

He's breathing, but his skin has turned white. I allow myself to listen. The clack of stilettos has come quite close. Because there's nowhere else to go, I scramble backward beneath Annabel's desk.

Okay.

I have the stake. I have nowhere else to hide. There's only one thing to do.

Wait for her to find me.

18

I'd Rather Die!

FROM MY VANTAGE point I see a pair of gorgeous black snakeskin ankle boots approach James. They aren't Lexa's.

Are they Lillian's?

I coil, stake in hand, ready to spring. Then I see the boots pass James. They stop in front of me; their owner crouches down to look under the desk where I'm hiding.

Her eyes are wide and dark and sad-looking. She's wearing a beautifully tailored jacket that's almost religious in its austerity and a simple black skirt, the elegant lines of which can only be French haute couture. Around her neck on a silver chain hangs a clay medallion I made in art class in the sixth grade.

It's Eva. My mother.

She holds a finger to her lips and stands up again.

Another pair of feet attached to spindly ankles enters my view.

"Who the bloody hell are you?" Lexa asks Eva.

"Do you attack people in the workplace?" Eva responds. "Are you *mad*? And why are you naked?"

"Sod off," Lexa says. "And move aside."

I can hear James groan. *Please be okay*, I pray. *Don't die on me.*

Lexa crouches, preparing to leap at Eva. I scramble out so quickly, I bang my head on the desk. Cross upraised, I'm ready to join the fray. To my surprise, however, Eva leaps into the air in a way that reminds me of a panther I once saw on the Nature Channel springing on its prey. She lands on Lexa before my boss has time for takeoff, and the two of them crash to the ground.

Locked together, they roll to one side of the corridor and slam into some mail bins. Then they reverse direction and roll to the other, where they bang into a filing cabinet.

At no point can I get a clear hit with the stake.

Though Lexa is fiendishly strong, my mom somehow manages to get a lock on her wrists. But then Lexa gets her wicked-stiletto-shod foot between their two bodies. With horror, I see the heel sinking into Eva, forcing her to release Lexa and scramble away. She gets to her feet so quickly, I can hardly track her movement.

Lexa uses her inhuman strength and speed to bounce to her feet like a gymnast, claws outstretched.

I'm desperate to win this fight—for James, for the Tasty Girls, to find out where my mom has been all these years (at the gym, it seems). But I've been reduced to spectator status.

Eva slaps Lexa across the face.

Lexa aims a roundhouse kick.

Eva is also using her beautiful sharp shoes as a weapon, getting in a few nasty high kicks.

"Kate, throw me the stake!" she cries.

I do so, amazed at how quickly my mom's hands grab it out of the air.

With another panther leap, she flings herself at Lexa. They both go flying backward into Annabel's workspace. My view is blocked, but I see Eva's delicate hand holding the stake high above her head and then stabbing it down with vicious force. There's a sickening crunch. Then a pop, then a long moment of panting breathing, then another pop and a sound like splintering wood.

Eva climbs off, gingerly.

On the left side of Lexa's chest, above her pale nipple, an inch or so of stake protrudes, bull's-eye on the heart.

There's no blood.

Eva has driven the stake so deep, she's pinned Lexa to the desk. I don't see how it's possible that Eva could have mustered that much force. I'm sickened and transfixed. It takes all my willpower not to vomit.

And then it gets worse. Lexa starts to writhe. Her legs in their cut-off leggings flex, attempting to find purchase on the ground. Her arms slap the desk. Before my eyes her flesh gets darker. She begins to blacken and shrivel like a Barbie on a campfire. Her perfect blonde curls wither and turn to ash. Her hands and feet become skeletal, crumbling and vaporizing. In a few seconds all that's left is a size-zero pair of cropped leggings with a black lace thong inside, and a pile of chunky jewelry.

"I got her in the heart," Eva says. "She won't be coming back."

I pull out my cell phone, hands shaking. "I'm calling nine-one-one."

She shrugs lightly. "Go ahead."

"I wasn't asking for your permission," I say, dialing.

I talk to the operator and am promised assistance within the next five minutes. Hoping that will be soon enough, I crouch over James to see if I can do anything to stop the bleeding. There isn't nearly as much blood as I expected, though.

"Someone's coming," Eva says, sniffing the air. "Someone human. We have to be quick."

She looks at me, seeming to drink me up with her dark eyes.

"Do you trust me, Kate?" she asks.

Trust her? She's my mother and I haven't seen her for six years.

"No," I say.

"Will you do what I ask now and let me explain later? It's very important."

I figure I owe her at least that much. "All right."

"What the fucking hell is going on here?"

I look up to see Lauren, fresh-scrubbed and carrying a venti iced coffee.

My god, it's Saturday morning. Managing editors really are dedicated.

JUST BEFORE seven A.M., Eva and I are ensconced in a booth at a diner not far from Beth Israel Hospital, where the EMTs took James. The place has a long counter in front, an extensive menu, and pink pleather booths in back. James is going to be fine; all he needed was some stitches. Sylvia's waiting for him at the hospital, giving Eva and me a chance to talk alone.

Lauren is still at the office talking to the police. She agreed to cover for us after Eva convinced her that there would be a scandal and a protracted investigation unless we put the police off track.

Our concocted story was simple: One of the senior editors, the notorious Lexa Larkin from the society pages, was dangerously unbalanced from too much dieting and had attacked James with an Agent Provocateur clawed gauntlet. I succeeded in dragging her off him, but she got away from me and left the building.

I asked if the police wouldn't see what really happened on the security cameras, but was told Oldham doesn't share its security footage with anyone.

Lauren agreed to snow-job the police on the condition that immediately after they left, we would explain to her what was really going on.

Facing Eva in our pink booth, I want a few things cleared up for myself.

"How did you get into the building?" I ask. "The guard wasn't letting anyone up without Oldham ID."

Eva looks tired. "I *persuaded* him," she says.

"And how did you get onto the floor? You need a pass code."

"Why don't you let me start at the beginning?"

"And what are these rumors about you and some guy named Gene Gantor?"

"Gene?" Eva looks baffled. "He was a fan of my work.

Nothing more. I loved your father deeply. I still do." She laughs ruefully. "If *only* that's what all this were about."

I choose to believe this, because I want to.

The waiter arrives to take our orders. I ask for an everything bagel with cream cheese and tomato. Eva requests black coffee and pulls her cigarettes out.

"You can't smoke in here."

She sighs. "New York has changed."

"I don't suppose I should ask you where you've been."

"Europe. I came back because Victoria got your message and was worried."

"She has your number?" I feel sick with betrayal.

My mother's expression is pained. "Please stop looking at me that way," she says. "I never wanted to leave you. I *had* to leave you, for your own safety. Everything I've done has been for you. I hope once you understand, you'll be able to forgive me."

"I don't understand. Why did you have to go away? And why did you come back?"

"Victoria told me that you'd run into members of the undead."

"You *know?*" Obviously, she knew just how to kill Lexa. And she didn't seem surprised when my former boss vanished.

Eva looks sorrowfully at me.

She's a vampire hunter! That's what she's been doing in Europe! She sure kicked and punched and wielded her heels in expert fashion doing battle with Lexa.

The waiter comes by with Eva's coffee.

She doesn't touch it.

Almost six years have passed since I've seen Eva, but in the

bright light of the diner, she looks exactly like I remember her.
Exactly.

Hysteria bubbles up in my chest. I want to kick or punch
something myself. Instead, I say, "Show me your incisors."

In her eyes, I read confirmation of my worst fears.

Eva smiles, revealing her tiny, perfect little white fangs.

My world shuts down to a pinhole. The diner goes dark.
Through the roaring in my ears I hear her saying, "I never
wanted you to know. I didn't want anyone to know."

The bite on my wrist throbs beneath its velvet band.

She is so full of shit.

I'm sharp again. "You ran away because you didn't want to
tell me you'd been bitten? You were ashamed that you were
tasty vampire food?"

I understand this state of mind pretty well, considering the
circumstances.

She nods. "All of that was part of it."

"You think we wouldn't have still loved you?" I ask her. I'm
fuming. Furious. "Me? Your daughter? And what about the
man whose heart you broke? I think he would have died if he
didn't have me to take care of."

"Please, hear me out," she begs. "My shame was only the
beginning. I would never have left you if shame had been the
only . . . Once they made me one of them, I learned that vampires are always seeking others who can join their ranks. They
have a pathological need for followers. That's why they're in
fashion. But very few humans can make the transformation.
There's a gene for it—"

"The style gene," I say. "Someone already told me."

"Exactly," Eva says. "And if I have it, *you* probably have it, too. From what I gather, it's matrilineal." She reaches across the table to seize my hand. Hers is bone cold. "Through me, my colleagues would have eventually found you. As long as I'm around, you're in danger. And nothing I can do will stop them from making you one of them."

I move my hand. "You didn't think of that before you agreed to become a vampire?"

"Becoming a vampire isn't something you agree to."

"That's not what I've been told. I heard that you have to give your consent."

"They're very good at twisting the truth. Vampires will only allow a certain type of person to join their clique. Your lifestyle, your values, and the person you are—all of those things 'consent' for you, without you knowing it. And *they* decide the moment is right, not you."

She takes a deep, shaky breath.

"If you had to go, why didn't you at least tell us *why*?"

"To prevent them from finding you. I knew that the only way to keep you safe in Monticello, far from the world of fashion, would be if you thought I'd left on my own, and were angry. Then you wouldn't come looking for me. I knew it would hurt—I've experienced that pain afresh every day since—but I also knew you would *survive*. I had to choose that. Don't you see why?"

"What about Victoria? If she knew you'd gone to all that trouble, why did she push me into this job?"

Eva sighs. "My sister has never believed in vampires, though God knows why, there are plenty in the art world. She chooses to think that I have made up a story to cover my inexplicable urge to run off and leave my family."

I guess this is more plausible than the truth.

"Arranging this internship for you was her way of proving my story a lie. She planned to call me at the end of the summer and say, 'See how crazy you are? Your daughter has been working at a fashion magazine all summer and she's happy as a clam.'" She smiles wearily. "She was so upset when she got your message. She loves you, too, you know."

But she lied to me, at least by omission, all these years.

"So," I say, "your plan didn't work. You destroyed our family for nothing."

"I had hoped that maybe you would be more understanding."

I don't say anything, just stare at my untouched bagel. She can keep hoping.

"Even if you can't forgive me, it's important that you at least tolerate me, Kate," she says. "We are going to need to work together to get you out of this."

"Hey," James says from behind me. I turn around to find him wearing a clean T-shirt I don't recognize and blood-spattered army pants. A bandage snakes from his neck down into the collar of the shirt, but he's standing more comfortably than you'd expect from a person with his injuries. People in pain look puffy and weird: You can usually see trauma on the face. But James is as hot as ever. Sylvia is at his elbow.

"Is this your mom?" he asks.

I jump up and give him a hug, and then a kiss. And another one. "Yes, this is Eva, my long-lost mother. You might not remember, but she killed Lexa." This is really hard. "She's a vampire, too."

Sylvia is wide-eyed with excitement. "Hi, Mrs. McGraw,

nice to meet you," she says, shaking Eva's hand and sliding into the booth across from her.

James looks startled. "What do you mean, 'too'?"

"Like Lexa and the rest of them. You should know what kind of family you're getting involved with. If you don't want to help me anymore, that's okay. I understand."

His expression is dark and thoughtful. "I figured your mom was a vampire," he says. "I wondered if she was going to tell you."

"You're not upset?"

He shrugs. "Why should I be?"

"Apparently this means I could turn into a vampire, too. Are you sure you want to be dating—or helping, or whatever—a potential vampire?"

"Do you want to be a vampire? Eternal youth, the best parties, great free clothes?"

"It's my worst nightmare! I'd rather die! Literally."

He kisses me on the head, the temple, and the lips again. "Then it won't happen. We won't let it."

Lauren approaches the booth with a look on her face that I'm sure she gets to use a lot at home, one that says, *'Fess up or I'm giving you a time-out.*

"How much do you want to tell her?" Eva asks tentatively.

"We're going to tell her everything," I reply firmly, adding under my breath, "It's always better to be honest with people."

James, Lauren, and I all squeeze into the booth.

I'm not looking forward to convincing our managing editor (not a job that attracts fanciful types) to believe in the bogeyman, but I've got Eva as Exhibit A.

"Mother, show her your teeth."

• • •

HALF AN hour later, I've told the whole story of the Tasty Girl Contest, our desperate late-night trip to the office, the confrontation with Lexa, and its horror-movie denouement. I've explained about the fashion murders and my conviction that they were Lexa's handiwork, although she denied it. And I've presented Lauren with hard evidence that several members of the staff are vampires, including showing her the bite on my wrist from Lillian.

Lauren takes it much better than I expect.

"Vampires," she says. "I always thought they were weird, but I just chalked it up to the industry. I wasn't really one of them, you know?"

"Yeah, we know," James and I chorus.

She sighs. "We're going to have to reschedule the Tasty Girl shoot. I'll have to crash something big into the October issue to make up for it. Who needs to be alerted?"

"Just the girls themselves," I say. "I think the photographer and the stylist must have been in on it."

"We'll call them anyway, to be safe," Lauren says.

"Oh, and Nin and Rachel, the other interns, are supposed to be meeting the models at the airport tomorrow. I can let them know the shoot is off."

"Good," Lauren says. "You do that. I'll have my assistant do the rest."

"I don't mind calling the Tasty Girls," I assure her. "That was our plan for the day, you know."

Lauren smiles. "Let me get someone working on it right away," she says, "so we can discuss the bigger picture."

While she's telephoning her assistant, I call Nin.

"What? How can they cancel it?" she wants to know. "Why? Lexa is going to lose her remainin' marble."

"I don't know. I'm just passing along the message. Can you call Rachel?"

"I'll tell her, darl. I'm meeting her for brunch right now. But she's not going to like it."

"Thanks, Nin."

"So," Lauren says, turning to Eva, "is there an exorcism we can do? The production schedule would be much smoother if half the payroll didn't sleep till noon every day."

"There's no way back," Eva says. "To release their souls from torment, we'll have to stake them all. But we're outnumbered, and they're very strong and fast, so it won't be easy."

I've seen how Eva kills and it isn't pretty.

As if she senses my distaste, her hand strays to the medallion around her neck.

"I'm not sure I believe in murder," I say. "Isn't there any other way?"

"It's not murder if they're already dead," James says reasonably.

"They seem pretty attached to their lives, or non-lives," I counter. "And we know they can survive without killing people. They can drink bottled blood or blood from animals—not that they should feed on pets, of course." I shoot a look at Sylvia. "I think any vampire who wants a chance to live in a sustainable, low-impact way should have it. Maybe some vampires *want* to be good." I glare at Eva.

"Theoretically, vampires can live that way," she tells me

evenly. "I do. But it's not accepted by vampire society at large. You would need a very strong and unusual leader to enforce those rules. And I know Lillian. She'll never agree to it, even if she were capable of controlling her staff, which she's obviously not."

On the diner table, my phone starts vibrating. I see that it's Rachel's cell phone number and ignore it. I deliberately called Nin because I knew Rachel would never let me off with such a vague explanation.

I take a deep breath. "Okay, so maybe we get rid of Lillian—persuade her to step down—and offer the rest of the staff a chance." I turn to Lauren. "You're not a vampire, and everyone is used to doing what you say. You could lay down the law for them."

"Lillian won't be persuaded," Eva says. "And there's another problem: With her alive and that wound on your wrist open, you're a blood donor. Now that's she's marked you, you're like a beacon. Our kind can sense you. And with each bite, your ability to evade an attack lessens. Most blood donors end up *wanting* it in the end. You'll see them shopping in Nolita, or at the tents in Bryant Park during Fashion Week, just waiting to be picked off."

I nod, thinking of the actor-auteur-provocateur turned human pincushion.

"The only way to reverse that is by killing the vampire who bit you."

"I can't see myself killing someone in cold blood," I say. "I hear what you're saying, but when I imagine doing it, even to save my own life, I don't think so. . . ."

"It's more than just your life," Eva tells me. "You've got the style gene. Once you die, after three days in the grave, you'll rise again."

I'm temporarily sidetracked by the implications of this. "You spent three days in a grave? You had a funeral and we weren't invited?"

I'm being rude, but Eva just looks sadder.

"I was dead. So I couldn't invite you. And they didn't know you existed. The vampire who makes you takes care of the funeral planning—and you know how they are about parties. They enjoy figuring out what you're going to wear in your coffin, and what they're going to wear as your grieving friends, and so on."

"And then they bury you? And you spend three days underground?" I ask.

I scan my memory for a time when she was away from home for three days and we didn't know where she was.

"Yes."

The thought of her lying in a coffin, still as sculpture, presents itself vividly to me. Her flesh would be cold and hard. I want to weep, thinking of her alone there.

But I can't cry now. I ask the first question I can think of.

"What happens when you wake up? How do you . . . rise?"

"The quickened vampire uses her newfound strength to smash open the coffin and crawl up through the loosened earth. We're in no danger of suffocating, so it's unpleasant but hardly a challenge." She says it lightly, but her eyes are haunted. I imagine the broken grave and the swim through the dark soil—and shudder.

"I'll kill Lillian." James turns to Eva. "I can do it."

"No," I say. "It's my life. I'll do it myself."

"I'm stronger than either one of you," Eva insists. "It should be me."

Sylvia says, "I have an idea that might give us an advantage."

19
Really, Really Juicy

CURL AGAINST James's body in the deep-blue vinyl back-seat of the taxi, willing the horrors of the previous night away. He looks gorgeous. His stubble has grown in golden around his mouth and dark on his curved cheeks. His hair is so messed up it's formed a kind of cowlicked fin on top. His brown eyes are a kaleidoscope of rust, gold, and green. A little smile plays around the corners of his juicy mouth. I really, really want to kiss that mouth. I want to see the fringe of his tiny eyelashes when he shuts his eyes. I want lots of things from him.

Sylvia, sitting on my other side, is busy text-messaging the West Coast. Turns out not only is she newly svelte, but the date with Nico's brother went well and my friend is in love. We left Eva outside the diner. She said she "wanted to spend some time" with me and I told her I'd call.

Out of the corner of my eye I see a black-clad scarf-swathed woman moving quite quickly—suspiciously quickly—along the sidewalk against the flow of traffic.

"I swear I just saw a vampire," I tell them. "She had that Lanvin crocodile-skin bag, the twenty-eight-thousand-dollar one. No human can afford that."

We're only a block away from my aunt's house. If it was a vampire, she probably wanted *me*. It's good we weren't home. "Someone's already found out about Lexa."

"How would they have found out?" Sylvia asks. "I've never heard of them having sensors that alert them when one of their kind has been staked."

"I don't know how. But it's Saturday afternoon. They should all be in bed. Even StakeOut should be sleeping it off somewhere. There's only one reason that someone would be up here."

"I don't like the sound of this," James says.

"Yeah, me neither. What are they up to?"

"No, I mean the sound, literally. I hear sirens."

"Oh my God. Me too." The noise is very faint but audible.

The cab turns down Seventy-second Street, which appears tranquil. We pay and jump out, but Miguel bars our way.

"I'm sorry, you can't go in there," he stammers. Then: "Miss McGraw," he says. "I'm so sorry. Your friends. They were waiting for you. I just went outside for a minute. . . ." He trails off, too distraught to speak.

"Which friends?" I whisper, heart slamming in my chest.

"Two girls. They didn't give their names."

"What happened to them?"

"I'm so sorry. I'm so sorry. I've never seen anything like it. . . ."

I dodge past him into the revolving door and he doesn't try to stop me.

I see the dead girls on the cowhide sofa in Victoria's lobby.

Both are covered with deep, suspiciously dry-looking gashes, as if their bodies have gone through some piece of industrial machinery. I have little doubt that the wounds conceal bites and that both bodies will be missing quite a bit of blood that can't be explained by the stains on their chic clothes and on the terrazzo floor of our lobby. It takes a minute to comprehend that the latest victims are Rachel and Nin.

And I'm responsible for their deaths. They must have come straight here after getting off the phone with me. If only I'd told them more.

James has come in behind me. "This is bad," he says.

I turn to him. I'm not aware of crying but my cheeks are wet.

"I guess Lexa wasn't the fashion murderer," Sylvia adds. Her eyes are animé-huge, staring at the two girls.

Lexa was just a copycat criminal, as unoriginal in death as she was in life.

"No," James agrees. "And the real murderer is trying to send Kate a message."

"But why? How do they know I'm a threat to them?"

"I don't know," he says. "But obviously they do."

I'm starting to feel a little wobbly on my feet. I knew Rachel and Nin. I sat in the same room with them all day, every day. I listened to their inane conversations about celebrities and office politics. We went to the cafeteria and people-watched together. We were office mates, almost work-friends. Well, not exactly. But I'm intensely sad for them nonetheless.

I pull out my cell phone and take a couple of quick snaps of the corpses. James looks at me curiously but merely asks, "Should we get out of here before the cops show up?"

We split up to decrease the chances of being recognized in case of police interest in our whereabouts—Miguel knows it was me that Rachel and Nin came to see—and agree to meet in an hour at the Plaza Gourmet III. It's the first place I can think of, and the last place anyone would look.

A surreal half-hour later, I arrive. James and Sylvia are already there when I walk in. Sylvia, I notice, went for the package of honey-fused sesame seeds that I always get. James is drinking black coffee.

It's funny that I don't feel more displaced—I can't go home, I'm probably wanted for questioning by the police—but the past few weeks seem to have prepared me for the sensation. I never did feel at home at Victoria's. And I suppose when we need someplace to sleep tonight, we'll check into a hotel or maybe call Eva after all. As long as it's not an address that Human Resources has on file for us, we should be okay.

"Have you called Rico?" I ask James.

"He picked up some boy and stayed at his place, so he's safe. I told him not to go home."

"I called Lauren. She was still at the office but said she'd go straight home. Her husband is instructed not to invite anyone in for any reason. She said not to worry about her."

I put my arm around Sylvia. "We're going to be okay." Her first real contact with vampires hasn't agreed with her as much as she thought it would. Her face looks pale. Once we've resolved things one way or another, we're going to have to worry about post-traumatic stress disorder.

"Those poor girls," she says. "They had their dream jobs. Everything was laid out for them in life. And they were so young."

"This has to end." I take out my cell phone. "I'm sending the pictures to StakeOut."

"*What*? Why?" James looks aghast. "Don't do that."

"Maybe it will motivate them to tell me who the fashion murderer is. I know they know, because they sent Beverly a text telling her that the person was right outside her building. If they're humans, they can't just let this keep happening."

"She won't do you any favors," James says.

I forward the pictures to StakeOut's mobile with a message that says:

> How can you just stand by? Did these girls deserve it, too?

"She's sleeping," James says. "It's noon on a Saturday and she parties all night."

But a few minutes later I get a message:

> Thanks for the scoop, dupe! And btw they did deserve it.
> Isn't that a Christian Louboutin shoe I see peeking out from beneath the carnage?

"See?" James says. "There's really no point in engaging with her."

"What assholes." I write:

> Tell me who it is. I know you know.

The reply:

> And ruin a good rubric?

During this exchange James looks increasingly more uncomfortable. "She won't help you," he says. "You can't trust her."

"You keep saying *her*. How do you know it's a her? Is that what Rico told you? You said he knows a tipster. Maybe he can help us."

James rests his elbows on his knees, looking at the ground.

"Actually, I have a better connection than he does."

"Really? Why'd you tell me you'd gotten my address through Rico?"

"I did. Kate . . . The girl who does StakeOut. Ah, shit. She's my ex-girlfriend. Shallay. The one who used to work at *Tasty* and made me want to never get involved with a work person again. She used to be Lillian's assistant."

Oh, I do not like this at all.

"The first time SO texted me was the night we kissed at Carnivoré. . . ."

"Right," he says. "That doesn't surprise me. She was there."

I think of the text I received from the bathroom line last night. "Was she at that photo opening, too?" I ask him. "Does she have red hair and was she wearing a black-and-white-striped top?"

James gives me a guilty-little-boy look. "Yeah," he says. "That was her."

Scandalized, I ask, "Do you generally talk to her when you run into her at parties?" James and I are hardly at the stage where I can demand he not speak to his exes (I'm not sure there's ever a point when that's appropriate), but I have to know.

"Usually. It was an ugly breakup, but we're friendly now."

I am liking this less and less. "So if you were going out with her, you must have known about the vampires a long time ago," I say.

"Shallay said awful shit about lots of people without me taking it very seriously."

I try to contain myself but can't. "What kind of name is Shallay?"

"I think she made it up. I never could get a look at her driver's license."

I'm already imagining James walking past Lillian's assistant's desk when the girl in the chair was the wickedly smart and funny Shallay, with the great boobs, and not me. I try to salvage things. "So we have an insider connection to Stake-Out. James, can't you call her and get her to tell you who the fashion murderer is?"

"She wouldn't tell me anything big like that. Shallay is all about who is useful to her, and I'm not that useful. That's what I was telling you. We've got to offer her something she wants. And you can't trust her for a minute."

"I can't believe you dated a girl like that."

"It was a mistake," he says.

I'm hoping for more detail but he doesn't offer any.

"All right," I say. "I have something she wants."

Burning with jealousy, I pick up the phone and dial. Sylvia buries her face in her hands. "I can't watch," she says.

Shallay picks it up on the first ring. Her voice is smoky and inviting. "Kate McGraw," she says.

I break out into a full-body sweat, feeling exquisitely awkward. "Shallay. I know who you are now," I say.

"Congratulations. But I'm not the only StakeOut writer, you know. We have a vampire-detection network here, in London, in Paris—"

"What's the point? You expose them but no one believes you."

"You aren't privy to all of our plans. Or any of our plans, come to think of it."

"You have plans? How many people are going to die before you act?" I ask her.

She continues smoothly, as if I haven't spoken. "You also

ought to be a little more ingratiating if you want something from me."

"I don't want something. I have a deal to offer you. You tell me who the murderer is. I go after her. I have the help of a senior non-vamp member of the staff, and together we're going to stop this craziness. Afterward, I'll tell you all about it. We can do an IM interview."

There is a pause.

"How about photographs?" she says. "Do you have anything with better res than a cell phone?"

"I can't promise pictures."

"Find a way," she says. "No photos, no deal."

"Okay," I agree, deciding that I'll sort it out later. Breaking a promise to StakeOut won't bother me that much. "Who is it?"

"Let me talk to my people and get back to you," Shallay purrs. "And by the way, Kate, no matter what he says, I dumped *him*."

When I hang up, Sylvia emerges from behind her hands and asks, "What did she say?"

"She's talking to her people."

"I don't like it," James says. "We can't trust her."

Fifteen minutes later I get a two-word text. I stare at it, sadly.

　　Lillian Hall.

It makes sense.

20

At Stake

JAMES, SYLVIA, EVA, and I are back on the black flagstone plaza in front of Oldham at five A.M. on Monday. We spent Sunday night strategizing in Eva's hotel room. Of course, when I called her, she was happy to help. Each one of us is armed with a twelve-inch-long, one-inch-thick wooden dowel with a razor-sharp pointed end and a red rhinestone-encrusted handle, supplied by Eva. Even a rank amateur should be able to stake a vampire with one of these, she assures us. In my bag, I have one for Lauren, who will be joining us shortly. Though I hope she won't have to use it.

The plan is for us to find the blood supply (which, based on my information, is somewhere in Shane Lincoln-Shane's office) and dose it with ground-up Xanax, courtesy of Sylvia. She got the idea from *Interview with the Vampire*, in the scene where Claudia poisons Lestat: She offered him two victims who had been heavily dosed with laudanum. We are going to do the same thing, but instead of rendering the editors and assistants unconscious, we want them feeling nice, mellow, and open to suggestion.

Eva and I will take care of Lillian—easier said than done, I know—and then Lauren is going to call a meeting and spring the regime change upon the staff. If things turn violent—well, the drugs will slow them down and we'll be forearmed.

It's not the greatest idea anyone ever came up with, but it's the best we can do.

LAUREN SHOWS up wearing a Jil Sander suit and spike heels. Shane Lincoln-Shane, who looks exquisitely handsome in a bespoke suit, accompanies her. A requisite inch of shirt cuff shows beneath his strictly tailored sleeve. A folded square of silk in the breast pocket probably picks up the color scheme of his shirt and his socks, but it's too dark out here to tell.

"What's *he* doing here?" Eva asks, tense beside me.

"I'm sorry I didn't give you any warning," Lauren says smoothly. "I knew you wouldn't want me to risk talking to him. Shane may be a vampire, but he's on our side."

"Hello, Eva," he says graciously. "It's been a long time."

She inclines her head slightly.

Shane extends a graceful, chilly hand to me. "You may speak to me tonight, but don't get used to it," he says coldly.

James looks stunned.

"You said we needed an unusual leader, one who will keep order. That's Shane," Lauren explains. "He's willing to do it in exchange for the title of creative director. And I'm going to help him, in exchange for becoming editor-in-chief."

"You can't appoint each other to those positions," James says, eyeing Shane with a strange expression on his face.

"But if we're mutually supportive, we have a good chance of convincing Corporate," Lauren counters. "We also need Shane to get access to that blood. And he can provide us with a list of known vampires, which will make things easier this morning."

This was a weak link. We'd been planning on using Eva to do the spotting—fashionistas know each other when they see each other. Lauren was going to take her around and introduce her as the new Web director so she could get a gander at the staff.

I can't think of an immediate protest and apparently no one else can, either, because we meekly follow them into the building.

LIKE LILLIAN, Shane has a strange-smelling box full of dirt in his office, which, I now imagine, is the vampire equivalent of Frette linens. High-ranking vampires must get a box of dirt in their office the way humans of rank get a sofa or conference-room table. There are all kinds of Red Cross paraphernalia around: pens and Post-it pads and a canvas tote. On his bulletin board, Shane has every violent-themed photo shoot from the past few years, starting with the Steven Meisel shoot for Italian *Vogue* where the model is manhandled by the police. The bloodier the photos are, the more Shane has marked them up with his trademark mauve pen, writing things like "Love this look!" or "Thanks for the memories!"

"I haven't been in here since Lillian took over," Lauren

admits, clearly appalled. "The *Shop Girl* art director used to keep fresh flowers and listened to Faith Hill."

I'll bet she didn't have an industrial-size refrigerator behind her desk, either.

"Who let you expense a refrigerator of this size?" Lauren asks, outraged.

Shane smiles silkily. "You were on maternity leave," he tells her.

He opens the fridge, revealing rack after rack of stiff, translucent bags of fresh blood. They gleam with the jewel-like brilliance of expensive luxury goods. We take out Sylvia's bottle of Xanax and begin to grind the pills.

Shane arranges himself at his desk and turns on his monitor.

"The peaceful solution is never going to work, you know," he tells us languidly. "Too many of these girls are loyal to Lillian."

"You better hope it works," Lauren tells him. Shane is an ally, but only up to a point. We have a certain sharp-ended stick reserved for anyone who doesn't go along with us. I really hope it doesn't come to that.

At twelve-thirty—half an hour after beverage distribution—it's time.

Eva and I walk together down the hall toward Lillian's enclosure. It's quiet as a grave. Lauren has gathered the remaining vampire staff in the conference room and sent everyone else to the fifteenth floor for a special lecture on rights and permissions. James, Sylvia, and, most important, Shane have her back.

Outside Lillian's door I nod to Eva. She mouths the

words "Be careful" and then I knock gently and push the door open.

Lillian is sitting at her desk, heavy-lidded, an empty cup in front of her. She looks smaller and somehow crumpled. She doesn't smile and say *Entrez!* when she sees me. And although of course I'm expecting it—our relationship has changed quite a bit in the past few days—it still hurts.

"I'm surprised you dare show your face," she says without energy.

"After what happened at my apartment this weekend? You thought I'd be afraid?" I'm already spiky with adrenaline, buzzing with the stress of confrontation.

Her red lips curve upward briefly, as if with a pleasant recollection.

"I saw what you did to Rachel and Nin."

"Are you accusing me of something?" she asks, still without heat.

"I'm not accusing you. I'm telling you that I know what you did. I saw you leaving my building."

"You did?" She looks marginally more interested. "Oh, of course. The taxi. I thought someone inside smelled familiar. . . ."

"So you admit it?" I ask her. "And it wasn't just Rachel and Nin, either, was it? You've been, uh . . . snacking for ages."

"I feel strange this morning," Lillian says, yawning. "I should rend you limb from limb, but I can't quite be bothered."

"Rending causes wrinkles," I say. Vampires yawn? "Have you heard that?"

"Very funny," she says. "Too bad you won't be around to be funny much longer."

"Lillian," I say, deviating from the plan. "You don't really want to hurt me, do you? We were kind of friends, weren't we? I've been thinking about you a lot—the low energy, the lack of enthusiasm, the turning to inappropriate food sources for comfort, and— Depression is an illness. If you've been acting out in inappropriate ways—*really* inappropriate, but still . . . Maybe we can get you some help. Is there a spa or a retreat you could go on?"

I'm imagining a brochure with the headline "Eternal Life Got You Down?" And a nice castle with bars on the windows. My mind prompts that bargaining with her is wrong. She's a killer. Vigilante justice is the only kind called for here. But my heart balks.

She stares at me without any trace of her former affection.

"You think we were friends?" she says. "You're even more naive than I thought. The only reason I took an interest in you was to get back at your mother. I hated Eva. Gene Gantor was my lover for centuries, and suddenly Eva came along and ruined everything."

"But she never had anything with him!" I blurt. "She was *married*. And she loved my dad." And she told me so, but I can't let Lillian know I've been talking to her.

"Relationships between creative people are very complicated," Lillian says. "Eva usurped me as Gene's inspiration. When I found out she had a daughter, I was thrilled. I was going to make you love *me*. I was going to be like a mother to you. I wanted to take you away from Eva just like she took Le Gantor from me."

I want to say that she didn't need to bother. I was already well "away" from Eva, but the words stick in my throat.

"But after you've stolen James from me, I don't *want* you around for all eternity. Or even for another half hour, come to think of it." She makes a move as if to get up from her desk but sinks back into her chair.

Yay, Xanax.

"What did you come to my house for yesterday?" I ask in a small voice.

"You thought I'd come to kiss and make up?" Lillian asks.

No. I didn't. But I didn't believe until now that she might have come to kill me.

"I had—what would you call it? An inappropriate food craving—and thought I'd pay you a little visit," she says. "And speaking of that, I find I'm still a bit hungry. There was something off about this morning's drink. Come over here."

Unwillingly, I move toward her. This is how I finally convinced Eva that it should be me to confront Lillian, despite my total lack of experience and downright reluctance: Lillian is old and strong, and she'd fight Eva from the second she walked in the door, but I can get close to her.

Slowly, I eke my way across the Oriental rug toward her desk. I knew that it had to be me to do this, but I'm not sure I'll be able to. Trembling, I circumnavigate the desk.

Lillian reaches out and grabs my wrist, still encircled with a velvet ribbon to hide the mark of her teeth.

"How is this healing?"

"It's not," I reply shortly. "But you know that."

"Show me."

I think she may be trying to use her mind control, but I've been careful to avoid looking into her eyes. Moreover, the Xanax should be diluting her strength. At this point in our previous encounters I've been immobilized, but right now I still have the energy to wrench my wrist away and run.

I can't, though. She needs to think that I'm helpless.

I put my bag down on her desk, just where I'll be able to reach into it. Then, one-handed, I untie the ribbon and allow it to fall to the floor, exposing the two deep puncture wounds on my wrist. They're black at the center, surrounded by red, puffy-looking skin.

"I'm so sorry," Lillian says insincerely. "Does it hurt?"

"It hurts a lot."

I tuck the arm behind my back, slowly, as if it's taking a great effort to resist her.

"Will you at least consider getting help?" I ask her.

"No," she says, looking a little surprised that I'm still able to talk back to her.

"Will you stop killing people?"

"My dear, I haven't even begun killing people," she says, smirking. "All those years I was careful, drinking only from donors, never taking too much. I didn't realize how easy it would be to break the rules. Or how thrilling."

She's already reaching for me. Her arms, bare beneath the cropped sleeves of her white Sisley jacket, are like marble, and the short nails on her blunt, almost masculine white hands are tipped with crimson. I'm squeezed between her and the desk, which is good, because otherwise I would have a very hard time not running away at this moment.

But I can't run. Not yet.

I allow her to draw me down onto her lap, though my flesh crawls with the contact. On a cellular level my body knows that she's abhorrent, unnatural, wrong.

The wound on my wrist, however, has its own ideas. It aches for the cleansing pain of her teeth. Ignoring the sudden urge to feed myself to her, I grope behind me for the Swarovski-encrusted handle of the stake.

"You may have tried to be a mother to me," I tell her, "but my real mother did everything she could to save me from this."

Lillian's face is ecstatic. She's clearly not listening to me.

"There's no reason to keep the donors hanging around," she says. "Especially donors I'm very, very disappointed with. Now bring back that little boo-boo."

My heart is hammering so loudly she must be able to hear it. It's probably an incitement to feed. My hand makes contact with the stake. I struggle with my emotions. She's not my mother, or even a mother figure, I tell myself. She's the woman who killed my fellow interns and a researcher, and numerous girls about town, and a little dog named Marc Jacobs. And if I don't stop her, no one will.

"Lillian," I whisper. "Look at me."

She raises her dark head, her face a mask of hunger and desire. My resolve quivers. I think of a scalpel, cutting into flesh to heal it. I can do that. Shaking with horror, I lock my elbow and bring the stake up from below in an upward thrust, at the same time falling forward to bring the full weight of my body behind the blow. Her razor-sharp teeth glance off my shoulder. Pain blooms brightly as her teeth break the skin. And the stake lands home in Lillian's chest.

I'm screaming as I do it, calling for Eva.

That was our prearranged signal. Not subtle, but it works.

Hissing, Lillian breaks away from me, but her movements are fumbling and slow. She looks down at her ruined jacket and the glittery red hilt protruding from her chest, confused. "What have you done?"

"I'm sorry." I want to squeeze my eyes shut but won't let myself.

She stumbles backward, away from me. Then she sees Eva.

"What's *she* doing here?"

"Protecting me," I tell her.

Lillian's mouth falls open. Her crystal blue eyes meet mine and there is nothing human in her dimming gaze. She looks slowly at the stake protruding from her chest, then back at me as if she can't believe it.

"I think I got her," I whisper to Eva.

"You did," my mother says, wrapping her arm around my shoulders. "You didn't even need my help."

Lillian collapses on the floor, beginning to tremble. Black patches appear on her shapely limbs, and then spread as if her flesh were paper held over a candle. Her beautiful snow-white face carbonizes and implodes with a sound like breaking glass. Rings and earrings thunk to the floor. The blackened limbs wither and disappear. The crisp Sisley jacket slowly deflates, white as the day it was made and not showing even a trace of soot. It's horrible to watch, but I don't turn my eyes away.

I'm not sure how long we've been standing there—it feels like a lifetime—when Eva tentatively brushes a strand of hair away from my forehead.

"Let's go," she says. "It's time to negotiate."

ONE OF Shane's minions has ordered flowers. A low, trough-sized arrangement of tree peonies crouches in the center of the table, wide open and already shedding perfumed slivers of soap-white petals. I inhale deeply, the perfume calming my nerves. A man who likes peonies can't be all evil.

Shane and three out of four designers are gathered around the table, as well as the photo editor—James's direct boss—and the two other photo assistants and a photo researcher. They were all vampires and he never got suspicious? Naturally, the fashion department is well represented. I see Kristen, the twins, several assistants. Noë from Beauty. The gorgeous model booker is a vampire, along with a svelte Italian woman from Features. Annabel sits with her arms folded across her chest, looking defensive. The chairs on either side of her are empty. Everyone but me—in my blue silk Vintage Vogue top—is wearing black.

I give Lauren the nod that our work with Lillian is done and she smiles supportively. Eva and I move to flank her, Sylvia, and James, until we're forming an impromptu phalanx blocking the door. James says "Congratulations" but his face is grim.

"Where's Felix?" I whisper. "He's not a vampire?"

"I guess not." He shrugs. The receptionist is merely annoying, not undead.

The mood in the room is expectant, but not too tense, thanks to the pharmaceutical industry.

Shane Lincoln-Shane clears his throat. "I have sad news. Lillian Hall has left the magazine to pursue other projects."

Even sedated, the girls can't help but rustle in surprise.

"Lexa Larkin has also been terminated," Shane says. He's seated casually sideways at the table—as suspected, his lavender socks pick up the speck of lavender in his tie—and he doodles while he talks. Nonetheless, he has the room's complete attention. "I'm making the announcement here rather than in the regular staff meeting because we have some . . . human resources issues to discuss. You all know what I'm talking about.

"Lillian believed what her staff consumed during off hours wasn't her business," he continues. "She was more interested in page count than body count. And that has had certain repercussions. Headlines in the newspapers have been stirring up the civilian population. That kind of thing." His voice is soft, with just a tiny tinge of a foreign accent.

"Lillian's carelessness, and the carelessness of her deputies"—his eyes rake Kristen, Noë, and the twins—"has led to a very perilous situation for all of us."

He pauses and looks around the room before continuing. "As a cautionary tale, I'd like to talk about the contest that Lexa Larkin conceived of. Against my better judgment, Lexa was allowed to hire her own photographer and stylist, and pick her own location." He turns to Annabel. "Why don't you share with us all what she planned to do?"

"I don't know what you're talking about," she says.

Her eyes dart to me for help. I had no idea Shane was going to put her on the spot like this. I want to rescue her, but I also want to know why she told Lexa I was on to her. In all the craziness, I'd forgotten that particular betrayal.

Shane's frightening, cold stare bores into Annabel.

"It was a simple shoot with an ultraviolent theme," she says. "I scouted the upstate location for her. You saw the pictures."

"And didn't a certain junior staff member come to you with

her concern that the models for the photo shoot were going to be mistreated?"

Hey. He means me.

"And instead of bringing the matter to the attention of your superiors, you informed Lexa of the junior staffer's suspicions?"

"Mistreated how?" Kristen asks. "What was that British hag planning?"

How quickly the stilettos are out in the open.

"Ten models. Mistreated the ultimate amount," Shane replies.

"Impossible!" Noë says. "A disaster like that would change everything for us."

"That's some serious overeating if you ask me," the model booker spits.

"They say that in Europe we have different standards, but we would never!" one of the twins protests.

"Ahem." The slightest sound from Shane cuts the babble like a razor blade through a line of facial powder.

"If I'd told Lillian, she would have done nothing!" Annabel says. Her face darkens. "You all needed to *see* what Lexa was *really* like."

"So, to experience the satisfaction of seeing your boss deposed, you put us all at risk?" Kristen asks, glancing at Shane. "That's outrageous."

"It is," Shane agrees. He gives them all the thousand-year cold stare. "We won't be having any more of that behavior."

There is a chorus of agreement. I catch Lauren's eye with relief: Our plan seems to be working.

"Annabel wasn't the only one who was asleep at the switch

here," Shane continues. "You were my liaison to Editorial on this project. Why didn't you tell me all was not well?"

He's talking to James. My James. Sometime during this conversation James has eased away from my side and is now standing closer to the door.

"I'm not a mind reader," James says mildly. "Lexa didn't tell me what she was up to. And when I found out, I took care of the problem."

"Did you? I thought my old friend Eva McGraw took care of it while you lay on the floor and played possum."

So it's all going to come out finally. I turn my head to catch James's eye. *I'm not surprised*—I beam the thoughts at him— *and I know what you are. I've known ever since your wounds healed so fast. Maybe even before that.*

"I'm sorry," he mouths.

I have so many questions but, obviously, they'll have to wait until later.

Shane pulls out a crystal-encrusted wooden stake. "Regular staff purges make a magazine stronger. It's an Oldham tradition." Suddenly the room is bristling with stakes. Everyone from Art and Photo seems to have come to this meeting with a sharpened, jewel-handled bar of wood. The stakes, carried by gorgeous black-clad people against an all-white background, are wonderful accessories. The camera would love this. I glance at James, wondering if he's seeing the same thing I am. But James has disappeared.

"We didn't agree to this!" Lauren cries.

"Trust me, it needs to happen," Shane says over his shoulder as he savagely impales Kristen Drane, the single vent of his jacket flaring. "Everyone close to Lillian has to go—for everybody's safety."

He pulls the stake out—foamy with fresh blood—licks it, then goes after Noë.

"I wasn't close to Lillian!" Annabel yells. She's holding a chair up, trying to ward off two designers, but she's obviously overmatched.

"But *you're* not a team player!" Shane replies, dropping Noë like a couture rag.

I'm ambivalent. Annabel was my friend, but she was also willing to let the Tasty Girls die. In fact, I wouldn't be surprised if Annabel—supportive, ass-kissing Annabel—hadn't encouraged Lexa in the idea to begin with. I remember how she brightened up at my dad's suggestion that she get her fired. Am I really willing to fight to defend her?

It seems that I am, because my feet have already carried me halfway around the conference table when Annabel suddenly throws the chair, lunges for the cord to the blackout blind, and yanks it open. The shade snaps up with a sound like the crack of doom. Sunlight floods the conference room. While everyone is blinking and hissing and trying to cover their exposed skin, Annabel picks up another chair and heaves it through the plate-glass window. Her movements are slower than usual, but she's got the element of surprise on her side. There's an explosion of noise, the crackle of falling glass, and then a tendril of fresh air wends its way onto the thirty-seventh floor. Annabel has disappeared. The room is suddenly silent, littered with shards of glass and a whole lot of empty designer clothes.

"Can she do that?" Sylvia asks.

Eva walks over to the gaping hole into the sky and pulls the blind back down over it. The vampires breathe sighs of relief. "She'll have quite the sunburn when she's done, but the answer is yes, we can survive in even the brightest sun for a brief period of time."

"Boss, do you want us to go after her?" Matilda asks. It's brave of her since everyone is still shaken and wincing from his or her brief contact with the light of day.

"She can run but she can't hide," Shane says. "And that goes for him, too."

"James didn't do anything wrong!" I say. My voice sounds shrill. "You shouldn't blame him."

Shane trains his cold stare on me. "I realize we've had an unusual day," he says, "but let's not forget the chain of command. Mr. Truax is fired—at the very least—for his part in this debacle."

"All right, people," Lauren says, clapping her hands. "Kate, let's deal with your personal matters on personal time. And everyone, let's get this conference room cleaned up before that rights and permissions lecture is over."

"Don't worry," Matilda jokes, "those things last an eternity."

Lauren eyes the little piles of deflated clothing. "Unfortunately, it looks like our fashion staff has been decimated. Who can help me return these clothes to the closet?" Her eye falls on Sylvia, who is obviously bursting with the desire to be of service, despite the fact that her skin is flecked with stray blood. "There might be a job in it for you."

Sylvia's radiant smile almost makes the whole thing worth it.

Epilogue

WALK OUT onto Victoria's terrace carrying a tray with a bottle of wine and two glasses—though there will be three of us present this evening. My aunt, wearing a Gucci gardening hat, is busy cutting white angel's trumpet—a perfumey night bloomer—for a bouquet. Eva sits at the little iron table, looking out over the twinkling lights of Manhattan.

"Well?" she asks me.

"Shane made creative director. Lauren didn't get the EIC spot. I think she'll quit. And HR offered both Sylvia and me full-time positions as fashion assistants." I can't help but grin.

Her smile is tinged with concern. "Are you going to take it?" she asks.

Eva still thinks it's dangerous for me to be in the business. I'm safe from Shane Lincoln-Shane and my immediate coworkers, but the entire industry is lousy with vampires.

"If I do take it, you don't have to move here to protect me."

We've discussed this as well. Eva has a custom-sewing shop in Milan, and she has started making just enough to keep her head above water. But if I'm going to hang out with known vampires, she wants to be close. And I wouldn't be surprised if Eva 4 Eva was planning a comeback. She's also making noises about contacting my father.

"Pour us some wine, dear." Victoria glides up and air-kisses me, with a disapproving glance toward Eva. "You really ought to have some," she tells her sister.

"Oh, later," Eva says vaguely.

Vic has chosen to deal with the presence of the supernatural by steadfastly denying its existence. My aunt needs to bury her head in the sand like this because Sterling, Eva tells me, is one of the tribe.

"Ching-ching!" Victoria holds up her glass. "You'd be crazy not to take the position."

"That's what I've been thinking," I answer her, adding quickly, "I'm still going to med school but I might defer a year."

"Defer as long as you like. Let me just get a vase for these and we'll toast again to all the wonderful free clothes you'll be getting."

When she leaves the terrace, I pull a folded-up magazine page out of my bag and flatten it out for Eva. "I found this today," I tell her. "Look here." I point to an item on a new Louis Vuitton boutique opening in Paris. In the crowd outside there's a blonde carrying a parasol, and next to her stands someone holding a camera. The picture is way too small for them to be recognizable, but I know in my gut it is James and Annabel. "If I take the job, I'll get to go to Paris Fashion Week in October."

Eva frowns at me unhappily. Naturally, she doesn't want me to date a vampire.

"I know he's all wrong for me," I tell her, "but if I'm going to be in Paris anyway . . . I just want to talk to him."

"No good ever came of chasing a man across two continents," Victoria says, returning with the flowers arranged in a Japanese coralene vase.

"I wouldn't be," I say sulkily. "I'd be working."

Inside my bag my phone beeps, but I don't bother to check it. The messages from Shallay have been coming all day, ever since she steered me toward this item. And they say:

> let's play a game called Where's Boytoy? can you figure it
> out before I do?

I just might do that.